The
Woman
Upstairs

BOOKS BY RUTH HEALD

The Mother's Mistake

The Woman Upstairs

RUTH HEALD

bookouture

Published by Bookouture in 2019

An imprint of StoryFire Ltd.

Carmelite House
50 Victoria Embankment
London EC4Y 0DZ

www.bookouture.com

ISBN: 978-1-78681-535-4
eBook ISBN: 978-1-78681-534-7

PROLOGUE

I crawl to the top of the stone stairs. Every bone in my body hurts, but I have to get out of here. I have to get help. I have to find Mum.

My vision blurs. I can see the two figures just above me, shadows in the doorway. Their backs to me. About to leave. About to lock the door behind them and leave me all alone.

I stand shakily, ready to follow them out of the dark.

They are angry with me, angry with each other. But I can't focus on their words. My vision is blurry and my ears ring. I feel panic building inside me, filling me up so there's no space left to even breathe.

Then the hands come towards me, palms facing outwards. I see them coming but I can't move out of the way. My broken body won't cooperate. They reach out and push me as hard as they can.

I tumble backward. I'm flying for a second. My last moment of freedom before I land and feel my head crack against the first stone step. My legs are above me, tumbling over me, my arms folding at impossible angles beneath me.

And then my world goes completely black.

CHAPTER ONE

I stare down at the two blue lines on the pregnancy test.

This can't be happening.

Closing my eyes, I sink down heavily onto the floor. I slump against the bath, tipping my head back until it rests on the cold acrylic edge, still wet from a flatmate's shower.

I shake the test but the lines remain. Confident and straight.

'Katie – are you in there?' A knock on the bathroom door startles me. 'Katie – I'm desperate here. There's only so much more pressure my bladder can take.'

Amy. My flatmate and best friend.

I look back down at the pregnancy test, hoping the lines have disappeared. They haven't.

I stand up unsteadily, feeling slightly sick. Morning sickness? The thought makes me feel sicker still. Am I really pregnant?

Shoving the test into the waistband of my skirt, I glance at my reflection in the mirror. I'm still in my barista uniform, milky stains down the front of the shirt. My thick brown hair's still tangled from my nap. I can't even take care of myself. How could I take care of a baby?

'Katie! What are you doing in there?'

I take a deep breath and open the door. Amy rushes past.

Looking back, I see the wrapper of the pregnancy test resting on top of the toilet and make a dive past Amy to grab it.

'What's that?' Amy asks, her eyes wide.

'Nothing,' I say, screwing it up in my hand.

'Oh my god – you're not?' The look in my eyes must confirm her suspicions. 'What are you going to do?'

Three minutes later, Amy is in my room, perched on the edge of my bed, her arm around my shaking body.

'Everything will be alright,' she reassures me.

I tell her all the reasons I shouldn't have a baby. I don't have a career, or any savings; I don't own my own place. I don't think Ian will want the baby. We're not even in a serious relationship.

Amy stops me mid-sentence. 'But do *you* want the baby?' she asks.

It's only a split second before the answer is clear to me.

'Yes,' I whisper, shocked.

'Well, then you'll make it work,' she says confidently.

I'm about to ask her how when my phone buzzes. It's Mum. She'll be here in half an hour.

I kick myself for offering to cook for her and my sister. Right now dinner with the pair of them is the last thing I need.

'Don't worry, I'll help you,' Amy says, fully aware of the huge anxiety Mum elicits in me.

Amy's worked in pub kitchens before and she powers through chopping the vegetables for the casserole, while I faff around pulling herbs out of the cupboard. I keep forgetting where things are. My mind's a jumble. I gag as I cut the chicken. I throw the ingredients haphazardly into the casserole dish and shove it in the oven.

I haven't even tidied up. I go to the front door and trace the path my mother will take through the flat, trying to see it through her eyes. There's an old rusty freezer by the front door that belongs to my flatmate Cliff, full of fish fingers and chicken nuggets. Muddy tyre tracks mark a path through the hallway, where Mike dragged his bike through earlier. I notice the unidentifiable stains on the walls, the cobwebs in the corners and a lonely Christmas paper chain out of reach, just below the high ceiling. It's been there at least three years. No wonder Mum hates coming here.

I run the vacuum cleaner over the hallway carpet, working myself up into a sweat. The mud is gone but the place still looks shabby, and I can see the dust along the edges of the carpet and on the skirting boards.

In the shared washroom, the pale bath mat is covered with dark hairs. The intercom rings as I'm pouring an overgenerous helping of bleach into the toilet bowl. I take the dirty mat and shove it in the cupboard in the hallway on my way to answer the intercom.

'Mum,' I say. 'Come up.' I buzz her in, and I just have time to rush to my room and run a brush though my hair before she knocks.

When I open the door, Mum's hand is poised as if to knock again, a delicate silver bracelet dangling from her slim wrist. Her mouth is pinched in concentration as if she's been bracing herself. Her frown disappears in a split second and we greet each other with matching forced smiles.

'Mum!'

'Something smells nice,' she says, slipping off her shoes and entering the flat. My sister, Melissa, follows behind her. I still have my trainers on from work and I self-consciously take them off.

'Chicken casserole,' I reply as I nudge my flatmate Mike's muddy football boots out of the way and Mum and Melissa follow me to the kitchen.

I notice the huge pile of washing-up that's been left in the sink at the same time as Mum sees it and frowns.

'Drink?' I offer.

'Just a lemonade,' says my sister. She hasn't had any alcohol for nearly ten years, ever since she and Graham first started trying to conceive.

'Wine for me,' my mother says.

I pour the drinks, helping myself to some water from the tap and hoping Mum doesn't ask why I'm not having wine. When I turn to hand her her drink, I notice she's looking me up and down. I wrap my arm round my stomach self-consciously. If anyone's going to notice I'm pregnant, it will be Mum. She's always watched my weight as closely as she's watched her own.

I rub the long, jagged scar on my upper arm, a habit from childhood which returns when I'm anxious, particularly when Mum's around. I brace myself for her questioning, my secret burning inside me.

'Haven't you had time to get changed?' she asks.

'Oh,' I say, surprised. I look down and remember I'm still in my barista uniform. I notice the milk stains and blush.

'No – I forgot,' I mumble.

She sighs. 'I wish you'd leave that place, Katie. You're thirty-six now, far too old to be serving coffee for a living.'

'I know how old I am, Mum.'

'All that money on music college,' she says, wistfully. 'I thought you'd make something of yourself.'

I wince, her words hurting me more than she can imagine. The work as a barista was supposed to support me until I got my big break. But I'm still auditioning fifteen years later, and the break hasn't happened. I write songs and do the occasional pub gig on my electronic keyboard, but that's as close as I get to fulfilling my ambitions these days.

'Mum—'

'All I wanted was for you to achieve what I couldn't.'

Mum played the piano professionally before she injured her hand in an accident.

'I think the casserole's ready,' I say, although I know it can't be. Amy and I have only just put it in.

I get up and check the oven, but Mum continues.

'I hoped you'd have settled down by now, have a career and a family.'

I hear a sharp intake of breath from Melissa. The career might have happened for her – she's a partner at a law firm – but the family hasn't worked out. At least not yet. I feel a stab of guilt that I'll almost certainly have a baby before she does.

'Mum, I'm happy here,' I say as I make a show of taking the casserole out of the oven and stirring it.

'But are you? Is this really the way you want to live?' She makes a sweeping gesture, taking in the whole messy kitchen.

I feel my emotions well up inside me. My life won't be this simple for much longer. In nine months everything could change. I shove the food back in the oven.

'It's no fun being single as you get older,' Mum carries on.

She's been single since Dad died when I was six. I still think of him all the time, how things might be if he was alive. In the photos I have of us, I look like a miniature version of him. We gaze at the camera with matching smiles. I imagine he'd understand me in a way that Mum doesn't. Perhaps Mum would be happier too if he was still around. I scratch at the scar on my arm.

'You did an amazing job on your own,' Melissa says to Mum, as I return to the table. I feel a familiar twinge of jealousy. Mum always seems to turn to Melissa for reassurance. After my father died, all I can remember is Mum and Melissa constantly together, hugging and whispering, shutting me out, telling me that I was too young to understand.

I wish I had clearer memories of Dad. I only have flashes of recollection: Dad listening to me play the piano. His calloused hand holding mine tightly as we walked to school. The slight smell of whisky as he kissed me when he got in from work.

I top up the drinks.

'How are your book club friends, Mum?' I ask, trying to change the subject.

She takes the opportunity to dissect the life choices of her friends' children. Claire's daughter is married to a banker and they're moving to Hong Kong. Sarah's daughter is running her own fashion business. Molly's daughter has worked her way up to partner at one of the big accountancy firms. But Grace's daughter is seeing a married man. And Pamela's daughter is still living at home, she says with a frown.

Sometimes I think it must be easy being my mum, seeing everything in black and white, dividing people so neatly into the successes and the failures. Me: failure. My sister, Melissa, with her brilliant job, high-flying husband and own house: success. Except for the failure to produce grandchildren.

'Even Pippa's daughter has got married now,' she continues. 'She gave up her lifestyle travelling the world and settled down. Just in time. They're expecting their first child in March.'

My sister smiles tightly and I'm plunged back into my thoughts about the baby. My baby. I can't really have a baby on my own, can I? For a moment I allow myself to imagine a world where Ian and I stay together, have the baby and live happily ever after. But that hardly seems realistic. I might want the relationship to develop into something more, but I'm sure he sees it as just a fling. What am I going to do?

The buzzer to the flat rings and I jump. It will probably be for Mike. He's always having people round to the flat; friends, acquaintances, people he met at the pub.

'Hello?'

'Katie – it's me.'

'Ian?' My stomach turns. Now is not a good time. We haven't met each other's families before. We're not that serious yet. Besides, I need more time to get used to the fact that I'm pregnant. If I see him I might just blurt it out.

'I thought I'd surprise you. I brought the Argentinian Malbec – your favourite.'

'Who's that?' Mum asks.

'No one, Mum.'

'Your mother's here?' Ian asks. 'I'd love to meet her.'

'Invite your friend up. I'm sure there's enough food to go round.'

I give in, under siege from both sides. 'OK then,' I say with a sigh. 'Come on up.' I know this is going to be a mistake.

A minute later, Ian greets me with a big smile, a bunch of flowers and the bottle of red wine.

Out of the corner of my eye, I see Mum's eyebrows rise as he kisses me lightly on the lips. She's taking in every detail: Ian's smooth dark hair, his chiselled features with slight wrinkles round the eyes. His sharp suit and manicured hands. The expensive wine and flowers. And the fact that he's closer to her age than mine.

'Come and join us,' she says.

'I'd love to,' Ian replies.

'So how do you know Katie?' Mum asks.

I'm not quick enough to think of a reply. I don't want to introduce him as my boyfriend. Not here. Not now.

'She hasn't mentioned me?' Ian says with a grin. My mother's eyebrows shoot higher as he puts his arm round me.

This is too much for me, and I have a childish urge to run from the room. Ian and I are just casual. But now he's meeting my mother. And I'm pregnant with his child. None of this was supposed to happen.

'Where did you meet?'

'At work,' I say quickly, dreading Ian offering up the word 'online' to Mum. 'At the coffee shop. Ian runs his own business and he sometimes comes in.'

'Your own business?' Mum's eyes light up and I wonder if this will go some way to compensating for the fact that he is so much older than me.

'I run a property business,' Ian says. 'We buy houses, do them up and then sell them or rent them out.'

Melissa frowns. 'Doesn't that inflate house prices and stop young families getting on the housing ladder?'

A part of me can see what she means. Melissa and Graham are both lawyers in the city, and Melissa resents the fact that it still took them years of scrimping and saving to afford a small terraced house in the outskirts of London. Despite this, I feel defensive on Ian's behalf.

But Ian hardly blinks. 'It's not quite like that. We buy houses that need a bit of care. We do them up to make them habitable for people before selling them on. Often people can afford a mortgage but can't afford big repairs to a house. We do the essential improvements so that young people can buy them.'

'I'm a psychiatric nurse,' my mother says suddenly, although no one's asked. Usually she just says she's a nurse, leaving out the psychiatric part, but when she wants to test someone she gives her full job title. She retrained after my father died.

Ian nods politely. 'That must be fascinating.'

'It is,' she says, disappointed not to get more of a reaction. 'Do you have a family yourself, Ian?' I slump down in my chair, embarrassed.

'No,' he says, with a smile. 'I've always been married to my work. I wanted to build the business to have the security before I started a family.'

'It's a bit late for you to start a family,' Mum says, and I blush.

I feel the weight of my secret, like a stone in my stomach. It's not too late at all.

'I think the casserole's ready,' I say, praying it actually is ready this time. I dread to think what question she might ask next.

'People start families later and later these days, Mum,' Melissa says. Melissa's forty and her husband Graham's forty-five, eight years younger than Ian.

'I didn't mean you, love.' Mum reaches her hand out and touches her shoulder, but Melissa shrugs it off.

'I keep myself fit and well,' Ian says. 'Anything's possible.' I can't bear to meet his eye.

'It can take a long time to get pregnant,' my sister says, and my heart aches for her.

Not always, I think, as I reach my hands into the oven to take out the dish. How the hell am I ever going to tell them all?

'Ow!' I've been so distracted I forgot to put the oven gloves on. The casserole pot is already halfway out of the oven and it falls to the floor before I can stop it, bits of chicken and broken china flying across the kitchen.

I burst into tears.

Ian rushes over and puts his arm round me. 'What's wrong?' he asks.

I glance up and meet my sister's eyes through my tears. Her gaze is so intense that for a moment I think she knows my secret. She can see right through me, like she could when we were children and we were so close I thought she could read my mind.

I can't keep it inside me anymore. It's too huge to contain. And sooner or later everyone in this room will know anyway.

'I'm pregnant,' I blurt out. I only mean to whisper, but the words shoot out louder than I intend, filling the kitchen.

As soon as I've spoken I regret it. Even my mother is silent. The clock in the kitchen ticks so loudly I wonder why I never noticed it before.

I hear my sister's chair scrape back suddenly on the kitchen tiles, and she bolts from the room.

When I finally dare to look up Ian is staring at me, speechless, his eyes full of questions.

CHAPTER TWO

SIX MONTHS LATER

I force the zip closed on my last suitcase. I'm all packed. After five years, I'm moving out of my flatshare. I'll miss the hustle and bustle of communal living, and my late-night chats with Amy. But there's no way I can stay. Not now. I smile as I touch my belly and feel one of my twins kick against my hand.

In just a couple of months my life will be completely different. I'll be a mother to two girls, in a big house in suburbia, living with my property developer partner. It sounds good on paper, but inside I'm terrified.

I was stunned when Ian turned out to be delighted about my pregnancy, and excited I was carrying twins. It was then I finally realised I was in love with him. Since we found out he keeps buying little gifts for the babies; tiny booties and delicate blankets, soft toys and rattles.

As soon as the sonographer showed us the twins wriggling about on the scan, we both instantly fell in love with them. They touched each other in the womb, hands reaching out and brushing each other, as if they already felt a connection. Ian's hand squeezed mine as we watched.

Even Mum's happy after the initial shock. She's been telling her friends about my big house, rich boyfriend and future children. I've switched from a cautionary tale to a success story overnight.

I survey the empty bedroom, ready and waiting for the next tenant to arrive this afternoon. Without my stuff cluttering every surface and my pictures on the walls, my old room looks soulless and bare.

I swallow my sadness and turn to leave, shutting the door behind me.

In the living room Amy gets up to say goodbye. I wrap her in a hug. 'I'm going to miss you,' I say.

'It's the end of an era,' she replies. Amy's lived here nearly as long as I have. While other housemates have passed through, the two of us have remained, closer than sisters.

'What am I going to do without you?'

'You'll have Ian.'

I half smile and she grins back at me.

'I'm glad he turned out to be alright after all,' she says.

When Ian and I first got together, he'd revealed so little about himself that Amy and I would entertain ourselves by making up stories about a secret double life he might lead. Middle-class drug dealer. Russian spy. Male escort.

'Do you think I'm doing the right thing?' I ask, doubts rising to the surface once more.

Amy raises her eyebrows. 'The right thing? Of course you are! I would die for an opportunity like this. It's like you've won the lottery. You're moving into a multimillion-pound house in a really nice area.'

I smile at her. Ian's commandeered one of the houses his company owns for us to live in. They bought it a couple of months ago, and luckily no one's moved in yet. As soon as I told Amy that Ian and I were moving in together she found the old listing for the house on Rightmove and showed me the pictures. The house is beautiful: three storeys and five bedrooms, a modern kitchen diner opening out on to huge gardens and a bathroom with a cast iron bath by a window overlooking a park. Amy was desperate for us to go together and check it out before I moved in, but then her friend had a crisis. He'd split up with his boyfriend and needed somewhere to stay. I'm moving out of the flat a bit earlier than planned so he can take my room. I'll be in the new house for a few days on my own before Ian joins me. His elderly mother is moving out of his place into sheltered accommodation in a few days' time, and he'll join me when she's settled.

'I'll miss this,' I say, indicating the tatty sofas and piles of newspapers in the corner.

'Seriously? You'll miss the mud on the carpet, Mike never cleaning the kitchen, Cliff playing the PlayStation until 2 a.m., and no one ever cleaning the toilet?'

'Well, when you put it like that.'

'Are you sure you'll be OK moving in on your own?' she asks. Ian wanted to take the day off to help me move, but he has too much work on.

I smile at Amy. 'Of course.'

'Are you certain you don't want me to come with you?'

'You've already done enough. I'll only have a suitcase to carry now you've organised that van.' Amy's mate's going to drive the rest of my things to my new house tomorrow afternoon after work.

Her expression turns serious. 'You're doing the right thing, honestly. But if you need me, I'm only a phone call away.'

'Yeah.' I think of all the nights we've sat opposite each other on the faded sofas, having heart to hearts about boyfriends and jobs and life. A phone call won't be the same.

'Don't cry,' Amy says, reaching out and gently wiping a tear from my cheek. 'You'll get me started.'

'Well, then,' I say. 'I'll see you soon.'

Amy smiles through her tears. 'Yes, at your baby shower. I can't wait. You can show me round the new place then.'

I give her one final hug. Neither of us want to let go, but I make myself pull away. I take my suitcase and then turn and leave the living room for the last time, tears running down my face. I remind myself I have to be strong. I have the twins to think about now. My future is with Ian and the babies.

Two hours, two hot Tubes and a taxi ride later, I turn into the street: Adelaide Road. I'm glad I decided to just bring one suitcase of essentials on the sweaty journey.

The street looks exactly as it did on Google Street View. Huge plane trees line the pavements and shield the three-storey houses from prying eyes. The domineering, detached, double-fronted houses cast me in shadow and I feel tiny. I imagine families playing together in the front rooms, haloed by the light from the wide bay windows. I look up in awe. Delicate balconies look out over the road from the top floors.

A young child whizzes past me on a scooter, in a sky-blue school blazer and matching hat. A woman follows behind him, young with long acrylic nails, chatting on her mobile in another language.

She pauses her conversation to shout after him.

'Frederick – wait at the crossing! Remember what your mother said.'

She must be his nanny. I wonder what world I'm moving into; who could live in these impossibly huge houses. Lawyers and bankers and high-flyers, I guess. And now me.

I swallow, feeling out of place in the summer dress I bought in the supermarket. The people round here must be swimming in wealth. I'm never going to fit in. I've always rejected the idea that money leads to happiness. My own seemingly idyllic, middle-class childhood, spent in a sizeable house in the suburbs, taught me that.

I go past the identical red-brick mansions, the bright green manicured gardens. The only slight expression of individuality comes from the cars on the driveways and the colours of the garages and front doors, which are varying shades of grey, blue and green. I'm looking for my house, the one Amy showed me on Rightmove, but I realise I don't remember the colour of the garage. I doubt I'll be able to distinguish it from all the others.

I glance at the address again. Number fourteen.

The road changes as it nears the high street. The trees shelter the occasional parked car and there's a coffee shop on the other side of the road. I must be nearly there now. I feel my first buzz of excitement. This will be the start of a new life for us.

I pass number twelve. In front of the racing-green garage, its gravel drive showcases a Porsche and an SUV, next to a perfectly maintained, characterless flower bed.

The next one must be number fourteen.

I stop and stare.

A huge overgrown hedge obscures the house from view. Bins overflow onto the concrete driveway, and a rusty washing machine sits among McDonald's wrappers and broken beer bottles. In one corner of the driveway there are ashes from a recent fire.

My heart sinks.

This can't be it.

I fight my way to the front door, past the boarded-up, graffiti-covered bay window, brambles scraping my bare knees under my summer dress and drawing blood. I can just make out the tiled path beneath the vegetation.

The paint has peeled off the front door, exposing the dark wood below. The ivy that covers the front of the house has stretched its fingers over the entrance, and I pull it away with my hands revealing the number.

Fourteen.

1

My sister lies next to me, the fear in her blue eyes reflecting mine as we listen to our parents fight from the safety of our bedroom. My pyjamas are drenched in sweat, clinging to my body.

It's so hot it feels like I'm drowning.

Drowning is one of the things that could kill us. My dad likes to list them sometimes. Drowning. Being run over by a car. Being stabbed by the kitchen knives. Sometimes when he lists them it sounds like he's trying to protect us, to make sure we're careful. But we know they're really a threat. Things that might happen if we're naughty. If we don't do as he says.

I want to get up and open the window, but I'd never be brave enough to tiptoe across the bedroom. I don't think I could without being heard.

A door slams.

I feel pressure in my head. Thump. Thump. Thump.

It's like the drum I like to play in the music class at school. Except the drum is inside me, beating louder and louder.

Another door slams. The shouting gets angrier. I wonder if one day Mum will snap and kill him. I'd like that, I think. Just me, Mum and my sister. I wouldn't be scared then. What would there be left to be scared of?

The shouting is closer now, and I cover my ears so I can't make out the words. I don't want to hear how much they hate each other. Outside the world is muffled. I can just make out the low roar of my father, like the dinosaur in the storybook Mum used to read me. Mum's response is a squeak, like the tiny field mouse.

My sister moves closer to me and puts her arm round my hot skin. She cocoons me with her body and pulls the sheets over us both. Under the covers, my eyes adjust until they meet hers.

'Everything will be alright,' she says, stroking my hair. 'We'll always have each other.'

I snuggle into her. She's right. As long as we're together, we'll always be safe.

CHAPTER THREE

This is it. Number fourteen. The house I'm supposed to be moving into. Today.

Beads of sweat run down my forehead and I scratch angrily at the old scar on my upper arm.

Maybe it's the wrong house.

I take my key out of my handbag and turn it over in my hand.

I pull the ivy off the door, take a deep breath and insert the key into the rusty lock. It fits. With a bit of force, it turns and I hear the bolt shift reluctantly. The door has expanded in the heat, and I have to shoulder-barge it before it opens. Then it catches the breeze and swings wildly, banging into the wall beyond and bouncing back towards me.

Pushing the door open, I peer into the wide hallway. A musty, rotten smell fills my senses and I can just make out a dusty pile of old post in the dark.

I stop and glance over my shoulder. Despite the glare of the sun, the house is in shadow. I realise I can't see the street beyond the tall hedges. No one could even see I'm here.

There must be some kind of a mistake. I feel sick. Ian can't expect me to stay here on my own.

I look at my suitcase on the doorstep beside me and blink back tears. So much for a fresh start. I dial Ian's number, my anger building.

No answer. As usual. He's always working. I try again. Still no answer. Where am I going to sleep tonight? I'll have to go back to the flatshare. But the thought of explaining why to Amy makes me flush with shame.

I take deep breaths and try to calm myself. Maybe I'm over-reacting. Maybe the house isn't as bad on the inside as it looks on the outside.

I take a single step onto the stained offcut of green-brown carpet which serves as a doormat and feel around for a light switch. The wall feels bumpy, as if the wallpaper is textured. Eventually I feel the dirty plastic of a switch. I flick it hopefully on and off, but of course, it doesn't work. The electricity has been cut off. In desperation I turn my phone torch on.

I tiptoe inside, sensing the need to be quiet, as if I don't want to disturb the house. I can feel the stagnant air moving with me as I make my way inside. This house is supposed to be our home, but I feel like an intruder. I can't imagine ever feeling like it belongs to us.

I glance up the dark staircase and see the rectangular patches of darker wallpaper, which must have been shielded at one time by pictures. I can just about make out the flowered pattern on the paper and I imagine family photos filling the walls. Who lived here? Who let it get into this state?

The thought of someone living in this place makes me shiver, even though it's hotter than hell. I remember the ashes on the driveway from a fire, the rubbish overflowing the bins, the graffiti. The cavernous house would be perfect for a squat. What if I'm not alone? What if there are already people living here?

I must pull myself together. If there was someone living here I would have heard them by now. My curiosity spurs me on across the bare floorboards, which creak and groan beneath my weight as I venture through the hallway. The walls are speckled with unrecognisable dark stains and a patch of black mould descends from the ceiling. I pass a bookcase overflowing with books and paperwork, a reminder that this was once someone's home.

I hesitantly push open the first door I come to, afraid of what I'll find. Empty. Except for the flies circling round an unidentifiable black shadow. Is there something dead there? A mouse? Or a rat? I swallow.

In the tiny galley kitchen, I'm relieved to see there's no sign of cooking on the ancient stove. Brambles block the back door entirely, so I can only see out of the top half of the window and vines have crept through a yellowing cat-flap and spread over the floor. The garden could be tiny or huge. I can't tell. I try the door handle and it gives a little, the screws loose. I push a bit harder and the door lurches outwards, detaching from the rotten wooden frame. It opens about half an inch, hemmed in by the vegetation. It hadn't been locked.

I think of Ian with rising anger. What was he thinking? There's no way I could sleep in an unlocked, derelict house on my own.

I try to return the door to the frame, but one of the hinges is loose and it hangs unevenly. I abandon my efforts. I've seen enough. It's time to leave.

When I step back out of the front door and into the daylight, I breathe in the fresh air desperately. I look at my lonely suitcase, still sitting on the step.

The coffee shop across the road is the only building that comes close to looking as run-down as the house. The sign outside offers a full English breakfast with coffee for £4.99, as it creaks in the wind. Inside, the smell of coffee competes with the smell of bacon, but loses the battle. I order and take a seat on a chipped wooden chair at a checked Formica table. The decor wouldn't look out of place in a hipster bar, but I think the tables here date from when they were fashionable the first time round. I've worked in places like this, serving workmen breakfasts early in the morning and stressed mums with screaming babies coffee later in the day.

The builders at the counter hand over fivers from paint-splattered hands and then leave, most likely to work on one of the loft conversions that seem to be taking place at every other house along the road. The café is quiet now, with just one other customer left. A woman on her own, reading the papers. The table I've chosen is next to hers, beside a rusty electric fan, which does little more than move the hot, sticky air around the room.

The reality of my situation is starting to sink in. The house isn't fit to live in. I've no idea what Ian was thinking, but he's let me down. The perfect life I'd imagined with him and our twins was just a fantasy. I feel sick. I must calm down. I take a sip of my coffee, burning my tongue, as I try to quell my anger.

I phone Amy.

'How's the house?' she asks excitedly, before I get the chance to speak.

'It's not the one we thought it was,' I say. 'It's so run-down…'

'Really? Well I'm sure you'll fix that in no time, you're so organised.' She sounds distracted, as if she wants to get me off the phone.

'Amy – has Jake moved in?'

'Yeah, he's unpacking now. Why?'

'I just thought I might come back.'

'Don't be so silly. I know you're nervous about moving out, but really, how can you reject a multimillion-pound house to come back here?'

'Seriously, it's not in a fit state to live in. It's not the house we thought it was.'

Amy pauses and I hear voices in the background. 'I know you're having your doubts about moving in with Ian,' she says. 'But just give it a go.' Someone interrupts the call, and she says she'll be there in a sec. 'Listen, I have to go and show Jake round. Call me if you need anything. You'll be fine. Just stay chilled. Love you. Bye.'

'Amy, I—'

But she's already hung up.

I try Ian again. It's still a few days before he's due to move into the house with me. I could stay at his place. I'd go there now but I don't have the address. His mother has dementia and visitors upset her, so we've always met at my flat or gone for weekends away.

If I can't get hold of Ian then I need to find somewhere to stay tonight. I hate Ian for putting me in this position.

I'm going to have to ring Mum. She's only an hour on the Tube from here. If she can put me up overnight, then maybe I can fix things with Ian in the morning. Maybe this is all some kind of mistake.

I take a deep breath and pick up my phone.

'Hello? Katie?' She sounds irritated, as if I'm interrupting, and I can hear the faint hum of voices in the background, which I assume are from the television.

'Hi Mum. Umm… I'm at the new house.'

'What's it like?'

I might as well just spit it out. 'I can't live here, Mum.'

'What do you mean, you can't live there?'

'It's so run-down—'

'What? Worse than that grotty flat you've just come from?'

I wince. 'Much worse.'

'Katie – it's a huge house in a lovely street. You told me that yourself.'

'Mum. It's not liveable.' I don't know how to get through to her.

'But didn't you see it before you moved in?'

I frown, embarrassed. How can I explain that Amy and I had looked at the wrong property on Rightmove? 'No, I—'

'It can't be that bad,' she says, with growing impatience.

'I can't live here.'

I want her to offer to let me stay with her, but instead I hear her sigh. I grit my teeth.

'Can I come and stay with you? Just for tonight?'

'What's Ian going to do? Can't you stay wherever he is?' I hear the criticism in her voice. I feel my tears starting to fall and I wipe them away, embarrassed.

'He's away at the moment,' I lie.

'Well, I'm not at home either. So you'll have to find somewhere else. You're thirty-six. Not a child. You need to grow up before you become a mother yourself.'

'Mum—' My voice breaks.

I hear the low rumble of a man's voice in the room with her, but I can't make out what he's saying.

'I have to go, dear. Good luck.'

CHAPTER FOUR

I stare into my coffee. What the hell am I going to do now? I'm furious with Ian. He'd probably think nothing of booking a hotel in my situation. He doesn't understand that most people don't have enough money to just splash out on luxuries whenever they feel like it. I don't have enough money for a night at a B&B, let alone a hotel. My finances have always been so carefully balanced. So I'm on my own. Homeless.

I think back to the run-down house. Would it really be so bad to stay there? I'd have to sleep on the floor, unless by some miracle the upstairs is furnished. I think of the dead rodent I saw in one of the rooms, flies circling. I only looked downstairs. I've no idea what else I might find in the rest of the house.

'Are you alright?' The woman on the next table offers me a tissue.

I nod, embarrassed, remembering I'm not alone in the coffee shop. 'I'm fine,' I mumble. I take the tissue and dab my eyes. 'Thanks.'

The woman smiles warmly and I look at her properly for the first time. She's as thin as a rake and dressed in a long black skirt, bright pink blouse and sensible black loafers. Her dark hair is scraped back into a ponytail, tied with a bright pink scrunchie with a Hello Kitty motif, even though she must be in her fifties.

'I couldn't help overhearing. You're having some house trouble.'

'I've just moved in. Across the road.' I point, even though you can't really see the house from here, just the driveway with the overflowing bins and the huge hedge.

'Oh…' she says, staring out the window. 'The one opposite?'

'Yeah. Behind the hedge. It's very run-down.'

'Yes, well. I suppose it could do with some care. It hasn't been looked after.'

'My partner bought it,' I say. 'I was supposed to move in today. But it doesn't even have electricity.'

'You've nowhere else you can go?' she asks, sounding worried.

'Doesn't look like it,' I reply, glaring at my phone and thinking about how Mum cut me off.

'How awful for you. I wish there was some way I could help.'

I look up at her, taking in her kind eyes. It's so nice of her to be concerned. Maybe this is what it's like once you get a bit away from central London. People looking out for each other.

'I'll be fine,' I say stoically.

'At least it's warm. I've even heard people are sleeping outside in this heatwave.'

She's right. A customer at my coffee shop told me he's sleeping in a tent in his garden because of the balmy nights. Perhaps I should think of this like camping. It can't be that different. But I still shiver at the thought of being alone in the house.

'I've got a torch you can borrow, if you like,' she continues. 'If you don't want to sleep in the dark.' She digs around in her huge handbag and laughs. 'I've been carrying around this Mary Poppins handbag for years. It's about time something in it came in useful.'

I smile at her. 'Thanks. I'd appreciate that.'

'It's only a house,' she says, smiling kindly. 'Just bricks and mortar. What can a house do to you?'

'There could be squatters,' I say, remembering the remains of the fire in the driveway.

'No one's been living there. Believe me, I'd know. I always take my afternoon coffee in this café and I haven't seen anyone go in or out in months.'

'I suppose I'm just being paranoid,' I reply, with an embarrassed smile.

'No, not at all. Better safe than sorry. And I'm sure your hormones are all over the place with a little one on the way.' She glances down towards my stomach.

I nod. Maybe she's right.

'I haven't even been upstairs,' I admit. 'I wasn't brave enough.'

'I could come with you if you like… If you think it would help.'

'Oh no, don't worry about me.'

'Are you sure? I wouldn't want anything to happen to you in there. Especially not after I'd reassured you that it would be fine.' She laughs a tinkling laugh.

I hesitate.

'I can see you're thinking about it,' she says. 'Let me come in with you. It'll make you feel better. And it's not like I've got anything better to do.' She indicates the newspaper lying closed on her table. 'I've finished the paper.'

'OK then,' I reply. 'I mean – thank you. I'd appreciate that.'

She holds out her hand. 'I'm so sorry, I forgot to introduce myself. I'm Paula. I know the area well, so anything you need to know, just ask.'

'Katie,' I say as I shake her hand.

With Paula beside me and her torch lighting the way, the house feels less daunting. It's just an empty shell. Lifeless. For a moment I allow myself to imagine making it my own, doing it up to match the others in the street. I could have a good life here, if Ian's willing to make the house habitable. Otherwise I don't know what I'll do. I glance at my phone. He still hasn't returned my calls.

We walk through the hallway, and I try the one remaining door downstairs. A musty smell fills my nose as Paula's torch illuminates a wide fireplace with sooty tiles. When I look closer, the bones of a dead bird lie in the grate. I recoil, thinking of the dead rodent in the other room. What else will I find?

'Look,' Paula says.

I turn and see a piano, the only piece of furniture I've seen in the house. The lid is broken and cracked, but I can see the quality of the craftsmanship. I lift the lid gently, a layer of dust coming off in my hand. Underneath the ivory keys are yellow.

'Wow,' I say, a flutter of pleasure running through my body. 'How could they have left this here?'

'I don't know,' replies Paula. 'It's beautiful, isn't it?'

I'm glad she appreciates it. Not everyone would.

I run my fingers over the keys, letting out a familiar melody. It's so long since I've played, and the dusty keys feel heavenly under my fingers. The piano is horribly out of tune, but I close my eyes and imagine how it should sound. For the first time I want this place to be my home.

When I open my eyes Paula is standing behind me. 'That was breathtaking.'

'I used to play a lot when I was younger. I'm a bit out of practice.'

I imagine a future in this house, getting the piano tuned and letting my fingers dance over the keys to my heart's content. No housemates or neighbours to worry about. I imagine the twins growing up to the sounds of Beethoven and Bach. I could teach them to play themselves.

I smile at Paula. 'Do you play too?' I ask.

'A little,' she says. 'I haven't for years.'

'I'd like to teach my girls when they're older.'

'Your girls?'

'Oh,' I say, realising I haven't told her. 'I'm having twins.'

'Two girls?' She turns to me and I catch the whites of her eyes widening in the dark.

'Yes,' I laugh. 'It was quite a shock when we found out.'

'It must have been. Can I feel them?' she asks softly. 'I'd love to feel them kick. To sense the life in them.'

I hesitate. I hate the way that my pregnancy has made my body public property, how strangers ask to touch my bump. I want to say no, but Paula is helping me out and I'm not sure she'll understand my objection.

'OK,' I say.

Paula puts the torch down on the piano top and its light disperses into one corner of peeling wallpaper, the rest of the room darkening. I don't see her hands coming and her sudden touch makes me jump and I step back, banging against the piano, the base keys sounding loudly.

'I'm sorry,' I mumble.

'Don't worry,' she says, as she gently caresses my stomach. 'I can feel them. How lovely. One's kicking.' She must be able to feel something I can't, because even though I'm concentrating hard I can't sense either of them moving. Tension runs through my spine.

She rubs her hands over my belly, over and over, stroking it. A part of me wants to tell her to stop, but it's too awkward to say anything; I would seem oversensitive. I clasp my hands together, palms sweating. It will be over soon.

She presses a bit harder, on my pelvis. It feels uncomfortable, but it's not that different to what the midwife did in my antenatal appointment last week, so it must be OK.

'I can feel a head,' Paula exclaims in delight.

'Great,' I whisper, my back against the piano. I move slightly to my left, hoping she'll take the hint.

But her hands delve further. 'There's the other head,' she says. 'Twins.'

And then her hands leave my body as fast as they arrived.

I step to the side and reach for the torch. I feel afraid, but I'm not sure why. I have an irrational desire to shine the torch on Paula's face to see her expression, but I resist. It's like communication has been lost between us. In the dark she couldn't have seen my expression either, couldn't have read the signs that I was uncomfortable.

I feel a desperate need to get out of the house, into the air. But I still haven't seen upstairs and the evening is closing in. It won't be long until I have to sleep here. I look at my phone again. Still nothing from Ian.

'Let's see the rest of the house,' I say, scratching at the scar on my upper arm and shining the torch into the hallway.

On the stairs I hand the torch back to Paula and hold the handrail, treading carefully, with Paula a step behind me. I can only hear the sounds of our breathing and our footsteps as Paula lights up the way ahead of me.

'Watch your step,' I say, pointing out a loose floorboard. She shines her torch down, stealing light from the staircase ahead, so I have to stop, unsure of what awaits me in the darkness above. I'm glad I'm not on my own. It would be so easy to trip and fall. It would be ages before someone found me. I stroke my bump, promising my twins that I'll protect them.

At the top of the stairs the landing is carpeted, dark brown and threadbare in the central thoroughfare and beige and thick at the less well-trodden edges. In the dilapidated bathroom, tiles hang off the walls over the old, grimy bath in 1970s avocado, perched precariously on rotting floorboards.

We go into three bedrooms; two doubles and a box room. The box room is crammed floor to ceiling with old furniture, dining chairs teetering on top of an old desk by the doorway. The other two rooms are almost empty, save for a mattress in the middle of the floor of one. Paula shines her torch round the room and I take in the big, thick curtains covering the windows and the patterned wallpaper. A stale smell fills the room and I wonder when the windows were last opened. I draw back the heavy, cobwebbed curtains and look out on to the rubbish-strewn driveway and the tall hedges that shield the house from the street beyond. As I struggle with the window latch, I realise they're painted shut.

'I guess this is where I'm sleeping tonight,' I say, but I can't manage to sound cheerful.

'Oh, sweetheart.' Paula reaches out and touches my arm. 'Don't worry. You'll be fine. When's your husband getting here?'

'My partner, not my husband,' I say, not wanting to over-claim my relationship with Ian, who has let me down so badly. 'He's coming over in a few days. He's busy with work at the moment.'

'What does he do?'

'He's a property developer.' The irony of my words strikes me and I feel embarrassed, not daring to turn and look at Paula. 'I don't think he can have seen the house himself,' I say quickly, making excuses for him. 'He can't have realised the state it's in.'

'It's been left to rot,' Paula says.

'I know.' I run my hand over the bumpy wallpaper absent-mindedly, feeling the repeating pattern under my fingers.

'I'm so glad the house has you to take care of it,' Paula says. 'That's just what it needs. A fresh start. New life running through it.' She pats my pregnant belly and I squirm uncomfortably.

I don't even know if Ian will do up the house, if we'll end up living here. Worry knots my stomach.

'Let's keep going,' I say. 'It's getting dark.'

We look round the rest of the house quickly, taking in the box room on this floor and then ascending the stairs to the second floor where there are two further small, damp bedrooms, filled with more old furniture. One leads out on to a tiny balcony with rickety railings and a view over the coffee shop opposite.

There's nothing to fear here. Only the dark and the damp.

We go back downstairs and I walk Paula to the door.

'No rush to give the torch back,' she says, handing it over.

'Thank you. And thanks for looking round with me. I feel much better now.' It's true. Now I feel I can get through the night here.

We say goodbye and she hugs me unexpectedly, encircling my bump.

'You'll be fine,' she says, reassuringly.

I watch as she walks away, stepping carefully over the brambles. She's been so kind.

I feel a light pressure on the skin on the top of my foot exposed by my sandal and glance down. I gasp and draw my foot away as a furry tail slithers away into the undergrowth. Another rat scurries by me. Then another. And another.

I hurry down the path away from the building, only catching my breath when I'm beyond the hedge and under the comforting amber glow of the streetlight.

I stare back at the house, still feeling shaky. They say you're never more than six feet from a rat in London. They're inside the walls and under the floorboards. But I've never seen more than one at a time.

And these rats weren't creeping in to seek shelter for the night. They were running in the other direction. Out of the house. They must have been there the entire time we were looking round.

2

Another day. Another fight. Do all parents fight the way ours do? It's hard to tell. I've asked friends at school and they all say their parents argue. But I think they mean they just shout, maybe smash a wine glass. On television and in books that sometimes happens: parents argue and something gets broken. But I haven't read a book or seen a programme where parents attack each other like mine do. I haven't seen anything where the mum comes out bloody and can hardly stand up afterwards. I suppose it could be one of those things that just isn't on children's television, but goes on in every household. On TV, they never show people in the bath or on the toilet. It might be something like that.

I cover my ears as the sounds get louder. I hold my sister's hand tightly, and she squeezes mine.

The sounds change. Dad's voice has gone silent and Mum's is a desperate squeak. There's a dull thud. Like a person falling against the wall. Then the screams come. If they weren't coming from my own home, from downstairs, I'd think they were from a dying animal.

I turn to my sister in bed, my eyes wide, mirroring hers. 'What should we do?' I whisper.

'Do?'

'We need to help her.'

'Why?'

'She...'

'She doesn't help us, does she?'

'No, but—'

My sister strokes my hair. 'Why don't we read a story together?'

I stare at her, trapped in the moment, every part of me knowing I should try and help Mum, but not wanting to move from under the covers, not wanting to confront Dad.

But I have to help. I slip out of bed, go to the doorway.

'Are you stupid?' my sister asks.

'No,' I say, hesitating with my hand on the door handle.

'He'll kill you.'

Silent tears fall down my cheeks. Mum's screams have stopped altogether now. I squeeze my eyes shut tightly and pray that means she's feeling better and not something much, much worse.

CHAPTER FIVE

I blink awake, confused and disorientated, drenched in sweat. I shift my cumbersome pregnant body on the mattress and gag at the smell that rises from it.

The cavernous room expands around me and threatens to submerge me in its darkness. I'm used to waking up early to the bright daylight seeping through the gaps in my thin curtains and the sound of the shower and the thumping of boots down the stairs as Mike leaves for his early shift on the London Underground.

But here it's pitch-black. The thick curtains block the light out entirely and the room is completely still. I have no idea what time it is.

I hear creaking. Slow, careful footsteps on the stairs.

Every muscle in my body tenses. It takes me a moment to remember where I am. In the house that Ian bought. On a mattress on the floor. Alone.

But now there's someone else in the house with me.

My mind turns to the remains of the fire on the driveway. Has someone been living here?

I tell myself they won't come into this room. I could hide in here until they've gone. Message someone, and wait for them to come and get me. I know Amy would come if I needed her. I start to write a text.

The footsteps get closer and my heart beats fast.

I sit up awkwardly on the mattress, the stale smell rising from its core as its springs moan under my weight. I stop still. What if they heard me?

Then I look down in horror.

The mattress. Why was the mattress in here?

I jump up. No other room had a mattress. If someone's been living here, they've been living in this room. Are they coming back now? Are they coming in here?

My eyes scan the room for some sort of weapon to defend myself.

More footsteps. I'm running out of time.

I reach out for the torch but I instead of getting a grip on it, I only manage to swipe it and I hear it rolling across the floorboards until it hits the wall with a clunk.

They must have heard that. They'll know I'm in here.

I desperately run my hands over the bare wooden floorboards, searching for my phone.

My hand skims across dust and dirt until it eventually clenches around the phone and I almost cry with relief.

I start to dial.

9–9–

Then I hear the doorknob turning.

The light changes as the door opens and I scream.

In the dim glow of my phone, the figure in the doorway is only a shadow, a dark shape against the grey hallway. I jump to my feet, forgetting about the twins for a moment. The weight of my belly almost unbalances me.

Then there's a light shining right in my face. I blink rapidly, trying to see beyond the glare.

'Katie – are you alright?'

Ian. It's his voice that gives him away. I can't make out his features in the dark. For a moment my relief that he's not a squatter makes me forget my anger, but then it rises up inside me, full pressure.

He tries to wrap his arms around me and I push him away, adrenaline coursing through my veins.

'You frightened me,' I said.

'I came as soon as I got your messages.'

'I called you last night,' I say angrily. 'Over and over. I had to sleep here on my own.'

'I'm so sorry, Katie. I was busy with work. I don't always check my phone.'

'How could you let me move in here when it's like this?'

'I had no idea it was like this. I—'

'Didn't you even look round before I moved in? Or are you too much of a big-shot property developer to even check the house your girlfriend and babies are going to move into?'

Ian runs his hand through his hair, a sign that, for once, he's flustered. 'Of course I was going to look round. But when you decided to move in earlier than planned, I didn't have time. I only got the keys from the office the day I gave them to you.'

I glare at him, furious. 'Surely you saw it when you bought it?'

Ian shakes his head. 'One of the other guys from the office looked at it. He never said anything about the state it's in. There'll be hell to pay when I see him. I never thought it would be like this.'

'I can't stay here.'

'I know. You absolutely can't. I'm sorry. I'll pay for a hotel.'

My anger is subsiding, and I feel like I might burst into tears.

'But for how long, Ian?' I indicate my belly. It's not long until there'll be four of us to accommodate.

'As long as it takes to make the house suitable for you. I'll give the office a ring now and get them on it immediately. I need to look round to see everything that needs doing, but I'd hope we could be back in time for your baby shower.'

'You know, we don't have to live in a huge house like this. Don't you have any other properties we could move into instead?'

'All our other properties are being rented out, or are undergoing renovations.' He puts his arms round me. 'Let me put you up in a hotel. I owe you that to say sorry. You could come to my place, but my mother's still there and you don't need the hassle of moving in and then moving out again in a couple of weeks. I'll find a hotel close to your work and you can have an easy life for a while. Let yourself have your bed made and your breakfast cooked.'

'OK,' I say. I feel uncertain, grateful for his offer, but anxious about delaying moving into the house. But I don't have much choice. The house isn't ready. And Ian's right; living in a hotel will enable me to get some rest. I've started to feel exhausted working all day in the heat while heavily pregnant.

I feel like we're putting everything on pause: the house, our relationship and the start of our life together with the babies. I want to feel secure. I want to know that me and the girls will be safe. I need to know Ian loves me as much as I love him. I need to know I can trust him.

I'm relieved to leave the house and start my journey to work. It's a ninety-minute commute, but luckily I'm on a late shift today, so I have time. Despite a generous application of deodorant, I feel dirty and embarrassed as I wait for the Tube. I slept in all my clothes, terrified that the rats I'd seen yesterday might scurry over my bare skin in the middle of the night. This morning I couldn't bring myself to shower in the rotting bathroom, so I've brought a towel and some shower gel so I can use the cold shower at work.

On the train people crush together in one communal pool of sweat, the carriage dense with the smell. It's so oppressive that I don't know where I end and the person next to me begins. I fight through the crowd inside, pushing my pregnant belly in front of the people in the priority seats until I'm offered the chance to sit down.

This summer is a killer. As the heat has risen, so has the death toll across Europe. I'm not sure how much longer I can stand working in the coffee shop with my cumbersome belly and my twin babies acting as mini hot-water bottles inside me.

I'm relieved to leave the Underground tunnels and climb up outside into the fresh air. I pass the park, the yellow grass dead and dry from the unrelenting sunshine. I walk on the shady side of the street, grateful to the tall office blocks that loom over me, blocking the sun. I envy the people working in the buildings above me, air con units fanning cold air generously around their offices.

I'm in position behind the counter at the café just in time, after a quick cold shower in the back room. I feel refreshed as I serve the first coffees and listen to the complaints about the heat. In the first flush of summer customers came in glowing, talking of sunbathing in the garden and staycations. Now they complain they can't sleep at night and their plants have died. At least it's midday and I didn't have to work the morning rush today. Lunchtimes and afternoons are quieter, despite our offers of iced coffee to help weary office workers cool down.

'Must be difficult for you in this weather,' a customer says, looking at my bump. I nod. I've heard it so many times before.

I used to love my job, chatting to customers and watching the ebb and flow of the world around me. But lately I've been struggling. As I work, my pregnant belly pushes down on my pelvis, my hips ache and sweat pools uncomfortably between my breasts and my bump. I've begun to look forward to finishing, although I know I'll miss it when I do. I won't be able to come back to work after maternity leave. My salary wouldn't cover childcare for one baby, let alone two. And besides, it's far too long a commute from my new home.

'Cheer up,' says Martin, my twenty-year-old manager. 'A smile costs nothing.'

I respond with a tight smile, and Mick, the maintenance guy, catches my eye and winks. He's in his sixties and has been like a father to me, giving me advice on life and relationships like I imagine my own father would have done if he was still alive. We've been working here longer than everyone else and have built up a whole host of in-jokes.

Martin sees Mick's wink and looks as if he regrets what he's said. Since I announced my pregnancy, he constantly consults the employee handbook to check he's not breaking the myriad of rules for taking care of pregnant staff.

'Are you too hot?' he asks. 'Do you want to do the tables?'

I nod and grab the cloth from the side. It's cooler on the café floor, and Martin intends for it to be an easier task for me. But when I lean over to clean the tables, my bump gets in the way and the buttons of my long-sleeved uniform strain uncomfortably over my breasts. These days, even wiping down tables requires a level of exertion that makes me red-faced and sweaty.

I've only managed to clear a few tables before Martin calls me back over. I frown at him. There's only one customer in the queue, her back to me, her straight dark hair falling nearly over her shoulders. Surely he can serve her himself.

'Just a sec,' I say, squeezing through the entrance to the area behind the counter.

The woman turns towards me and my mouth drops open. It's my sister. We haven't seen each other for months.

'Melissa!'

'How are you, Katie? You're looking so much bigger.'

'I'm OK,' I say a bit too brightly, aware of the beads of sweat forming on my brow.

Melissa looks so well put together in her neatly ironed designer dress, but her eyes are watery. 'I'm sorry I haven't been in touch,' she says. 'Work's been crazy.'

Melissa's law firm is just a few streets away from the coffee shop, but she rarely sees daylight, bent over her computer late into the night most evenings.

Two businessmen come in the door and form a queue behind her. I'll need to serve her so I can get to the next customers. We have a target for customer waiting times.

'Do you want a coffee?' I ask her.

'I don't drink coffee.'

'Of course – I'm sorry.' I kick myself for being so insensitive. For the last ten years Melissa's cut out everything that she thinks might affect her chances of conceiving.

'I didn't come for a drink. I came to talk to you.' I hope she's about to tell me she's finally pregnant, but I can tell from her eyes that she hasn't come with happy news.

I glance at Martin, who's hovering behind us, listening to our conversation. He nods. 'Why don't you take your break now?' he suggests, moving forward to serve the men behind my sister.

Melissa leads me to a table in a corner, one I haven't cleaned yet, and I grab the cloth from the side to give it a quick wipe.

'It's good to see you,' she says softly, staring at my pregnant belly, more visible now I've moved from behind the counter.

'You too,' I reply, placing my hand over my stomach, once again feeling guilty that it's me who's pregnant, not Melissa.

'I'm sorry I didn't reply to the pictures you sent me of the scan.'

'It's OK,' I say. 'I understand.' I'd been hurt at the time, but I know how hard it is for her.

'The pictures sent me into a bit of a tailspin. I was just coming to terms with you having one baby. But when I found out you were having two… It's like you were getting a ready-made family. The one I'd always wanted, the one I'd worked so hard for.'

'I'm sorry,' I reply. 'I didn't think about how you'd feel.' But a part of me had known she'd be angry. She'd cut off her best friend completely when she'd had a baby. I'd hoped it would be different with me. That she could be happy for her own sister. I'd wanted everyone to see the photos. I didn't want to hide my twins away to avoid upsetting her.

'It's not your fault. I just need to accept that I'm destined to be an auntie, not a mother.' She starts to cry and I reach out and grip her hand.

'I don't know what to say.' I remember when we were little. She was the one who always comforted me.

'Mum said I should come and see you,' she says quietly. 'She didn't want us to fall out over this.'

I can't imagine Mum as a peacekeeper. I think of last night when she wouldn't let me stay at her house and frown.

'What's wrong?' she asks.

'I asked Mum if I could stay with her and she said no.'

'But why did you need somewhere to stay?' Melissa looks confused. 'I thought Ian had bought you a house.'

'It needs doing up.'

'Surely you can live there while it's being done up?'

'It's really run-down.'

She looks at me doubtfully. 'God, can't you just be grateful? You know you're living in a far bigger house than me or Mum could ever afford. And you've never even saved a penny towards it.'

'I've worked hard,' I say, defensively. But she's right. I've never made enough money to save any. I always imagined I'd rent forever. 'Look, I needed somewhere to stay and Mum wouldn't have me. Don't you think that's a bit mean of her?' I remember how scared I was sleeping in the house. How Paula helped me.

Melissa laughs. 'You can't expect Mum to bail you out. You're thirty-six, Katie. Not twelve.'

I sigh. Melissa never gets it. She always defends Mum. But then she's always been her favourite.

'So where are you going to stay then?'

'In a hotel.'

'A hotel? Seriously? Then you didn't need her help, did you?'

'I did last night. I had nowhere—'

'Last night? You called her last night?'

'Yeah. I would never have called her unless I really needed her help.'

'You know she was in hospital yesterday?'

I'm taken aback. 'In hospital?' I scratch at the scar on my arm, afraid of what I'm about to hear.

'She didn't tell you?'

'No,' I say, alarmed. 'Is something wrong?'

Melissa sighs. 'She's always trying to protect you. It's like you're still her baby.'

'Protect me?' I feel a rising panic. 'Melissa – what's wrong with her?'

'Nothing for you to worry about. She just had a scan. Her headaches have been getting worse.'

Mum's had headaches for as long as I can remember. When we were children she sometimes had to go to bed in the day for hours at a time. But she's never really mentioned them since I left home. I'd assumed they had stopped.

'What do you mean, they've been getting worse? Do they think there's something wrong with her?' My eyes widen as my mind rushes through a series of devastating reasons for the headaches getting worse.

'They don't know. She's had them for so long, it's unlikely to be anything serious, but they're worried enough to make her have a scan at the hospital.'

Why didn't they tell me? I feel faint, and I grip the edge of the table to calm myself. I don't always get on with Mum, but since my father died there's only been the three of us. I couldn't bear it if something awful happened to her too.

CHAPTER SIX

Later in the afternoon, I receive a message from Ian to say that the rest of my things have arrived in the van and that work has already started on the house. He's booked me into a hotel in the city centre, just round the corner from the coffee shop.

I walk to the hotel, the weight of my belly slowing me down. The huge glass offices that line the street reflect the sun's rays around me, trapping the heat. I long to sink into a cool bath and wash the grime and sweat of the day off me. I hope the weather cools soon. It's so hot and humid that I've begun to wish for rain, a huge storm to clear the air.

All through my shift I've been thinking about what Melissa said. I can't believe no one told me Mum was in hospital. What if the headaches are a sign of something serious? I'm desperate to speak to her to check she's OK. I wanted to call her from work, but we were run off our feet and I couldn't take another break.

When I arrive at the hotel, I ascend the carpeted steps and the doorman holds the door open for me. I walk across the expansive foyer to the check-in desk. The receptionist stares at my slightly-too-small barista uniform and raises her eyebrows, before checking my reservation and handing over the key.

When I get to the room I collapse onto the freshly laundered sheets on the bed and breathe in the clean smell gratefully. I pull my phone from my handbag, take a deep breath and call Mum.

She picks up on the second ring.

'Katie.'

'Hi, Mum.'

'You survived the night in your new house, then?' She laughs and I feel a twinge of irritation, despite everything.

'Yes, it was fine.'

'There you go. I told you it wouldn't be so bad.'

I take another deep breath.

'Mum – Melissa said you'd been in hospital.'

'Oh.' She pauses. 'Just for a check-up.'

'About your headaches?'

'Yes. What exactly did Melissa say?'

'She said you were in hospital, having a scan.' I can hear the panic in my voice.

'Yes, that's right. It was just routine. Nothing to worry about. You need to relax. Stress is bad for the babies. Look, I've got to go. We'll catch up soon, won't we? I want to hear all about the new house.'

'Mum—'

'Bye, darling.'

I stare at my phone. She's hung up.

After a week at the hotel I start to get restless. The lie-ins, cooked breakfasts and the short walk to work have helped me recuperate, but I still feel like I'm in limbo, stuck between my new life and my old life. I can feel my babies kicking inside me impatiently and I want to be ready for their arrival. There's so much to do and so much to buy. A double pram. Cots. Clothes. Blankets. Toys. I can hear the clock ticking whenever I even start to think about it.

Ian gives me regular updates on the house renovations. His team have fitted a top-of-the-range kitchen, repainted the bedroom and living room and replumbed the downstairs toilet. He tells me every tiny detail: the integrated wine fridge in the kitchen, the complexities of Victorian plumbing and the precise shades of paint for the bedroom. But I'm still worried it won't be finished in time for the babies' arrival.

One day after work I take the Tube and the bus over to the house.

As I turn into the street I feel a sense of foreboding, the huge houses casting the street in shadow. I remember how much of an outsider this road made me feel, even before I saw the house.

I berate myself. This is a lovely street, a street lots of people would work their whole lives to be able to afford to live on. So why don't I feel I could be happy here?

I brace myself as I approach the house. Our house. The hedge is still tall and overgrown and I feel a rising sense of panic. I reach the driveway and the disappointment hits me like a punch. It looks exactly the same: the rusty washing machine still sits in the middle of the driveway, the garden is still overgrown and the living room windows are still boarded up. Is it possible that Ian's just been working on the inside and hasn't thought to address the outside?

I hear a noise behind me in the undergrowth and I jump. I catch sight of green eyes staring up at me.

Just a cat. It disappears again. But I can't get rid of the image in my head of the rats running from the house. I shiver.

I take out my key and open the front door, a sense of dread rising up in me.

The hallway is as dark as ever despite the daylight outside and I shine the torch I borrowed from Paula into the house.

Just as I expected. The post has been cleared out of the hallway, but apart from that it looks exactly the same. My heart sinks.

I reach for the light switch, knowing nothing will happen when I press it. But to my surprise, light floods the hallway from the bare bulb on the landing. Ian has at least managed to turn on the electricity.

I hesitate, not sure if I should go in any further.

'Hello?' I call out.

I worry that Ian might be inside, that I'll have to explain I'm checking up on him.

I hear men's voices in the kitchen, but they don't sound like Ian. I walk through to see a brand-new kitchen, freshly fitted, just like he said. Two workmen stand in the middle of it, drinking tea. We exchange pleasantries and then I continue my journey round the house. I start to feel guilty as I notice all the work that's been done in just a week. Behind the boarded-up windows, the living room has been painted. The downstairs bathroom has been replumbed. I should never have doubted Ian.

Outside, a driver is unloading boxes from his van. I expect they're for the house. I try to walk discreetly by, but the man calls out.

'Do you live at number fourteen, miss?'

'Yes,' I say. 'But I'm off out now.'

'Can you just sign for these?'

I look down at the packages and see a line drawing of a cot on the cardboard. There are two identical boxes. Ian must have ordered them to surprise me. I feel a ripple of excitement and put my hand to my belly. It's all starting to feel more real.

'Could you take them inside?' I ask, keen to get away in case Ian returns and sees me here. 'There are men inside who'll sign for it.'

'Do you need some help, Katie?'

I look up, surprised. It's Paula.

'No, no. I'm fine,' I say. 'Thanks, though.'

'I'll take these inside, then,' the man says, and sets off down the driveway.

'I was just at the coffee shop and I saw the van arrive. I thought you might need help with carrying in the packages.'

'Thanks,' I say. 'But it's OK. I was just leaving.'

'It looks like you're making quick work of doing up the house.'

'Yes.' I smile at her, remembering how helpful she was when I first came to the house a week ago. 'Thanks for lending me the torch.'

'No problem.'

I rack my brains to think where I left it. I just had it in the house. 'I'm not quite sure where it is…' I say, embarrassed. 'Do you need it now?' I don't want to go back inside and look for it. Ian could be back any time.

'Just give it back to me when you're sorted. I'm always at the coffee shop anyway, when I'm between clients.'

I'd assumed she was retired. 'What do you do?' I ask, curious.

'I'm a doula. I look after pregnant women before, during and after the birth. I've just finished a longer-term role with a local lady. I spent a few months helping her look after her new baby. Her husband worked in the city and was never there, so she needed my support.'

'Oh,' I say. I touch my own belly, feeling my twins kick. I remember her handling my stomach in the house. That must have been why. It's her job.

'I just love babies,' Paula continues. 'Always have done. But don't let me hold you up. I only came over to see if you needed any help.'

'Thanks again,' I say.

Paula smiles at me. 'Any time you need help with anything, just give me a call.' She pulls a card out of her wallet. 'My details are on here. If you have any questions about birth, or anything at all, I'm happy to help.'

I take the card and make my excuses. I'm not sure I'll need the services of a doula, and there's no way I'd be able to afford to pay for it myself. I walk with Paula to the coffee shop across the road and we part with polite smiles. The sky has clouded over for the first time in weeks, and I feel a rush of relief at the thought of a break from the relentless heat.

I'm about to hurry away to get to the station before the rain, but something makes me stop and turn back round towards the coffee shop. Paula gives me a little wave from the table by the window and I lift my hand in return. I'm about to walk off when I stop stock-still, staring back towards the café.

There's a well-dressed blonde woman in her late fifties with dark glasses standing on the street outside the coffee shop, fanning herself with her wide-brimmed sunhat. She looks like she might be a neighbour, but she doesn't seem to be going anywhere. Instead she's standing by the blackboard outside the café, completely still. But she's not looking at the board. Her face is tilted upwards towards our house, her hand up across her forehead, shielding her skin from the hot sun.

Suddenly she turns in my direction. I can't see her eyes behind her sunglasses, but I can feel them boring into me. I meet her gaze. She looks back without moving a muscle and it gets so intense that I have to turn away. As I move off down the street I can still feel her eyes burning into my back, and I have a sudden desire to break into a run.

3

Dad's home from work. He's in the kitchen, waiting impatiently for his dinner. I stand in the doorway watching, too afraid to move. I've come down to get a book my teacher gave me to read at home. But it's on the other side of the kitchen, out of reach.

I know he's angry. He seems taller than usual, a looming shadow over Mum. She's cooking, stirring some kind of casserole. The wooden spoon bangs into the sides of the pot over and over again as if Mum is angry too.

He's right up behind her. She knows it. He knows it. And I know it.

I see his arms reach out towards her. I think he's going to hit her or grab her, but instead they wrap around her waist. She jumps.

He embraces her and for a moment they sway together. Then she lets go of the spoon, turns her head slightly and he kisses her.

I watch, shocked. I've never seen any sign of this before between my parents. But it looks like the love we see in films. Kissing. Cuddling. Could it be that they truly love each other?

I don't know how to feel. A part of me feels like finally things are right, that they are acting the way they're supposed to. I'm relieved. They must really be in love, not just pretending. But another part of me feels icky. As if I've suddenly become aware of some horrible truth. That this is what real love looks like. Not presents and flowers and chocolates. Not frogs kissing princesses and turning into princes. If my parents are truly in love, then the fights and the bruises on Mum's pale skin are real love. The anger and the pain are real love.

I'm flooded with disappointment. I want to go back to my room, to run away from my confused thoughts. But I don't. Instead, I just watch.

I watch as he turns her around, I watch as their bodies hug each other tight, see her wince as his arms squeeze against her injuries. Then he starts to rip off her clothes, his hands pushing up her skirt, pulling down her tights. It's all so fast, and she lets out a squeal of pain as he shoves her up against the wall.

Then he's pushing against her, her head banging against the wall. She's out of breath, her face red, his redder. He's squashing her. He's killing her.

'No!' I scream, running out of the doorway. 'Don't hurt her. No!'

'It's OK,' Mum says, her eyes wild, looking from me to him and then back again.

He continues, hurting her, and I reach out and grab the back of his shirt. 'Get off her!'

'Go away,' she screams at me. 'Just go away!'

Tears slide down my cheeks.

My father lets out a low grunt and then pulls away from her.

He pulls up his trousers, and turns to me.

'Little brat!' he screams. 'You ruin everything.'

I run as fast as I can. As I dart through the door something cold strikes the back of my head and knocks me to the floor.

CHAPTER SEVEN

When Ian and I return to the house together a week later the driveway has been cleared of rubbish, the skip is overflowing, the garden has been cut back and the front door and garage have been painted cornflower blue. The house is transformed, now indistinguishable from the others on the street. I can't stop smiling, and my heart's full with hope for our future together. Suddenly it feels like a happy life with Ian and the twins is within my grasp.

Ian insists on carrying me over the threshold, manoeuvring sideways through the door to accommodate my pregnant belly. Inside, the hallway is freshly painted, with a large pendant light hanging down from the ceiling. In the living room, the boards have been removed from the huge bay windows and light floods through the gaps in the venetian blinds, highlighting the soft new cream-coloured carpet and the restored Victorian fireplace.

'We still need to do the dining room,' Ian says, as I peer in. 'I was waiting to ask you what you wanted to use it for. I thought maybe it could be a children's playroom.'

I smile at the image, imagining our twins aged four or five, playing with their toys. It's hard to believe that that will be my life, living in this huge house with Ian and our two girls. The image is picture-postcard perfect. Yet despite everything, I feel uneasy. It's as if I've been picked up and transported into someone else's life.

I swallow the feelings down. Once I settle in, I'll be fine. Everything's just been so rushed, it's no wonder it seems like a big adjustment.

When I see the old piano, I smile. I'm so glad it's still here. I have a sudden urge to sit down and play my worries away. But Ian wants to continue the tour, and I exclaim at the new kitchen, not willing to admit that I've already seen it. Upstairs the bathroom has been done up and a new shower fitted. Our bedroom is carpeted and painted, with new curtains and the two tiny cribs assembled next to the bed. Ian's put a bed in the second double, but otherwise the rest of the upstairs is untouched.

'I thought you'd want to choose the paint colours for the nursery,' he says. 'And anyway, the babies will be in with us for the first six months, so we'll have plenty of time to do up the rest of the bedrooms.'

'It's perfect, Ian,' I say. 'Thank you.' I feel a rush of emotion and I'm not sure if it's love or relief. I lean in towards him, wrap my arms around him and kiss him full on the lips.

Two days later I'm getting ready for my baby shower and I'm filled with nerves. Two weeks ago, I was dreading this day, embarrassed by the derelict house. But now I have the opposite concern: that perhaps the house is too ostentatious, that my friends will think I've had a personality transplant and become completely materialistic.

In the kitchen, I take the new champagne flutes Ian has bought out of the packaging. Ian's stocked up our fridge with alcohol and insisted on buying an expensive pink cake from the local baker's. I'll be drinking the sparkling elderflower juice that Amy's bringing.

I look in the cupboards and realise we don't have any napkins or kitchen roll.

'Don't worry,' Ian says. 'There's a supermarket up the road. I'll get some. I'll be back in fifteen minutes.'

When Ian returns, a bag of napkins tucked under his arm, I've put my make-up on and I'm pacing back and forth in the hallway.

'Katie, stop worrying.' Ian puts his hand on my shoulder to stop me pacing, then drops his arm round me, stroking my hair with his other hand as he looks straight into my eyes. 'I'll look after everyone. I'll serve the food and drink and direct people to the toilet. You just sit in the living room and relax.'

'OK.' I smile.

'And don't worry about what anyone thinks. This baby shower is about you and the twins. It's about you carrying two babies around all day, every day for nine months. It's about celebrating motherhood.' He tucks my hair behind my ear. 'Don't let anyone ruin it for you.'

The doorbell rings and I find Amy standing outside, a look of wonder on her face. She's come early to help me set up.

'Wow, this place is even bigger than it looked in the pictures.'

'I know,' I reply, almost apologetically.

'Nice chandelier,' she says, looking up at the extravagant light fitting on the upstairs landing.

'Thanks.'

She looks at me and grins. 'And why exactly did you phone me and say you wanted to come back and live in the flat? This place is amazing.'

'It wasn't like this before. It was completely derelict.'

'Derelict? Sure. Admit it – you just wanted to come back because you missed me.' She wraps me in a tight hug.

'Well, I have missed you,' I reply.

'You don't need to make excuses to come back and see me. You can come over any time.'

I smile, but I don't think Amy has any inkling how hard it would be to make the trip across London with newborn twins. I'm not sure I do either. It was only when I started looking at double buggies the other day that it dawned on me just how difficult it will be to get around. There's no way I could carry one down the steps to the Tube on my own.

'Come inside.' I give her a quick tour of the house, watching her eyes widen in amazement with each new feature.

'So Ian turned out to be a catch after all?' Amy says loudly.

'Shhh… He's just downstairs.'

She laughs.

I nod and change the subject. 'There're still a few bits we need to do for the baby shower before everyone arrives.'

We go downstairs and Ian presents her with a glass of champagne, which she carries outside to the front of the house and continues to hold as she stands on a chair to pin up a banner. I feel the hot sun on my face as I watch her wobbling, leaning into the hedge as she ties the banner with one hand and spills her drink with the other.

'Isn't that a bit much?' I say, looking doubtfully at the huge letters which announce my baby shower. 'I mean, it's not like it's an open event. The people I've invited know the address.'

'Don't be such a killjoy. It's your baby shower. You're only going to get one, unless you're planning on having more kids after your twins?' She looks down at me from the chair, eyebrows raised, champagne glass held askew.

'No,' I say quickly.

'Well, the house is big enough for loads of children. You could run a nursery here.'

I laugh. 'Don't get carried away.'

We go back inside to discover that Ian has already put the food out. Amy grabs a handful of crisps and then pulls a collection of pink balloons and more banners out of her bag. Half an hour later, the living room is covered in decorations.

Amy looks at my stomach. 'Not long to go now,' she says. 'How do you feel about the birth?'

'Terrified.' Lately my anxiety has been building. I've heard all sorts of horror stories from friends with children.

'Yeah, I'm not surprised. I'd be terrified too. I don't know why anyone wouldn't be. Pushing something that size out of you.'

'OK,' I say, covering my ears. 'Enough. It's going to happen, and if it gets too much I'll just have to take the drugs.'

'Oh, I'm so sorry, I didn't mean to worry you. You can deal with pain, anyway. I remember when you broke your wrist and still went into work.'

'Yeah, that was stupid of me, wasn't it?'

The doorbell interrupts our conversation and I open it to see Mum, a bemused look on her face. Melissa and her husband Graham are just behind her.

'What on earth were you talking about, Katie, when you said you wanted to come and live with me?' Mum says.

Amy grins at her. 'You got the sob story too, did you? Poor Katie in her big house in the buggy belt…'

Mum and Amy both laugh.

'Come on, Katie,' Amy says, seeing my frown. 'I was only joking.'

'Are you OK?' I ask my mother, as she slips off her shoes. 'How are your headaches?'

'I told you, I'm fine. It was just a check-up.' My mother puts her hand on the radiator to steady herself and for a moment she looks fragile. My heart lurches. She'd had dizzy spells when we were younger, as well as the headaches. I wonder if it's all coming back.

'Hi, Katie.' My sister leans forward to kiss me on each cheek. Graham, her husband, does the same and out of the corner of my eye I see Mum disappear into the house. Melissa leans on Graham for support as she carefully takes off her heels.

'You look glowing,' she says, smiling.

I smile back at her. I'm so happy she's here. I know how difficult it is for her. The celebration must remind her of the baby she's wanted for so long. She didn't even attend her best friend's baby shower.

'I'm so glad to see you,' I say.

Inside the house, Ian presents Mum with a glass of champagne, my sister with a glass of sparkling elderflower and Graham with a beer. Ian's always been good at remembering the little things: how Mum takes her tea, my sister's preference for a non-alcoholic drink, my favourite cocktail at the bar just down the road from work.

After Mum, Melissa and Graham have come inside, the doorbell doesn't stop ringing and soon a crowd of us are assembled in the living room. There are people from all different times in my life: some of the girls from work, a couple of friends from music college and a few more I've known since school.

Amy introduces some games and soon everyone is laughing as they try to put nappies on a doll blindfolded. I'm opening the presents when the doorbell rings again. I look up in surprise. I'm not expecting anyone else.

I open the door and see Paula.

'Hi,' I say.

'Hi. I'm sorry to bother you. I just wondered if you had my torch? I wouldn't ask, except I've got a bit of DIY to do today.'

'I'm so sorry. I think I've misplaced it.' I look helplessly back into the house as whoops of laughter come from the living room. I've got no idea how long it would take me to find the torch, and I can't really leave my own shower to look for it.

'We're just having my baby shower,' I continue apologetically, although she can't have missed the banner outside. 'Can I give it back to you another time?'

Amy wanders out from the living room. 'Hi,' she says to Paula. 'Are you coming in?'

It seems rude not to invite her in now. 'Why don't you join us? We've got champagne,' I say. 'And we could use your expertise.'

I wonder for a second if I've misspoken. Perhaps the last place a doula would want to be is at a baby shower. Too much like her job.

But she smiles brightly. 'I'd love to join you,' she says, stepping inside.

I offer her a glass of champagne which she readily accepts, and introduce her to Ian, who's pouring more drinks in the kitchen.

'You've done so much work on the house,' Paula says. 'It's like a completely different place.'

I hear a hint of accusation in her voice which Ian clearly doesn't catch. 'Yes,' he replies. 'It needed gutting so we could start again.'

She turns to Ian. 'It's amazing. You've really ripped out its heart.'

'This kitchen is all new,' Ian states proudly. 'We've tried to make the most of a small space.'

'We've kept the original features,' I say, carefully. 'The Victorian tiles, the fireplaces…'

'Oh, I'm sure you have. That's what they go on about on property programmes, isn't it? Original features?'

'It is,' I say, and laugh.

'So how do you know Katie?' Ian asks Paula.

'Actually we met when I moved here. Paula helped me out with a torch before you fixed up the house. She came round to get it back.'

'In which case, I owe you a debt of gratitude, Paula. Thanks for helping the mother of my children in her hour of need.'

'No problem,' Paula says.

We walk back through to the living room, and I introduce everyone to Paula.

'Paula's a doula,' I say brightly.

'That will come in handy,' Amy laughs. 'Imagine if you went into labour today. At your own baby shower. You'd have an expert on hand to help.'

I laugh too. 'I don't think that's going to happen.'

Amy smiles and then goes to the kitchen to get more champagne. She walks round the room and tops up any half-empty glasses.

'What's a doula when it's at home?' Mum asks Paula.

'I help pregnant women with labour and often afterwards too, helping their recovery.'

'So you're a midwife?'

'No, not a midwife. I thought about that but decided against it. Midwives are so overstretched these days, they can't give women the care they deserve. I can offer much more of my time and care, to help a mother have the birth she wants.'

'We didn't have doulas in my day,' Mum says.

'I expect you didn't need to,' Melissa replies reasonably. 'There was a lot more money in maternity care back then. You'd have had more attention.'

'You could do with a doula, Katie,' Ian says, turning to me.

'Oh, I don't know,' I say quickly.

Ian turns to Paula. 'Katie's a bit anxious about giving birth to twins.' I flush, embarrassed. Giving birth is something women all over the world do every day. I shouldn't feel afraid, but I do.

'I could teach you some breathing exercises,' Paula says kindly.

'Breathing exercises!' Mum snorts with laughter. 'I don't think breathing exercises are going to cut it when it comes to the pain of birth.'

'A lot of the women I've helped have managed their births without any pain relief by using the correct breathing. It's all about having the right frame of mind. The problem is that these days most women are scared to give birth. They think they can't do it without medical help. But of course they can. Women have been giving birth for generations.'

'Didn't a lot of women used to die in childbirth?' Mum says, caustically.

I scratch my arm anxiously and my sister reaches out to give me a comforting pat on the back. 'Ignore her,' she whispers.

Paula gives Mum a withering look. 'It's important to listen to what the woman wants,' she says carefully. 'And that's my job. To help women have natural, joyful births.'

'Well, why don't you try out Paula's breathing exercises, Katie?' Ian suggests. 'You might as well give it a go. It might make you feel more prepared.' He turns to Paula. 'How much does it cost?'

Paula senses my reluctance.

'I can give you a free trial if you like. Just half an hour. I live round here, so it will be no trouble at all.'

'You can't say no to a free trial,' Amy says. 'After all, you're not doing NCT classes.'

I nod. Perhaps she's right. I haven't signed up for any classes because by the time I knew where I'd be living, all the local ones had been booked up.

I smile at Paula. 'Thanks.'

Ian grins. 'And if that works out, then you can always help with the birth as well.'

'Let's see how it goes,' I say quickly.

Paula looks at my belly. 'You haven't got too long. Believe me, the last few weeks whizz by. You should start thinking about birth partners, if you haven't already.'

'Well, I'll be there,' Ian says. 'I wouldn't miss the birth of my twins for the world.' He rubs my belly affectionately, but I can't help feeling a nagging worry. He's difficult to get hold of when he's at work; there's no guarantee he'll get there in time.

We go back into the living room and open the presents. I'm humbled by everyone's generosity and I start to feel emotional. The tiny babygrows and little rattles make everything seem suddenly real. I imagine holding my babies in my arms.

Amy and Paula come with me into the kitchen to get the cake, and Amy takes the opportunity to top up her champagne. 'You know,' she says, slurring her words slightly, 'I could be your birth partner, if you're not sure about Ian.'

She must have seen my doubtful look when Ian said he'd be at the birth. But Amy lives miles away, and there's no guarantee she'd get there in time either.

'I'm sure Ian will be there,' I reply hesitantly.

'It might be a good idea to have someone else on call just in case you go into labour and Ian's not around,' Paula says.

'Yes,' Amy smiles. 'And I'd be perfect.'

I nod. 'Of course you would,' I say, despite my concerns. 'I'd love it if you'd be my reserve birth partner.'

Amy laughs. 'When you put it like that, how can I refuse?'

After we've devoured most of the cake, people start to drift off home, until only my family and Paula and Amy remain. They tell me to relax, and that they'll clear up. I sink into the sofa and try to find a comfortable position that accommodates my pregnant belly.

Ian starts taking down the banners in the living room and I look at him happily. 'That went really well,' I say.

'I can't believe we'll be meeting our babies soon,' he replies, coming over to the sofa and stroking my bump.

'I know.' We stare into each other's eyes, connected now and forever through the babies growing inside me.

I feel a baby kick Ian's hand and we both smile.

'You'll be a great mother,' he says.

My sister comes in. 'He's right, you know, Katie. The babies are lucky to have you.'

'Thanks,' I reply gratefully, knowing how difficult it must have been for her to say that.

'I brought you a present,' she says. 'But I didn't want to give it to you in front of everyone. I thought I might cry.' She looks tearful now as she presents the gift, wrapped in pink tissue paper. I open it carefully.

Inside is a tiny red and blue striped hat. 'I knitted it myself,' she says. 'I was keeping it for our first baby. But I'd like you to have it.'

I feel tears well up in my eyes. I ease myself off the sofa to hug her and we stand still for a moment in the embrace. Perhaps there's a chance that having the twins will bring us closer together rather than pushing us further apart.

But our hug is interrupted by a scream. Then a loud crash. We pull apart, shocked. I run into the hallway, Melissa behind me.

We're just in time to see Amy tumbling down the stairs. Her leg bends at an unnatural angle as her body lands on top of it and I hear it crunch into the floor. Then her head bounces off the tiles with a sickening crack.

CHAPTER EIGHT

'Amy!' I cry out, running over.

Ian is already next to her, bending over to check her breathing.

'Be careful,' Paula says. 'She has a head injury.'

I sit down on the floor beside her and stroke her hair. 'Amy?'

She lets out a tiny groan and moves her left arm ever so slightly.

'Amy, can you hear me?'

'Katie?' Her voice is a whisper.

'We need to get her to the hospital,' Ian says.

'Don't worry,' I say softly to Amy. 'You're going to be fine.'

She starts to sit up unsteadily. 'Ow,' she cries out.

'Stay where you are for a moment,' Ian says.

'What happened?' Amy mumbles.

'She's slurring her speech,' Paula says. 'That can be really serious.'

'It's the drink,' Ian replies. 'She's just drunk.'

I nod, partially reassured. She'd been slurring before she fell.

Amy tries to stand and Ian quickly puts his arm underneath her to catch her as her legs give way and she collapses back down to the floor.

'What happened?' she asks again.

'You fell down the stairs.'

'I tripped,' she replies.

'Oh my god,' Paula says. 'There was stuff at the top of the stairs. A box of screwdrivers. I nearly tripped on them myself. I should have moved them…'

'It's not your fault,' I say.

'Let's just get Amy to the hospital,' Ian says quickly.

'I'll drive,' I offer. 'I haven't been drinking.'

I turn to Paula, Mum and Melissa. 'Can you let yourselves out?' I ask hurriedly.

'No problem,' Melissa replies. 'You get to the hospital.'

By the time we reach the hospital Amy is more coherent. After a couple of hours in A&E, it's confirmed that Amy has broken her leg. She'll be stuck working from home for the next few weeks, with her leg in a cast. Ian pays for her to get a taxi home, and then I drive us back.

Back at the house, Paula's left me a note reminding me of her phone number and thanking me for the hospitality. *Give me a ring to book in those breathing exercises*, the message says, and a few days later, she comes to the house.

'Not long to go now,' she says when she arrives.

'Yes,' I say. 'Our lives are about to be turned upside down.' I laugh, but inside I'm nervous about how I'll cope.

'They do say two at the same time can be difficult. You only have one pair of hands.'

'I hope I can handle it.'

'Of course you can. You'll just need some help. I'm sure Ian will step up.'

'I hope so.' I'd thought his work would calm down as it got nearer to our babies' births, but it hasn't. He's distracted by it and it's making him careless. Like the way he left the screwdrivers at the top of the stairs, causing Amy's fall.

'So what exactly does a doula do?' I ask, as I lead her into the living room.

'Well, usually I help the mother prepare for the birth, teaching breathing exercises, explaining clearly what will happen. The antenatal appointments with your midwife should really cover all of this, but so often they don't.'

I nod as I think of my own antenatal appointments. I've been in and out in ten minutes each time.

'And then during the labour itself, I act as an advocate for the woman, making sure her wishes are respected, and there are no unnecessary interventions,' Paula continues.

'The women are lucky to have you,' I say, honestly.

'Are you giving birth at the hospital down by the station?' Paula asks.

'Yes,' I reply.

I notice Paula's furrowed brow. 'What's wrong?' I ask, concerned. 'Isn't it a good hospital?'

'I've had mixed experiences there,' Paula says. 'It depends which staff you get on the day.'

I place a protective hand over my belly.

'Should I change hospital?' I ask. There's still time.

'No, no. In all honesty, you never know who you're going to get on the day in any hospital. The best thing to do is to be fully prepared, write a birth plan and have someone by your side who you trust to stick up for you.'

'OK,' I say, a knot of anxiety growing in my stomach. I'm not sure I trust Ian to arrive in time, and Amy's not an option anymore either, since she had her accident. 'I'll have to work that out then.'

'Can Amy still make it?'

'No, she's broken her leg. She won't be able to dash across London.'

'Gosh, poor thing. Is there anyone else?'

I sigh. 'I'd ask my mother, but I think she'd just stress me out. She has such strong opinions, and because she's a nurse she thinks she's always right.'

'Take some time to think about who you might want to have with you. I can help you with a birth plan. Have you thought about it at all?'

'I want to try and do it naturally,' I say, 'but if it gets too much then I'll have pain relief.'

Paula laughs lightly. 'There's your problem right there,' she says. 'You're already thinking of it as pain. And pain is a negative thing. The trick is to change your thinking. Don't think of it as pain, think of it as an enormous natural energy, pushing your baby out of your body. Every contraction takes you one step closer to your babies being born. And that's what you want, isn't it?'

'Yeah,' I say, uncertainly. 'But I've heard the pain can be horrendous.'

'You can breathe through any pain. Honestly, I've helped so many women breathe through the contractions. No one regrets having a natural birth. But often people regret having a medicalised one.'

I nod. She's probably right. I'm just nervous.

Paula takes my hand in hers. 'You don't need to worry. Soon you'll meet your babies. And I can already tell you're going to be a great mother.'

4

At school, a policeman comes in to give an assembly about how we can keep ourselves safe. He says there are bad people in the world. They're called strangers. And they might offer you sweets or ask if you want to see a puppy in the back of a van. Whatever you do you mustn't go with them. They might hurt you. You can't even talk to them, or you'll be in huge trouble.

We listen intently to the policeman's talk, our legs identically crossed on the dark tiles of the school hall. We understand that hurting people is wrong. We understand that strangers hurt people. But we want to know about other people that hurt us. We wait hopefully for the answers we need, for the policeman to tell us what to do when people who are supposed to love you hurt you. We don't need to go off with a stranger to be hit round the head or clipped round the ear. We only have to go home.

But he never mentions fathers. Even if he did, we wouldn't say anything. If our teacher asked us if anyone hurt us, my sister and I would never tell her. Because she'd never believe us. She likes Mum and chats happily to her as if she knows her. She'd never think that she'd let my dad beat her up. That she'd let him beat us up too.

People are always complimenting Mum on her hair, long and flowing and full of volume, like a shampoo advert. But there's a reason she always wears her hair down. It's to cover the colours on the back of her neck; the reds and the browns and the purples. My sister and I can wear our hair any way we like. Because when he hits us, he makes sure it's over the head. Our dark hair covers the injuries better than any plaster.

CHAPTER NINE

Melissa comes to see me at the coffee shop a few days later, just after 5 p.m., as my shift is finishing. For some people that would be the end of the working day, but not for my sister. This is her 'late lunch', and the first time she's been able to take a break all day. She's going back to the office straight after.

'Did you want a drink?' I say, as I take off my apron.

'No, let's get out of here. I need to grab a sandwich anyway.'

'They make sandwiches here.'

She laughs. 'Yeah, I've tried one before. No thanks.'

'Alright then.' I shout out goodbye to Martin and the others, and we leave the café and go to an artisan bakery a few doors down.

I watch my sister nibble at her houmous and carrot wrap. 'What's going on?' I ask. There must be something up for her to visit me. Then I feel a stab of worry. 'Is it Mum?'

'No, it's not Mum. I just wanted to check you were alright,' she says.

'Huh? What do you mean?'

'It must be a big change for you. The house. The twins. You didn't quite seem yourself at the baby shower.'

I raise my eyebrows, feeling suddenly exposed. 'I'm fine.'

'OK. It's just that you always seemed happy in the flatshare. At the baby shower you seemed a bit subdued.'

'But I'm happy now,' I insist. 'How could I not be?' I think of how beautiful our house is, but I can't help feeling empty.

'You just don't seem like you anymore. You're living the kind of life I aspired to, but I never thought it was what you wanted.'

I nod. She'd be right at home on my street.

'I'm fine,' I say. 'I know I'm lucky.'

'You can turn to me whenever you need to,' Melissa says. 'We need to look out for each other. We're sisters.'

Her comment reminds me of our childhood. I don't have many memories from when I was little, but I remember how close we used to be. When did that change? When we were teenagers? Or before, when our father died? I remember how, after he passed away, she spent all her time with Mum and it felt like I was always on the outside.

'Thanks,' I say. 'That's kind of you.'

She takes a sip of her smoothie. 'I'd love us to be close again.'

'Me too,' I say, earnestly. I can't remember the last time we had a conversation as frank as this one.

'Have you decided on names?' she asks.

'Yes,' I say, smiling. 'Frances and Alice.' I'm excited to finally tell her.

'Frances?' Her face pales.

'Yes, after our father.' I grin. I wish my father was still around to meet the twins and this seems like the perfect way to remember him. I'm sure my sister will agree.

But Melissa pushes her chair back rapidly. She knocks the table and her glass wobbles, bright green smoothie spilling out onto the glass tabletop. She runs out, leaving her unfinished sandwich behind.

I stare after my sister, shocked. I've no idea why the babies' names have upset her. I scratch at the scar on my arm and dash outside onto the street. It's started to rain, and she's already disappeared amid the jumble of umbrellas.

Ten minutes later I'm on the Tube home, still confused by Melissa's reaction. The carriage's like a sauna, moisture rising from discarded raincoats and wet umbrellas. When I get off and emerge into the air, the queue for the bus home snakes down the street. There are no seats in the shelter and I decide to walk, avoiding a bus that will almost certainly be late and overcrowded. My flimsy umbrella provides little defence against the rain, and soon my wet uniform clings to my skin and starts to itch. My bump aches.

When I get back to the house, Ian opens the door before I've turned my key in the lock.

'Hello,' I say, surprised at his eagerness to see me.

'Hi. You're looking lovely.'

I frown. I look anything but lovely. My belly is huge, I'm wet from the rain, and at the same time I'm hot and sweaty.

'I don't feel it,' I say.

He wraps his arms around me.

'Honestly, you look beautiful.'

I kick off my sensible slip-on shoes, bought when my belly grew so big I could no longer bend over to do up my trainers.

Ian takes my head in his hands and wipes a raindrop from my cheek, then runs his hands through my hair.

'You know how much I love you, don't you?'

His lips meet mine and he kisses me passionately, almost desperately. The sex that follows is rushed, both of us suddenly needy for the chemistry we've lost as my body's grown bigger and energy levels have dropped. We remain in the living room, shedding our clothes quickly on the sofa, laughing as we shift positions until we find a way to fit together again.

Sex was the foundation of the beginning of our relationship; quickies in expensive hotels on our lunch breaks and dirty weekends away in Europe. It's a relief to find we're still as attracted to each other as we ever were.

We pull apart, sweaty and satisfied. He smiles at me, and then kisses me on the lips.

'I love you, Katie.'

'I love you too,' I say, letting myself forget my anxieties about our future together just for a moment.

'I'm afraid I'm not going to be able to stay for dinner tonight,' Ian says as he pulls on his trousers. 'I've got to work.'

'Oh,' I say, disappointed. I just want to relax in the warmth of his arms; I don't want to lose him to his work. It happens too often.

A shadow passes over the window and I'm not sure if the sun has simply hidden behind a cloud, or if there's someone behind the shutters. I suddenly feel exposed, pregnant and naked. I start to pull my dirty barista uniform back on.

'As long as you take some time off work when the twins arrive,' I say.

'Of course. Actually I'm going to be away for a short while.'

He goes to the kitchen while I dress and brings me a glass of water.

'There's an amazing opportunity at work,' he continues.

'Really? How long will you be away?'

'A week.' He reaches over and strokes my hair. 'I'm going to hate being away from you.' His hands caress my belly. 'And the girls.'

'A week? Where? Can't you pop back and see us?'

'That's the thing. It's in Thailand. A new client. Building a whole hotel complex. Billions involved. And they want us to be one of the prime contractors. It's not an opportunity I can turn down. It's in a beautiful, undeveloped part of the country. Next to the beach, backed by mountains.'

'In Thailand?' I sit up straighter. Thailand's so far away. What if something happens with the babies while he's away? 'When did you find out?' I ask, wondering how long he's kept this from me.

'It was confirmed this morning. I knew it was coming but I was hoping it would happen a few months down the line, once you were settled with the twins. I'm sorry, I know the timing is awful.'

'Can't you send someone else?'

'I'm afraid I can't send a junior for a job like this. It has to be me. I need to meet the management company, see the site, assess the opportunity.'

I realise I don't have a choice. He's going. We've got so much left to do to prepare for the babies, and I'll have to do it all on my own.

'When are you leaving?' I ask.

'My flight's booked for tonight.' He glances at his watch and smiles apologetically. 'I'm afraid if I don't leave soon, I'll miss it.'

After Ian's gone I don't know what to do with myself. There's not much in the fridge, and I go out to Sainsbury's to get myself a ready meal, which I heat up in the microwave and consume on the sofa on my own. I feel a stab of loneliness. I wish Ian wasn't going to the other side of the world so close to my due date. He'll be on his flight by now. I feel unsettled in the house on my own, remembering the shadow that passed by the window earlier, and the woman by the café watching the house a couple of weeks ago.

After dinner I take the bin bag out of the kitchen and go outside down the unlit path to the bins. I lift the lid off the dustbin and see an unsightly mush in the bottom. I'll have to get that cleaned out, but for now I just chuck the bag in.

'Hi,' a voice behind me says, making me jump.

I turn to see a man towering over me in dark clothes.

'Hi,' I say, goosebumps rising on my skin, despite the balmy night. I eye up the path from the bins back to my front door. It will take less than a minute to get back inside.

'Oh, sorry, I didn't mean to scare you.' He reaches out and puts his hand on my shoulder. I recoil. 'I'm Cameron, your next-door neighbour.' I let out the breath I'd been holding as he points to the immaculate house next door. He's the guy with the Porsche.

'Katie,' I say, regaining control. 'Nice to meet you.' I hold out my hand, grateful when he removes his from my shoulder to shake mine. It's pitch-black tonight, the moon covered by dark clouds.

'I just wanted to introduce myself. I saw that you'd moved in and wanted to say hello. You've done a great job tidying up the front of the house.'

'Thanks,' I say. 'But my partner did all the work.' I feel an urge to mention Ian, so he knows I don't live alone.

'Has he done the inside too?'

'Yes.'

'Oh, that's good. That house had been left for too long. I'm glad someone like you moved in. Someone who'll take care of it.'

I nod, thinking of the appalling state of the place when I first moved in. 'What happened to the previous owner?' I ask.

'You don't know?'

I look at him, surprised by the concern in his voice. 'What happened?' I ask again.

'He…' Cameron glances down, sees my heavily pregnant belly and starts again. 'He died recently. He'd lived in the house for years, since he first got married. Although the last few years he was in a home and the house was empty.'

'That's sad,' I say, thinking of the elderly man moving to a home, away from the house he'd lived in for so many years. 'I suppose it used to be a family home.'

'Yes,' he says, frowning. 'A long time ago.'

'Well, it will be again soon. Once my two are out.' I pat my belly.

'Two?' he asks, his eyebrows shooting upwards.

'Yes, twins.' People are always shocked, and I have to wait a moment for him to recover from the surprise.

'That's lovely,' he says eventually. 'I'm so glad a family are moving in. It's a fresh start for the house. God knows it needs one.'

CHAPTER TEN

The next morning I drag myself out of bed, wash in the rainforest shower in our freshly done-up bathroom, then towel myself off with one of my old scratchy towels. I dress quickly, surveying my bump in the mirror, running my hand over the stretch marks. My babies kick, and I watch in fascination as I see my skin ripple in the mirror, a tiny foot pushing out.

The house feels empty without Ian. When I'm on my own I seem to only go in certain rooms, like a mouse repeating the same route again and again, leaving the same tracks. Ian hasn't done much more work on the house since the baby shower. The hallway, the living room, kitchen, bathroom and our bedroom could be straight out of the pages of an interior design magazine. But the other rooms are trapped in the past. When I step from one room to another, it's like stepping back in time to the 1950s.

A car horn honks outside and I glance out the window to see Mum's Peugeot, looking out of place on the huge driveway. I go downstairs and climb into the car, pulling the seat belt round my pregnant belly.

'How are you feeling?' she asks.

'Fine, thanks,' I say. 'How about you? How are your headaches?'

'Oh, not too bad,' she says as she pulls out of the driveway.

'Have you had the results of the scan?'

'Yes, they don't think there's anything to worry about, but they're going to run some more tests.'

'Tests for what?'

'Nothing serious. My appointment's not for months. If they were worried they'd be seeing me a lot sooner.' She quickly changes the subject back to pregnancy. 'You know, I was dreadfully ill when I was pregnant with you. Sick right until the end.'

I nod. 'I'm lucky. I haven't had that.'

'You look glowing,' she says.

'It's the blusher,' I reply, and then feel bad about batting away her compliment.

We walk round the shops together for hours. I rarely enjoy time with my mother, but today it feels almost companionable. She isn't questioning my life choices or telling me to get my act together. She seems to have softened now she has grandchildren on the way.

I'm so huge now, that I feel like I'm ready to split at the seams. Strangers continuously stop us to ask when I'm due. I'm overwhelmed by all the baby clothes and equipment in the shops. Babygrows and sleepsuits. Booties and socks. Hats and scratch mittens. Sheets for the crib and sleeping bags. Soon my mother and I are laden with bags. Mum wanted to pay for a lot of it, but I've insisted we put it all on Ian's credit card. He gave it to me before he went away with instructions to buy only the best for our babies.

Mum's bought the babies one toy each: a beautiful hand-knitted caterpillar and a stuffed elephant.

'Will you need a double buggy?' Mum asks.

'Yes,' I say, although I still can't imagine myself pushing one around. It all feels unreal.

'They can be expensive, you know. I'm happy to buy it for you.'

'It's OK,' I say. 'We can afford it.'

'You don't have to push me away, Katie. They're my grandchildren and I want to provide for them.'

'Honestly, it's OK,' I say. 'Thank you, though.'

'Melissa said she spoke to you the other day about the babies' names.'

'She did.'

'She's very hurt, Katie. She didn't want you to use the name Frances.'

'But I don't understand why,' I say. I've tried calling Melissa to discuss it with her but she's refused to answer the phone. 'I want to name the baby after Dad.'

'I know, sweetheart. It's just, Melissa wanted to use that name too. If she ever has children. Are you sure there's not another name you like? Why don't you have Frances as a middle name?'

Melissa never told me she wanted to use the name. I feel a stab of guilt and I wonder if I should give in. But then my resolve strengthens. He was my father too.

'No, Mum. I've already decided.' I feel tearful all of a sudden. Why can't she be pleased for me?

'OK, then. I'll speak to Melissa. She was very close to her father.'

'I was close to him too. Just because I didn't have as many years with him as Melissa had, doesn't mean I loved him any less.'

'I know you loved him,' she says. 'I've always known that. I'm sorry. I just told Melissa I'd talk to you about it. I wasn't sure how fixed you were on the name. But of course, you have every right to use it.'

'OK,' I reply. But the conversation leaves a bad taste in my mouth. Why does she always have to put Melissa first?

We head over to the department store and, after much deliberation, I choose a double buggy.

'Are you sure you don't want me to get it?' Mum asks. 'I'd like to buy you something useful.'

'No, Mum, it's too much money. We'll get it.'

I hand Ian's credit card to the till assistant. She gives me the card machine and I type in the pin.

'Do you know what you're having?' she asks conversationally, as she waits for the card to go through.

'Two girls.'

'How exciting.' The card reader beeps and a receipt comes out. The till assistant stares at it for a second.

'I'm sorry. Your card's been declined.' She starts typing into the card reader again, and then holds it out to me. 'Do you want to try again?'

I retype the pin. This time the woman watches the machine as it processes, tapping her foot impatiently. 'I'm sorry, it's declined again.'

I stare at her, alarmed. Have I maxed out Ian's credit card? He'd said I could spend as much as I liked. Maybe I've spent more than I thought.

'Use mine,' Mum says, reaching into her wallet.

She hands her card to the shop assistant and the payment goes through. She turns to me. 'You can pay me back if you like, but I'd prefer it to be a gift.'

'Thanks, Mum,' I say, thinking of all the other things I was planning to buy for the babies while Ian was away. Nappies, wipes, nappy rash cream. Will I be able to afford them on my own?

That night a storm comes, the dark clouds letting go of their rage, built up like a pressure cooker over the long hot summer. I've always relished the anger and destruction of a storm. But this time it feels different. I don't want to climb the stairs into the dark upper floors of the house and go to bed; don't want to fall asleep.

Instead I go to the kitchen and make myself a cup of tea, listening to the rain lashing against the windows. Sometimes I feel afraid in this house, even in the daylight. I'm not sure if it's because I'm now responsible for the two new lives growing inside me, or something more. The feeling haunts me, following me around my shiny new kitchen. I stare out into the dark overgrown back garden. Ian hasn't had time to look at it yet and brambles scrape against the brand-new back door. Even now, in the bright light of my state-of-the-art kitchen, I can't shake the feeling that someone's watching.

I finish my tea and make myself go upstairs, listening to the storm pummelling the house. As I lie awake in bed, I hear the winds rush through the roof tiles and wonder if Ian did any work up there, or if his work was all superficial, decorating over the cracks, ignoring the sagging roof.

I feel irritated with him for a moment. He's flown off to Thailand, while I'm stuck here. Being a family is such a huge commitment, and I'm not sure either of us is ready. Ian always used to say he was married to his job. I hope he'll have time for us.

The storm rages outside, picking up garden furniture in its clumsy grip and throwing it back down in anger, ripping fences from their foundations. I hear a scraping sound and then a crash from above my head. I freeze. Is it a tile falling off the roof and tumbling to the ground? What if there's a squatter in the attic sheltering from the rain? I've never been up there, nervous about climbing a ladder with my front-heavy, unfamiliar body.

I put the thought out of my mind. Of course no one's living up there, but it's easy to imagine. And I'm on my own now. If something happened to me, how long would it be before someone found me?

I put my hand on my pregnant belly, hoping to feel my babies move, hoping their movements will calm me. But there's nothing. They are sleeping right through it. At least, I hope that's what they're doing.

Fear grips me. When did I last feel them move? I can't remember any movement since this morning. I was so busy shopping with Mum that I didn't notice any kicks.

I'm awash with guilt. It's my responsibility to look after them and I haven't even been monitoring their kicks like the midwife told me to. What if they're in trouble?

Crash.

My whole body tenses. What was that?

It wasn't thunder. The sound was closer than that. It was inside the house. I lie completely still, terrified.

Another crash. This time louder. I sit up in the bed.

The whole house vibrates, and above the thunder and the pounding rain I hear crumbling from inside the house.

I brace myself. I wish I wasn't alone – there's no one but me to find out what that was.

5

'You know what the policeman said,' my sister says encouragingly, pushing me forward a bit. 'If someone's hurting us, then we have to tell.'

'He was talking about strangers,' I say doubtfully. 'And besides, he said we should tell our parents.'

'Or a teacher.' We both look across at Miss Kingdom on the other side of the playground. My sister has decided that she's the best person to tell. She's not our class teacher who likes our mother. She's a new teacher at the school, younger than the others. She has no connection to our parents or to us, and she seems nice. We've watched her for a couple of weeks, to check she's OK. We've watched her arrive at the school and get out of her car. We've watched her in the playground at break time. We've seen her giving cuddles to other children when they've been upset. When Benny was crying she picked him up off the ground and stroked his hair.

Now she's on her own doing playground duty, supervising all the children as they run around. She frowns as she watches a group of boys play football. She has a whistle round her neck so she can tell children off for running or fighting, but she hardly ever uses it, except to let us know it's the end of break.

It can't be long until the end of break now. We've been watching her for ages.

'Go on,' my sister says. 'Just ask her.'

We creep closer. A boy with a bleeding knee gets to her first and we watch her give him a hug and then send him inside to the nurse.

We must hurry, or we'll miss our chance. Tomorrow it will be a different teacher on duty.

'You ask her,' I say.

My sister suddenly lets go of my hand and marches up to Miss Kingdom. I scurry behind her, my heart beating fast. I'm excited and afraid. This could be the start of things getting better.

'She has something to tell you,' my sister says, pointing at me.

'I...' I stare at my shoes. 'I...'

My sister gives me a little kick. 'Go on.'

Miss Kingdom frowns and looks at her watch. 'What is it, girls?'

'Our father...'

'Your father? What's he got to do with anything?'

'He isn't a nice man.'

'What are you trying to say?'

She's already losing patience. This wasn't what we'd hoped for. I look at my sister with panic in my eyes, wondering whether we should stop now.

'He hit her,' my sister says.

'A smack?'

'No. Not a smack. He hit her properly. On the head.'

'Why would he do that?'

'Umm...'

She checks her watch again and then blows the whistle so everyone stands still.

'The policeman said to tell teachers about bad men,' my sister says hurriedly, sensing our time is up.

'Shhh...' Miss Kingdom says, indicating the whistle. *We look at each other, worried. I don't think we've explained ourselves properly.*

She blows the whistle again and everyone starts filing back towards the school.

'The policeman said...' my sister repeats.

'OK,' Miss Kingdom says. 'Leave it with me. Now get back to class.'

CHAPTER ELEVEN

I sit up in bed, stock-still, the sound of the crash echoing in my ears. I'm waiting for something to happen, something biblical.

But the storm continues to batter the house, and there's only the sound of the rain pounding on the windows and the wind whistling through the trees. No more crashing.

I tell myself that maybe I imagined it all. Mum always said I had an overactive imagination. But I know in my heart that what I heard was real. And I won't be able to sleep until I know what's happened.

I listen intently. I can't hear anything above the noise of the thunder. Perhaps the crashing sound wasn't in the house at all. Perhaps it came from outside. A tree could have easily come down in the storm, tearing through one of the neat and tidy houses.

Lightning flashes through a gap in the curtains, illuminating the two tiny cribs, ready and waiting beside the bed. I must be braver. I'm the adult here. I flick the lights on. It makes everything feel more normal, under my control. I can do this. I can cope in the house without Ian. After all, I've been single for most of my life. I'm used to looking after myself.

I think of Amy in our flatshare. She's probably fast asleep, seeing out the storm in a flat full of the bustle of other people. I never felt alone there. What would Amy say if she saw me like this? I was always the brave one in the house, removing spiders from the bathroom and telling messy housemates to clean up after themselves.

I pull myself together and get out of bed. I open the bedroom door slowly, the delay only adding to my fear. The hallway feels like a foreign land. I flick the light on.

There's nothing there.

But away from the storm hammering the bedroom windows, I can just about make out another sound. Water. A slow, steady drip.

I follow the sound to the second bedroom and open the door gingerly.

It's dark inside, but the dripping is louder. I automatically reach for the light switch and press it. There's a fizzing sound as the bulb lets out a spark, illuminating a crumbling ceiling and a puddle of dark, dirty water on the floor. Then all the lights go out and I'm thrown into darkness.

I step back into the pitch-black hallway. I must have blown a fuse. Lightning flashes through the house as I retreat quickly to my bedroom and find my phone. Using it as a torch, I go downstairs and find the fuse box in a dusty, dirty cupboard under the stairs. I fight my way past boxes of old magazines and newspapers to flick the mains switch.

The house floods with light and I go back upstairs, thunder bellowing. I return to the second bedroom and shine the torch inside. Water is steadily dripping through the ceiling, splashing into a small puddle.

I stare up at the crumbling plaster and wonder if the whole ceiling might come down.

I go back downstairs to fetch a bucket. Struggling to push the bed into the corner of the room, as far away from the leak as possible, I place the bucket under the drip. Above my head I hear the rain pounding on the roof, blown this way and that by the wind.

I google emergency repairs on my phone, but none of the lines are open until the morning. I leave several messages and then return to bed. But I can't sleep. As the storm rages, I get up every hour to check the bucket isn't overflowing and to empty it into the bathroom sink.

Eventually the thunder dies away and then, much later, the rain stops altogether. I fall into a fitful sleep.

On Sunday, when the sun rises, I wake with a sense of dread. I rush into the spare room, and I'm relieved to see the bucket is only half-full. But in the daylight I can see the full extent of the damage. The carpet is sodden and plaster has crumbled off the ceiling. Water is dripping down the back wall and the wallpaper's peeling.

I check my phone. None of the emergency repairs people have called me back. They must be having a busy day today. I look out of the window and see broken tree branches and rubbish from overturned bins littering the road. On the other side of the street, a fence has come down. I wonder what our house looks like from the outside; if the damage to the roof is visible or if it looks just the same as yesterday.

I go up the stairs to the top floor and into the small room that leads to the roof terrace where the leak must be originating from. I squeeze past the old wooden dressers, chests of drawers and broken chairs and look out of the double doors that lead outside onto the terrace. The black felt covering has caved in and I can see water running down and forming a puddle in the middle. I daren't go closer, otherwise I'm sure I'll fall through. I put my hand on my belly protectively. I couldn't risk the babies. I'll have to wait for the experts to come and fix the roof.

Neither of the twins move under my hand. When was the last time I felt kicks? I remember I was worried about them yesterday. I'd forgotten about that completely when I heard the crash. What if they're in trouble? What if I've left it too late to seek help?

I feel sick. I don't know what to do. I transferred my maternity care to the closest hospital when I moved and I don't even have the phone number for the midwives there. Tears well up in my eyes. I'm so angry with myself for not being organised. I pick up my phone and ring Paula.

'I'm worried about the twins,' I blurt out. 'They haven't been moving.' I wish Ian was here now to put my mind at rest.

'When was the last time they moved?'

'I don't know,' I say, panicking. 'Yesterday morning's the last time I remember. Do you have the phone number for the midwives? Should I go to the hospital?'

'No, no. Don't do that. You could be waiting ages to be seen. I'll come over. We had an appointment at ten anyway, didn't we?'

'Yes.' After my first session with Paula I'd booked in a second to go through my birth plan.

'Well, I can just come over a bit earlier. I can come round now.'

'Are you sure that's OK?'

'Yes, of course. I'll be over in half an hour. Quicker than you could get to the hospital.'

'Thank you,' I say. 'Thank you.'

While I'm waiting I google all the things you're supposed to do when the babies don't move, all the reasons that there might be for it. I get increasingly alarmed. What if I've ignored them too long?

I lie down on the sofa, hands on my stomach, praying the babies will move.

After five minutes, I'm rewarded. A tiny kick. And then another one.

Paula arrives carrying a big holdall.

'I came as quickly as I could. How are you? Are you feeling any movements now?'

'I've just felt a few,' I say. 'Sorry for alarming you. I think I was distracted. Maybe I didn't notice them earlier.'

'Hmm… but you said you hadn't felt any in twenty-four hours. A slowdown in movements is always a concern. I think I should examine you.' Paula is opening her bag, taking out wet wipes and gloves.

'OK,' I say. 'That sounds like a good idea.'

'Lie down on the sofa and push your dress up over your bump.'

I lie down while Paula closes the blinds.

I pull my dress up. My bump's huge, stretch marks littered across it like a child's attempt at a drawing. It doesn't look like a part of my body anymore. I lay my hands on it and one of the babies wriggles underneath them. The movement reassures me.

Paula comes over. 'My hands are a bit cold,' she says as she touches my skin. She's right. Her fingers feel freezing as she pushes down on the top of my bump. 'There's baby number one,' she says, and I feel my baby squirm out of the way of her grasp. She presses on the other side. 'And there's baby number two. I think that's the smaller one.'

'The smaller one's Frances,' I say. 'The bigger one's Alice.'

A bubble of worry rises in me. It feels wrong to say their names out loud, like I might be jinxing them.

She feels lower down, pulling the tops of my knickers down to feel my pelvis.

'Gosh, one of the heads has lowered. Frances's, I think. She's getting ready for her exit.'

'Really?' I say, alarmed. 'Do you think it will be soon?' My heart flutters. I haven't bought all the baby things yet. And Ian's away.

'Not necessarily. But I'd like to do an internal examination. Just to check everything's OK. I can't be certain from just feeling your bump.'

'Oh.' I can hardly get the words out, I'm so scared. 'Do you think there's something wrong?'

'I don't think so. But I just want to be 100 per cent sure.'

I worry that Paula might be downplaying the situation. The midwife at the antenatal clinic told me they avoid internal checks unless they have concerns.

I strip down my lower half obediently, scratching the scar on my upper arm so hard that I draw blood.

When her fingers touch me, I wince. I feel uncomfortable with Paula performing the examination, even though I keep telling myself it's her job.

Paula glances up at me and meets my eyes. 'Don't tense up now.'

'Ow,' I cry out. The pain is excruciating.

'If this hurts, you can practise your breathing,' Paula says. 'I'm just checking how everything is.'

I try to breathe through the pain but I can hardly catch a single breath.

When Paula removes her hand, her glove is bloodstained. I feel sick with panic.

'I'm bleeding?' I say, my voice high. 'Are the twins OK? What does that mean?' I remember how the midwives told me that twins are a higher-risk pregnancy.

'Oh, nothing at this stage, don't worry. You can get dressed. But I think you'll go into labour soon.'

'How soon?' I say as I pull my clothes back on. I feel a rush of excitement, followed quickly by fear. This wasn't supposed to happen while Ian was away. Can I do it on my own?

'Maybe in a few days. Maybe sooner. It's always hard to tell. I'd like to stay with you a bit longer, just in case. Do you want me to get you a glass of water?'

'Yes, please,' I say weakly. I'm still hurting but if I can't even cope with the pain of that, how on earth will I cope with labour?

I feel a tightening in my stomach, but I think it's just nerves.

Paula brings me the water.

'How are you feeling?'

'Does labour feel like period pains?' I ask.

'It could just be Braxton Hicks – kind of practice contractions.'

'Oh, right,' I say. But I feel the pain come again. It's definitely something. I rest my hand on my stomach, feeling my bump harden. 'I think this might be it,' I say.

Paula puts her hand on my belly. 'I felt that,' she says. 'That's a contraction. An early one, but still a contraction.'

'Am I going into labour?'

'Yes,' Paula says, smiling. 'I think you are.'

CHAPTER TWELVE

On the way to the hospital, Paula and I go over my birth plan. I want to have as natural a birth as possible. Paula is encouraging, telling me she has helped lots of women do exactly that. I don't want an epidural. I don't want any interventions.

Sitting in the back of the taxi, another contraction washes over me and I rock forward and then back as I count it out, the seat belt straining against me. The pain is manageable, I tell myself. I can do this.

I feel more relaxed than I imagined I would. I wish Ian was here with me now, going through this with me, but I know I'm lucky to have Paula. She knows exactly what she's doing. Before we left for the hospital she made me take a lukewarm bath to help with the pain. She examined me again just before we got into the taxi, and reassured me that everything is going smoothly. I'm in safe hands.

In between contractions, I reach into my pocket for my phone. I try to call Ian, but it goes straight to voicemail. I hang up as another contraction seizes me and I double over in the back seat.

'How are you feeling?' Paula asks.

'I'm coping,' I say, when I get my breath back.

Paula rubs my leg. 'You can do this. This is what your body was made for. Do you want me to call anyone for you?' She indicates the phone in my hand.

'No,' I say. Amy's still housebound, and it would be too stressful to have my mother there.

So it's just me and Paula. And I'm actually pleased about that. I can just focus on myself and my babies.

In my room on the labour ward, the midwife turns to Paula. 'Are you a relative?' she asks.

'No, I'm a doula.'

The midwife frowns at her and then turns to me. 'Anything you're concerned about?'

I glance at Paula, remembering her examining me. 'I've had a bit of bleeding.'

'Probably nothing to worry about. I'll check you over anyway.'

I nod, unable to speak as another contraction rocks through me, taking my breath away.

Paula reaches out and touches my arm. 'I know it's scary, but it will be alright. I've done this lots of times before.'

I think of Ian in Thailand. By the time he's back, the babies will be here. I reach into my pocket for my phone to try and call him again, but then the midwife starts hooking me up to the monitor. I'm afraid and excited. The pains are getting stronger now. Can I really do this?

'Is that completely necessary?' Paula asks the woman attaching the monitor.

'Sorry?' she says distractedly, as she fiddles with the buttons and the machine and then repositions the monitoring pads on my belly.

'Does she really need to be monitored? It's very restrictive. And it increases the chance of interventions.'

'It's a twin pregnancy. It's standard.'

'It's OK,' I say. 'I can cope.' But then I have to grit my teeth and try not to shout out as another contraction comes, even stronger.

The midwife leaves the room and Paula turns to me. 'I can't believe she hasn't even looked at your birth plan. They just don't have enough time to do everything.'

'It's OK,' I say, struggling to concentrate.

The midwife drifts in and out. A couple of hours later, when she's out of the room, Paula removes the pads from my stomach and lets me walk around, unplugging the monitor to stop it beeping.

The midwife reappears almost instantly and berates Paula as she reattaches me. Four hours pass by in a haze. I focus on my breathing but I'm getting exhausted. My contractions are coming so thick and fast and I can hardly bear it. I can feel the babies moving inside me, my body forcing them downwards.

'Keep breathing,' Paula says, stroking my back. 'Keep breathing. You're doing a great job.'

The hours merge into each other until the midwife checks my dilation once more and tells me we're ready to push.

I grip Paula's hand so tight as I push and push and push. My body burns as it opens up. And then, there she is. A tiny, perfectly formed baby girl.

My baby screams, and it's the best noise I've ever heard. My baby. I stare down the end of the bed at the red blotchy mess in the midwife's arms. I can't believe she's mine. I long to reach for her, to hold her against my chest, to put her on my breast. I just want to touch her, to stare into her eyes, to love her.

The midwives perform their checks and declare she's passed with flying colours.

'Six pounds,' the midwife says. 'She's perfect.'

The bigger of the two of them. Alice.

They pass her to me, but I only get to hold her for a second. Because then they look at the heart rate monitor for the other twin and see nothing on the trace.

A midwife rushes to my side and stands over the monitor, moving it around on my stomach to find the other baby. Alice tries to latch onto my breast, but the midwife moves her away to search for her twin's heartbeat.

She whisks Alice away from me and hands her to Paula. 'You can hold her later. We need to get her sister out of you. She's in distress.'

Alice screams, but when Paula holds her close to her bosom she calms and starts rooting. Paula wraps her blood-covered body in a shawl and rocks her from side to side, staring into her eyes. I feel a flash of jealousy at their first moments together.

But there's another baby inside me. Frances. And the midwife is still trying to find the heartbeat. Fear builds into a crescendo inside me. And then she finds it. It's only taken her a few minutes, but they felt like hours.

There are more people in the room now. Doctors. Midwives. I'm not sure who they all are. 'How are your contractions?' one asks me. I can't feel anything anymore, except an overwhelming sense of love for the baby that's just been born.

I can't even feel Frances moving inside me. My body is numb. I'm not contracting. My body's given up. Panic sears through me.

'I'm not getting any,' I say.

'Right, we're going to induce you, bring your contractions back on and get this baby out of you. If nothing happens quickly, we'll do an emergency C-section.'

A midwife comes in wheeling a drip, searches for a vein in my arm, then inserts the cannula and attaches it.

'She didn't want any interventions,' Paula says firmly.

'We need to get this baby out. There's no choice.'

Paula stands in front of the drip, blocking a doctor.

'Excuse me,' the doctor says. 'Let me do my job. Or I'm going to have to ask you to leave.'

Paula steps aside reluctantly.

'I don't want the drip,' I say.

'We need to restart your contractions,' the doctor says, cutting me down. 'Your baby's at risk.'

They start the drip. At first the period pains start up again, and they hardly hurt.

They present me with gas and air and I refuse it.

'Do you want any pain relief?' they ask.

'No.' Why haven't they read the birth plan?

But as the midwives go over to the drip and increase the dosage, everything blurs. I don't know where I end and the bed begins. My body convulses and contracts and there's no space, no air, no time to draw breath. I'm being torn apart from the inside. Two midwives stand over me and tell me to breathe. But I can't even think straight. All I know is that the pain is too much. I scream and scream and scream, my lungs raw.

But no one helps me.

'Paula!' I manage to shout her name when the pain eases slightly.

When the doctors' backs are turned, I see her go over to the drip and fiddle with it. She must be reducing the dose.

But it doesn't help.

I can barely hear their murmurs as I fade in and out of my body. They are saying I must stay still so they can find the heartbeat. That I must stop moving. But I can't. My body is moving on its own, shaking on the bed. I can no longer speak.

And they don't care. I can see their fuzzy images, in blue and white uniforms, going diligently over to the bag of fluid in the drip and increasing the dose of the hormone. I want them to stop. I need them to stop. I look at Paula as I scream, my eyes wide with panic. She holds my hand and I squeeze so tight I think I might break her fingers. I writhe away from her, my head jerking back and forth.

The room gets bigger and then smaller again around me and I feel like I'm not even there. Time loses all meaning. I'm not human; not even a body. In the room around me, the medical staff are going about their business as normal. They're ignoring me, they just want the baby. Frances. The baby that's trying to kill me.

The midwives hover at the edge of the bed, staring at me. I can feel the baby sliding down through my birth canal, my pelvis expanding to an unnatural width, my body expelling it as the baby stretches my body, ripping me in half.

They shout at me to push, to push, to push. And I do, pushing so hard that I feel like I'll break, that this will break me, destroy my body and my mind. The baby seems stuck, but I keep pushing. A doctor appears, frowning at the end of the bed.

Paula wipes back my sweaty hair from my head and I scream louder than I knew was possible.

I keep pushing, keep pushing.

The midwife is speaking. 'We're going to cut you now, widen the path.'

I'm hardly aware of what they're saying.

Then I feel the scalpel, cutting through my flesh. They put the forceps inside me and twist the baby out of me. Everything hurts. Every piece of my body. I'm completely broken.

I scream in agony and Alice screams with me.

And then her sister is dragged out of me. Frances.

6

In the evenings, when Dad has gone out to the pub, we sit down with Mum and she plays the piano. It's the only time we can really relax, the three of us together. I sit on the floor, cross my legs and close my eyes, letting the music take me over. I feel truly free, without fear. Dad won't be home for hours. There will be no violence and pain, only noise and laughter. Even Mum laughs when he's out. She looks younger when she laughs.

I know every note of the song Mum is playing. She's been playing the same tune to us since we were babies. A gentle lullaby before we go upstairs for our baths and she reads to us in bed.

I look at her now, her eyes closed, long hair flowing down over her shoulders, completely lost in the music. I come up behind her and wrap my arms round her, breathing in the lavender scent of her shampoo, feeling her cosy woollen jumper against my cheeks. She doesn't even wince when I touch her. Not like when Dad's in the house. Then she jumps when anyone touches her.

Her fingers keep dancing over the piano keys, as she tilts her head so her face is against mine and our hair tangles together. I smile at the warmth of her skin. I feel safe.

My sister reaches out her hand and I take it. We start to dance together, wildly, swinging each other round and laughing. Mum switches the tune and starts to sing, her voice clear and strong. I'm hand in hand with my sister, two peas in a pod. Dancing, jumping, joyful.

We cling to these moments. The moments when our mother loves us.
Because when Dad comes home, we will listen to him hit her.
And tomorrow she will stand by and do the dishes, turning her face
away as he hits us.

CHAPTER THIRTEEN

'Five pounds two,' the midwife announces, holding up Frances. 'Two perfect babies.'

'You did an amazing job,' Paula says to me.

I'm shaking on the bed. I just want to curl up and go to sleep. They pass Frances over to me and I stare at her tiny form. I feel nothing at all.

She starts to scream and I look across at Paula, still holding Alice, looking lovingly into her eyes.

I don't know what to do with the baby. At my feet, the doctors are peering at me.

'We need to stitch you up. Do you want to hold the babies while we do it? We'll give you a local anaesthetic.'

'No,' I say, and I try to pass the baby over. I don't want to hold any babies. I just want to rest. To recover. I can't process what's just happened.

Paula reaches out and takes Frances. She sits in the chair holding both babies, cooing at them. I turn away from her and start to cry, as I feel the needle piece my skin and the doctor starts stitching.

An hour later, I'm directed to the shower and I wash the blood off me. I let the tears flow out of me with the water. I'm still shaking, completely overwhelmed by Frances's birth. I've sat with the babies on my chest for the last half hour, but my feelings have numbed and I can't seem to connect with them. The rush of love I'd felt when I first held Alice in my arms has been taken over by a huge emptiness inside me.

The midwives have tried to help me with breastfeeding, but neither of the twins seem interested. Alice just cries, her face red and angry, and Frances just falls asleep.

When we get up to the postnatal ward, the midwife asks Paula to leave. 'Only partners are allowed to stay. No other visitors until the morning,' she says firmly.

'Don't go,' I say, reaching out to grab Paula's arm. I have no idea how I'm going to cope on my own. But after the midwife has put the babies in their cots beside the bed, she leaves, escorting Paula out with her.

I don't know what I'm supposed to do now. I've been told how important it is for newborns to have milk in their first hours, but neither of the babies have fed. I look at them both, fast asleep. Should I wake them and try and feed them again? I wish Paula was here to help me.

I need to contact Ian. Tell him about the babies.

My phone is in my bag next to the bed. I sit up slowly, stomach muscles straining and start to ease myself out of the bed. I'm not sure if my legs will support me, or if they'll give way.

Beside me Frances starts to scream, a mewling sound that rips at my heart. I stare at her, completely overwhelmed. It hits me that I'm responsible for her now. Her and Alice. I have to look after them forever.

I lift Frances out of the cot and rock her back and forth. She keeps screaming. I should try and feed her. I sit on the edge of the bed, lift up my top and put her to my breast. She doesn't respond. Alice joins in the screams. I stare at her too. How am I supposed to hold both of them? I feel sick. What am I doing? I can't be a mother.

I put Frances down and lift Alice up. When I put her to my breast she starts to suckle, and I flush with a sense of achievement.

I've done something right. I think about how easy her birth was compared to Frances's. I wonder if she'll be an easier baby too.

When both babies are calm and back in their cots, I ease myself out of bed, wincing as I feel my stitches tugging, and go over to my bag and pull out my phone. My heart sinks when I check it. Ian hasn't returned my calls. I try once more, and when he doesn't answer, I send him the briefest text message to say the twins have been born and then lie back down on the bed, hoping to get some rest.

But I can't sleep. Babies scream, midwives chat and new parents coo over their babies. I keep checking my phone, but Ian hasn't replied to any of my calls or messages. I wish I'd taken another contact number for him in Thailand. I don't even know which hotel he's staying at. His office will know, but it's too late to call them. I just wish he was with me now, supporting me through all the stress, telling me he loves me. Instead I'm all alone.

I stay up watching the twins sleep in the cots beside me and waiting for Ian to call me back. As I stare down at my babies, I'm suddenly overwhelmed by intense, crippling love. They're perfect. My love for them clamps round my heart and I reach out and hold my finger to Alice. She clasps her tiny hand around it and I marvel at how perfect each finger is, each tiny fingernail.

But I can't help feeling on edge, because a part of the picture's missing. In the bay across from mine, a father sits in the chair next to the bed, rocking his screaming baby while its mother sleeps. Without Ian, our family isn't complete. My heart thumps loudly in my chest as I watch my babies sleep and look at the empty chair by the hospital bed where he should be.

Paula arrives on the dot of 8 a.m. the next morning, the start of visiting hours. She helps me to breastfeed Alice and then turns to Frances and changes her nappy.

At the beds around us more relatives are arriving, clutching flowers. I feel a pang of jealousy.

'Alice looks just like you,' Paula says. I smile. While Alice has my features, Frances looks like a tiny version of Ian, with her broad forehead, high cheekbones and intense eyes.

'Can you pass me my phone?' I ask Paula. 'I need to call Ian.' She hands it over.

The call goes to answerphone again and I feel a wave of disappointment. I leave a garbled message about the births and how beautiful our girls are and how Frances looks just like him.

'What time is it in Thailand?' Paula says.

'I've no idea.' It could be the middle of the night for all I know. But I've called him so many times, he should know it's important.

'I'm sure he'll call back when he gets your message.'

In the bed opposite, the husband is taking photo after photo of his wife and new baby.

'Can you take a photo of me and the twins?' I ask Paula.

I hand her my phone and she clicks away.

'Can I have one with them too?' she asks after she finishes.

I place a twin in each of her arms and then take a photo and show it to her. She could easily be mistaken for a proud relative. I wonder if she has children of her own. If she does, they must be grown up by now. She's never mentioned any.

'Have you let everyone know the twins have arrived?' Paula asks.

'No.' I've thought about telling my mother and Melissa, but I really wanted Ian to be the first to know. 'I should tell them, shouldn't I?'

'Are you ready for visitors?'

'Umm… I don't know.' I feel like my body's been torn apart. I have no idea how to look after my twins. And Ian's abroad. 'I think I'd like to adjust to everything first. Before I see anyone. And I want Ian to come back and meet the babies before anyone else.'

'I'm sure he'll fly back as soon as he gets the message.'

I nod. 'And then Mum and Melissa can visit once he's back. I think I'd feel more comfortable then.'

'Maybe best to let them know about the babies when Ian's back, then?'

I nod. 'Yeah. I think I'll wait.' I feel a bit guilty about it, but it only seems fair for Ian to meet his daughters first. And I need a bit of time to recover before I'm faced with my family.

'It won't hurt to leave it a day or two for Ian to get back. I usually recommend parents have a whole week to bond with their children before they have any visitors. Unwanted guests can really disrupt establishing a routine.'

'I just think I'll need some help with the babies,' I admit. 'Is there any chance…?' I trail off, too embarrassed to ask her directly if she'll help me. Ian and I had agreed that Paula would help me prepare for the births, but we hadn't talked about afterwards. We'd assumed he'd be at home with us.

'Do you want me to stay with you for a few days to help you adjust?'

'Yes please. But I'm afraid I won't be able to pay you until Ian's back.' I look down at my feet, embarrassed.

'No problem. I'll just need to check my calendar.'

She pulls out her phone and I see her eyes scanning her appointments. I hold my breath. I've got no idea how I'll cope if she can't help me.

She smiles. 'I haven't got any clients this week. I'm free to help. I can come home with you from the hospital and get you settled.'

It's the nights I'm worried about most, alone with two screaming, hungry newborns. 'Can you stay overnight?' I ask.

'Of course.'

Relief floods me.

I'm discharged that afternoon, and by the time we get back to the house I'm exhausted. After we'd tracked down a taxi with two baby seats, I spent the journey wedged between my newborns, their screams reverberating around the car, with me powerless to comfort them. Now I'm back home, they're still screaming and I don't know where to start; whether to feed them, or change their nappies, or just hold them. I'm suddenly furious that Ian hasn't been in contact. How could he not get back to me? Why on earth did he go to Thailand so close to my due date?

Luckily Paula takes control and I go upstairs to wash while she looks after the babies. The shower drowns out the screaming and I clean the remaining specks of dried blood off my legs, the sweat out of my hair. I'm so glad Paula will be staying tonight. My fury's replaced with a twinge of longing for Ian, but I push it back down, and it's quickly replaced by worry. What if something's happened to him? What if he's not coming back?

I tell myself not to be so ridiculous. He's probably just lost mobile reception in some remote area of Thailand. He'll get back to me as soon as he gets my messages. And besides, with Paula's help, I've got things under control. I can manage for now.

I step out of the shower and wrap the warm towel around me, feeling so much better now I'm clean. I know my babies are safe with Paula downstairs.

I pad down the corridor to my bedroom, taking in the two tiny cots beside the bed. Tonight my babies will be sleeping next to me. I feel overwhelmed but excited. I can hardly believe this is my life. I'm a mum to twins. No matter how many times I say it to myself, it still doesn't sound real.

I brush my hair quickly, keen to get back to my babies. On the way to the stairs, I pass the spare room where Paula will sleep and stop still in front of the door.

The leak. I'd forgotten about the leak. I didn't have time to get it fixed before I went into labour.

I push open the door and stare into the room, gagging at the damp smell. The ceiling has a pale yellow stain spread across it and the corner looks like it might collapse. Crumbs of plaster have fallen down onto the floor below and the bucket I put out has overflowed, a sodden circle of carpet around it. There's no way Paula can sleep in there.

I go down the corridor and peer into the box room. Full of junk. The two bedrooms upstairs are the same. It would take days to clear them.

There's nowhere in this house for Paula to sleep. I'm going to have to ask her to go home. I'm going to have to spend the night on my own with two screaming babies I have no idea how to look after.

CHAPTER FOURTEEN

'Maybe it's best you don't stay,' I say to Paula when I get back downstairs. I try to sound casual, but my voice is choked. 'I can manage on my own tonight, and then see you tomorrow.' Frances starts screaming and I falter and then continue. 'I'll pay you the same, of course.'

'Oh,' Paula says, confused. 'You've changed your mind?' She picks up Frances and holds her close.

'There's nowhere for you to sleep. There's been a leak in the second bedroom.' I flush, ashamed that in this huge house, there is nowhere to put a guest.

'I don't mind that. I won't be sleeping much anyway. I'll be looking after the babies. They tend to scream a lot at night.'

I wince, imagining the night ahead of me. But I can't let Paula sleep in that room. She doesn't realise how bad it is. 'Honestly, I wouldn't want you to sleep there. It's not in a fit state.'

Paula frowns. 'You know, I'd really prefer to stay in the house with you. You're very vulnerable when you've just given birth. What if you had an accident? New mothers get so exhausted, it's easy for these things to happen. I'd like to be here to look after you, just for a night or two, to get you settled.'

'I'm sure Ian will be back soon,' I say, sounding braver than I feel. 'Then he can help me out.' But I have no idea when or if he will be back. I feel a bit sick when I think about it.

Paula continues to rock Frances and she calms. 'Babies are always the most difficult at the beginning,' she continues, smiling down at my daughter. 'And Frances in particular had a traumatic entry into the world. I'm happy to stay wherever suits you.' She waves her hand to indicate the house. 'There must be somewhere.'

Alice starts to scream, and her cries are even louder than Frances's. I'm not convinced I can cope on my own. I think quickly. 'You'll have to stay in the main bedroom. I'll sleep in the spare room.'

'But you said there'd been a leak…'

I think longingly of the king-size bed in the main bedroom, the two little cots beside it.

'It's only a small leak,' I say reassuringly. 'I'll be fine.'

'Well, if it's only a small leak then I can sleep there,' Paula says, reaching out to touch my shoulder to reassure me.

'I'll be fine,' I say. 'Really, it's not a problem. You're helping me out so much. It's the least I can do.'

Upstairs, my bedroom is a mess. I tidy up a bit and strip the bed, replacing the sheets. As I bend over, I feel my stitches tug and I wince. My body is battered and bruised. I grab some clothes out of the cupboard, take my toiletries off the dressing table and chuck everything in the second bedroom.

I start to move the tiny bedside cribs, but I realise that's a crazy idea. My babies can't sleep in a room with a leak. The damp air could damage their lungs. Or even worse, the crumbling ceiling might cave in on them. I'd never forgive myself if anything happened.

I sit down on the edge of the bed and my tears flow freely. Nothing has turned out as I planned. I had imagined the babies being next to me from the beginning, Ian's comfortingly warm body beside me.

I'll have to sleep downstairs in the living room. I can sleep on the sofa, then the babies can be in their cribs beside me. I'll get the leak fixed first thing tomorrow and then we can switch round the bedrooms. I go downstairs and explain the plan to Paula.

'Are you sure that's a good idea? Your body's been through so much. You need to sleep in a bed.'

'But the girls can't sleep in a damp room.'

'They can sleep in with me. I often do that for new mums, sleep next to their babies to allow the mum to get some rest.'

'But I want to sleep beside them, to be there when they cry.'

'I understand. But why don't you let me do some of it? I can sort out nappy changes in the night, and I'll bring them to you when they're hungry. How does that sound?'

'That sounds good,' I say, relieved I'll still be there if they need me.

Paula puts her hand on my shoulder. 'Don't worry. It will only be one night. You'll get the leak fixed, and then be back with the girls in no time. You can get some rest tonight and be refreshed for looking after them tomorrow.' She puts the babies down and gives me a hug. 'It'll be fine. Remember, caring for new mothers and looking after babies is my job. That's what I'm here for.'

That night I toss and turn, unable to sleep despite my exhaustion. I feel empty without my babies beside me and I miss Ian more than ever. Why hasn't he called? It's been over twenty-four hours. Even if he has no mobile reception, surely he should have found some way to check his messages or contact me by now. He must have been so busy with work that he hasn't found time. He probably doesn't even know his babies have been born. So much has happened in the last twenty-four hours it feels like a lifetime, but for him it will have seemed like just another day.

I stare up at the crumbling ceiling and wonder if it's likely to cave in on me. None of the emergency repair people I rang before I went into labour ever called me back. I phoned and left more messages for them before I went to bed this evening, explaining that it's urgent.

When I shift my position on the bed, damp rises up from the mattress and catches in my nose. I cough. I keep my face close to the single pillow I took from my bedroom, so that the smell of washing powder blocks the smell of damp. Outside the open window I can hear two neighbourhood cats fighting.

My stitches sting and I go to the bathroom and splash cold water on them to stop them getting infected, as the midwife suggested. On my way back from the bathroom, I go over to Paula's room and stand by the door. It's shut. I long to see my babies, but I can't go in and wake them all. The house is silent, and I feel even more alone than I did before the twins were born.

I tiptoe back to my room and stare up at the ceiling. Water drips down the wall behind my bed and the wallpaper is starting to peel. Behind it I can see small line markings. I sit up and look closer. I can see they are pencil drawings of stick people. A picture of a family. A mother, a father and two girls holding hands. I wonder when they were drawn. What those girls' lives were like. When they lived here. The house has been standing since Victorian times. The children could be long dead. The drawings make me feel uncomfortable. I think of what the neighbour said about the man who lived here, the man who became ill and died. The house has a long history, and I'm just a tiny part of it. At one time there was a family here. Two little girls in this room. Like my two little girls down the corridor.

I wake to desperate, agonised screams. Alice. Her lungs are strong, whereas Frances's cries are more like a weak mewling. I stare at the door, expecting Paula to bring Alice in so I can comfort her. My whole body is tense, and I can't rest until I know she's OK. When my bedroom door doesn't open I get up, go to Paula's door and pause outside. The cries continue. I can't hear any words of comfort or movement. Why isn't she responding to them?

With rising alarm, I knock on the door and then quickly push it open.

Paula holds a screaming Alice to her bosom, rocking her back and forth.

'I'm sorry to interrupt, I—' I stop, not sure what I'm apologising for.

'It's OK,' she says, as she stares down at Alice. I feel a pang of jealousy. I want to hold my baby.

'Do they need feeding?' I ask, going over to the remaining crib and looking in at Frances. She's so tiny, her chest rising and falling in sleep.

'No,' Paula says. 'Alice is starting to calm down. And Frances is asleep. You should never wake a sleeping baby. If they're asleep, they're fine.'

'Should I hold Alice? Perhaps she wants her mother?' I ask uncertainly. I've read that babies recognise their mother's smell and it calms them.

'I've got things under control. She'll be back asleep in no time. You get some rest. You'll need it for the morning.'

'OK,' I say, staring into Frances's crib, reluctant to leave. I just want to pick her up and give her one cuddle.

'Don't worry. You'll get the hang of things soon enough.'

'You'll bring them to me when they need feeding?' I ask.

'Of course,' Paula says. 'I'll wake you up. Now go back to bed. Get some rest.'

I wake up to a hand on my shoulder.

Ian? Is he back?

I come to groggily, for a moment unsure where I am.

'Katie? Katie – wake up.'

When I see Paula, I quickly sit up. She strokes my hair back from my face gently and places Frances in my arms.

'You looked so peaceful asleep, but I knew you wanted to be woken up when they needed a feed.'

I pull down my nightdress and put Frances to my breast.

'I'll leave you in peace,' Paula says. 'Let you have some bonding time.'

I nod gratefully. As soon as Paula leaves, Frances's eyes drop closed and she seems to fall asleep. I try again once more, pushing her firmly to my body, but her eyes are still closed.

I stare at her, unsure what to do. Around me the house creaks and the radiators clunk. Frances begins to scream. For the next hour I alternate between rocking her and trying to feed her. But nothing works. She won't take any milk. We can't seem to bond at all. Tears of frustration and exhaustion are running down my cheeks by the time Paula comes back in with Alice.

'How did it go?' she asks.

'I can't seem to do it.'

'Maybe she's not hungry after all.' Paula takes Frances from me. 'Do you want to try feeding Alice?'

I already feel defeated, but I take Alice in my arms anyway. Paula advises me on how to position her, but she still won't latch.

'She fed in the hospital, didn't she?'

I nod. 'They both did.'

'It might not be working because you're too stressed. The babies can sense it. Why don't we try again in the morning?'

I frown. I'm sure the midwife said I needed to feed them every four hours. But I might be wrong. Everything's a blur. 'Will they be OK until the morning?' I ask.

'Of course they will. I'll be right beside them if they need anything.'

Paula takes a screaming Alice into her arms, lifts Frances up from the bed and returns to her bedroom with my twins. Once again, I'm alone.

7

The knock on the door is quiet, as if whoever's knocking isn't really sure they want to knock at all.

Only the postman ever knocks. And only when he has a parcel. But it's mid-afternoon and my sister and I have just returned from school. It can't be the postman. We creep to the top of the stairs and peek down.

'Answer the door,' Dad screams at Mum.

A second knock comes, even more timid than the first.

'Answer the bloody door!'

Mum scurries from the kitchen, removing her washing-up gloves. A smattering of soap suds lands on the floor. She'll be in trouble for that later.

She opens the door. My sister and I peer down, but we can't see more than the shadow of a jacket behind Mum. We can just about make out the sound of a male voice.

Dad stomps into view and we scramble back to our room, keeping the door open to try and catch the conversation.

We can't hear the words, but we can hear the tone. Dad's voice is angry, Mum's worried. The other man sounds nervous, his voice high, as if he's afraid.

The door shuts and we hear footsteps going through the hall and into the kitchen. Dad's let him into the house.

My sister and I look at each other. Who is he? Is this one of the occasions where we're supposed to be polite and go down and introduce ourselves, or should we stay upstairs? We never know what's the right thing to do. We agree without speaking that we'll stay where we are. We're excited and afraid. I see the thought occur to my sister too. What if Miss Kingdom's told the police about us and he's a policeman coming to help us? What if we're about to be rescued?

CHAPTER FIFTEEN

Light streams through the windows as Paula pulls the curtains back.

'What time is it?' I ask.

'Ten o'clock.'

'Ten?' I say, panicking. The twins will be long overdue a feed. How can I possibly have slept so long?

'You needed your sleep, so I let you have a rest.'

'What about the girls?'

'They're fine. There's no need to worry. I've fed them, changed their nappies and kept them happy.'

'You've fed them?'

'I gave them some formula.'

'Oh,' I say, disappointed. 'I wanted to breastfeed.'

Paula smiles at me sympathetically. 'A little bit of formula won't do any harm. Just topping them up until you're ready to feed them yourself. It was more important for you to rest.'

I tense up, concerned I'm already going against the midwives' advice to breastfeed. 'I feel like I've messed things up already.'

'Of course you haven't. I saw how hard you were trying last night. And besides, you have two babies. Most people have just one. Do you really think your breasts are going to be able to make enough milk for two? You're being far too hard on yourself. Do you want to try again now?'

'Yes,' I say, relieved.

'Right, I'll help you. Do you mind if I have a look?'

I oblige, pulling down my top to expose my breast. She takes a look, poking and prodding as I wince at the pain. 'Can't see anything wrong,' she says. 'It must be your technique.' She strips Alice to her nappy and hands her to me, but when I put her to the breast she pulls away and starts to scream.

'You need to be a bit firmer with her.' Paula pushes Alice's head forcefully onto my breast, cutting off her screams. She squirms but Paula holds her tight, and then she finally starts to suck vigorously.

I smile at Paula gratefully.

Then the doorbell rings.

My heart leaps. Could it be Ian?

Then it sinks again. Surely he'd let himself in with his key? I shift on the sofa, about to get up.

'You stay there,' Paula says. 'Keep going with the feed. Don't worry, I'll tell whoever it is to go away.'

I hear Paula open the door, and then a voice I'd recognise anywhere. Mum's.

Suddenly I remember. I was supposed to go for afternoon tea with her today. A pre-birth, mother-daughter bonding session and an attempt to build bridges. She's come to pick me up.

Oh god. I look around me in a panic. I'm exposed on the sofa and I haven't even told her the babies have been born. She's going to be furious.

In the hallway, I hear Paula explaining to Mum. 'I'm her doula.'

'Yes, we've met. But why are you here now?' Mum sounds confused.

'To look after the babies,' I hear Paula say calmly. My heart aches for Mum then. I remember how much she wanted to meet her grandchildren, how upset she'll be that I haven't told her they've arrived.

'You mean help with preparations for the birth?' Mum says, not understanding.

'No,' Paula says. 'I mean help with the babies. Katie gave birth to them yesterday.'

'What?' I can hear the shock in Mum's voice. 'But… they weren't due for another three weeks… Is everything OK? Is Katie OK? Why hasn't she told me?' Her voice is getting higher and higher and is now almost a squeak.

I take Alice off my breast and she takes my nipple with her and then starts to scream when it springs back out of her mouth. Ignoring the pain, I put her down and readjust my top. I need to talk to Mum, to explain.

'Everything's fine,' Paula says. 'The babies are healthy. Katie just didn't want any visitors for the first few days. She wanted some time for the babies to settle in.'

'But you're here. Aren't you a visitor?'

'I'm helping with her postnatal care.'

I pick a screaming Alice back up and rush into the hallway.

'It's OK, Mum,' I say.

'Katie!' She stares at me, then down at Alice in my arms. 'It's really true. You've had the babies.'

'Yes, Mum. I'm sorry I didn't call. It's been so crazy. I only got home from the hospital last night.' I'm rambling now, trying to explain my behaviour. I feel the guilt rising inside me as I see the expression on Mum's face.

'You didn't want to tell me?' she asks.

Paula interrupts. 'Now's not a good time. Katie was breastfeeding.'

'I could help,' Mum says. 'With the babies, or with the housework. It's so overwhelming when they're first born.'

'She just needs some peace.'

We're all still by the front door. A stand-off. I can see Mum wants to come in. But Alice's screams are insistent, demanding that I take action. I can't concentrate when she screams like this.

'Mum, I'm sorry but I really need to feed her.'

Mum stares at the baby in my arms. 'Can I hold her?' she asks.

'She's hungry. I just interrupted her feed. She needs her milk,' I say, feeling a kind of primal urgency as Alice's screams get louder.

'Could you come back another day?' Paula asks.

Mum looks stunned. 'I could wait here,' she says. 'Until she's been fed.'

'I'll message you, arrange something,' I reply, raising my voice above Alice's screams.

'Look,' Paula says. 'Katie's been quite clear. She's in the middle of feeding her babies. She doesn't want you here right now. She can message you when she's ready for visitors.'

Paula starts to shut the door and Mum meets my eyes, an expression of bewilderment and hurt on her face.

CHAPTER SIXTEEN

When Mum's gone, I immediately feel guilty. Alice is still screaming so loudly that I can hardly think, and I return to the sofa and perch on the edge, struggling to sit down on my stitches. I put Alice to my breast and she takes a shaky breath and then sucks angrily. Frances is still asleep on her mat. She rarely seems to be awake to feed, and I'm worried she's not taking enough milk.

I was too stressed to deal with Mum, on top of everything else. I still feel dazed from the birth. But did she really deserve to have the door shut in her face? She hadn't meant any harm. She was only coming to see me because we'd arranged it. And she'd wanted to see her grandchildren. And why shouldn't she? I feel so bad about the way Paula and I treated her. We were just starting to get on better. And now I've ruined things.

I pick up my phone from the coffee table and do what I always do when I'm feeling ashamed of my behaviour. I call Amy for reassurance.

She picks up on the second ring.

'Katie! I've been meaning to call you. I'm still stuck in the house. The doctors said I've still got to rest my leg. I've been so bored. And I wanted to talk to someone about it, but I just thought you'd be so busy with the pregnancy… Anyway, how are you? How are the little babies?'

'They've arrived,' I say, with a smile in my voice.

'What? What do mean, they've arrived?'

'I had them. Yesterday.'

'What? Why didn't you call me?'

'I was kind of busy.'

She laughs. 'So how was it?'

'Pretty awful,' I say. I go into the details of the birth. How Alice was a dream birth and Frances was a nightmare.

'Wow. That sounds horrific. Did Ian witness it all? Did he faint?' Amy laughs.

'He couldn't make it. He's in Thailand. On business.'

'On business! What was he thinking?'

'It was an important deal.' I don't know why I'm making excuses for him.

'Is he on his way back?'

'Not yet.'

'What do you mean, not yet?'

'I haven't even heard from him, Amy.' I feel the pressure building up inside my head, the beginnings of a migraine. Alice must sense my stress levels rising because she pulls away from my breast.

'Oh my god. Are you alright? Do you think something's happened to him?'

'I've got no idea. I don't know what's going on. He hasn't contacted me since the babies were born.' My stomach knots with worry. What if something terrible has happened to Ian? Or what if he's left me?

'Oh my god, you poor thing. So you're looking after the babies on your own? I could get a taxi over now. Come and help you. Although I can't do much with a broken leg. I could keep you company, though.'

I know she can't really afford a taxi and I don't want her to waste her money.

'It's OK. Paula's here.'

'Paula? Oh, the doula? That's good she's still there with you. But I can come too if you like. You need a friend.'

'It's OK,' I say. 'I'm coping.' I want to tell Amy about Paula shooing Mum away, but I can see Paula's shadow in the hallway and I'm not sure how much of the conversation she can hear.

'Mum came round too,' I say. 'But I'd forgotten she was coming. I told her it wasn't a good time. Everything was hurting and I just couldn't deal with her. I feel awful about it. She only wanted to see her grandchildren.'

'I'm sure she understands. You've just given birth. You're bound to be a bit emotional.'

'Yeah, I suppose so. Thanks.'

'Are you sure you don't want me to come round?'

'Don't worry. We can wait for your leg to heal.' Alice is starting to get heavy on my arm and I adjust my position on the sofa to get more comfortable, and then grimace in pain as I put pressure on my stitches.

'It could be weeks,' Amy says miserably. 'Look, this is important. You're on your own with twins. I'm just going to get a taxi over and put it on the credit card.'

'I thought you were maxed out?'

'I've got a new one.'

'You can't do that. Look – come over in a few days. I'm sure Ian will be back by then. Then he can pay for your taxi. It's the least he can do.'

'OK,' she says. 'I could come on Monday. Would that work?'

'Yeah.' I want to talk more, to tell Amy everything that's happened and confess all my worries about Ian, but Frances starts to scream and the rest of our conversation is a series of sorrys and pardons as we struggle to hear, until we give up and say hurried goodbyes.

When I get off the phone I see I have a missed call from a roof repair company. Paula takes Frances from me to comfort her while I ring them back.

'I can come round in an hour,' says the man at the other end of the line, 'and have a look. It sounds like the kind of thing that can be fixed today. Pretty straightforward.'

'Thanks so much.' I imagine myself sleeping beside my twins tonight and relief rushes through me.

'I just need to take the call-out fee over the phone. It's seventy pounds.' My heart sinks. I kick myself for maxing out Ian's credit card on baby clothes. I really didn't need so many. My own credit card is just shy of its limit and my current account's close to empty. My maternity pay hasn't come in yet. If I pay for this now, I'll be completely broke. And that's just the call-out fee.

'How much do you think the work will cost?' I ask hesitantly.

'Depends what I find when I get there. But I reckon a minimum of five hundred pounds. Possibly a bit more, depending on the extent of the damage.'

There's no way I can afford that.

'I'm sorry,' I say. 'I don't think I can go ahead.' I hang up the phone. I'm going to sleep in the leaking bedroom until Ian comes back and fixes it.

'I've cooked lamb for dinner. Keep your iron levels up,' Paula says that evening.

'You shouldn't be doing that. You're here to help with the twins, not cook.'

'It's nothing.'

I feel a nagging worry. I'm really not sure how I'm going to pay Paula if Ian doesn't return soon. He still isn't answering his phone and neither is anyone at his office. Perhaps they're in Thailand with him, helping him secure the deal. I've left so many messages. Why hasn't he got in touch?

I take Alice through to the kitchen and put her in the baby chair as I try to find a comfortable position on a designer kitchen stool.

I neck a couple of painkillers and then I eat quickly, desperate be able to return to a softer chair.

'Are you alright?' asks Paula, seeing my discomfort.

'Yes, it's just the stitches.'

'That doctor was a barbarian. You never needed to be cut in the first place.'

I wince. 'I know. I wish she hadn't.'

'You were doing so well in labour before they put you on that drip. Your breathing techniques were really working. You could have pushed Frances out, no problem. But she wanted to cut you. Probably in a hurry to take her break.'

'It's done now.' I don't want to think about it. I hadn't realised how much pain I'd be in after the birth.

Paula reaches out and strokes my hair. 'You've been so brave through all of this. I've been so impressed. But you don't have to be, you know. After dinner, I can run you a bath with Epsom salts and you can relax while I look after the babies. That should help heal your wounds.'

In the bath, I let my head sink under the water, enjoying the warmth on my face, my hair fanning out. Under the water I can only hear the gurgles through my ears, only feel the porcelain of the bath and my own chest rising and falling.

But I can't escape my thoughts. If Ian doesn't come back, what am I going to do? I'll be a single mother, struggling to look after twins on my own. I won't have any money. How will I even afford nappies?

I hear the bathroom door open and I rise up quickly, head surfacing from under the water. I instinctively put my arms over my breasts. But it's just Paula.

'How are you feeling?' she asks.

'Much better.'

She passes me a towel, and I gratefully wrap it round me. 'Thanks.'

'How are your stitches?'

They feel better, calmed by the salts, but I really can't say how they're healing. I have no way of looking at them without a mirror, and I haven't dared take one out to study the damage that's been done to my body by the birth.

'The salts have helped,' I say.

'I could have a look at them if you like? Apply some ointment to cool them.'

I hesitate for a moment, embarrassed by what they might look like.

'Don't worry, I've seen it all before.'

'Sure,' I say. 'Thanks.' I wonder at this moment if the indignity of giving birth has transformed me permanently from someone who changed under a towel at the gym, to someone who lets it all hang out in the swimming pool changing room, not caring who sees.

'Come into the main bedroom and dry off. It's easier there.'

'OK,' I say. She's right. It's awkward changing in my small double room, with the crumbling plaster and festering damp. I'll feel dirty again as soon as I enter.

I towel off in her room and throw on a T-shirt, while Paula potters around downstairs looking for the ointment.

'Are you ready?' Paula calls through the door.

'Yes,' I say.

'Lie down on the bed.'

I lay the towel out on the bed to catch the blood and lie down, feeling only moderately embarrassed about my semi-nudity. I shiver in the cold and goosebumps rise on every inch of my skin. Paula washes her hands in the basin in the room and then comes over.

I feel her fingers touch the stitches and I wince.

'Have you had a look at this?' she asks.

'No,' I admit.

'Maybe best not to. They haven't done a great job. It looks a little infected.'

'Infected?' This is the last thing I need.

'It's OK,' Paula says. 'I've got some cream that will help.'

Paula rubs it over and over into my skin and I bite my tongue to stop myself from crying out.

'There,' Paula says. 'That'll get better in no time. But it does make me angry that doctors can leave you like this and there's no way for you to know what they've done. They really haven't done a good job. What do people do when they don't have anyone to check them?'

'Thank you, Paula,' I say, rising from the bed and wrapping my towel around my waist. 'I really don't know what I'd do without you.'

'Do you know when Ian's coming back?' Paula asks me out of the blue the next day, as she changes Alice's nappy.

My body tenses. Does Paula suspect he's not coming back too?

'I'm not sure. He might need to stay out a bit longer.' I feel my face flush. I've tried to sound like I'm OK, but I'm going out of my mind with worry. If he's left me, then what am I going to do?

'How much longer?' Paula asks.

'A few more days,' I say vaguely. I'm so ashamed he hasn't been in contact. I can't admit that to Paula.

'I was just wondering if you'd thought about registering the births. You need to do it to qualify for child benefit.'

'Yeah, that's a good idea.' I need that child benefit money more than anything. I don't know how much longer I'll be able to afford nappies, let alone anything for me. But what about Ian? He should be on the birth certificate. 'But I should wait, shouldn't I? For Ian?'

'You don't have to. It might be best to do it without him. You don't want to leave it too late.'

'I'm not sure.' It seems so final to go without him. What if he reappears with a reasonable explanation for everything? After all, it's only a few days since the twins were born. That's not long if he hasn't been getting my messages.

'Let's give him a bit more time.' I blink back tears.

'Time for what?'

'He'll be back soon,' I lie. 'He's just trying to find a flight.'

Paula raises her eyebrows. 'There are lots of flights from Thailand.'

'He's in a remote part. He needs to get back to Bangkok before he can catch a flight.' I want to stop this conversation before the lies get more intricate, before I get caught in their web and I can never come back from them and admit the truth.

'OK,' says Paula. 'I just don't want you waiting around for him forever. He's not worth it.'

8

We want to hear what the man's saying to our parents, but we can't. They've gone to the kitchen and their voices don't carry up to our room. We think about creeping down from our bedroom but we can't risk it.

'He looked like a policeman to me,' my sister says confidently.

'I don't think he was wearing a uniform.'

'Not all policemen wear uniforms. Some go around pretending they're just normal people. And then they catch out the bad guys.'

'Do you think that's what he's doing?'

'Maybe. I mean, Dad let him in, didn't he? If he'd looked like a policeman he'd never have let him in.'

'Yeah.'

'And then Dad will relax and confess.'

'Confess to what?'

'To hurting us. To hurting Mum. You know, I bet Miss Kingdom sent him.'

I feel hope filling me up and I grin. 'Do you think he'll take him away?'

'I think so. He'll be put in jail.'

I smile at the image of Dad in jail, handcuffed, unable to hurt anyone.

Then I frown, remembering seeing the man at the door. He'd been shorter than Mum. How would he take Dad to jail?

Suddenly we hear the front door shut. I run into the hall and look out the window over the driveway. He's walking away from the house.

'Has he gone?' My sister asks, coming up behind me.
'Yes,' I say, sadly.
I sink down onto the carpet. We're not being rescued.

CHAPTER SEVENTEEN

When I get up in the morning, Paula already has the breakfast cooking. She's changed the nappies and put the babies side by side in the baby chairs Ian bought them. Frances is screaming as Paula scrambles the eggs and chops the mushrooms.

'Maybe she needs more milk,' I say. I'm so worried about Frances's milk intake, I want to grab any opportunity to try and feed her.

As I bend to pick Frances up Paula reaches for my arm and pulls me back. 'You should eat first. She can wait for her feed. It's better if babies know who's in charge.'

'Is it?' I thought you should always attempt to soothe a crying baby. At least that's what the book that Amy gave me on attachment parenting says.

'Of course it is. If you let them do what they want now, what do you think's going to happen when they're teenagers?'

I look doubtfully down at my baby's scrunched-up, blotchy face. Every mothering instinct I have tells me to pick her up and comfort her.

'I could just give her a quick cuddle…'

'No.' Paula says firmly. 'If you do that then you're undermining your credibility. Honestly, I've looked after babies for years and the disobedient, emotional ones are always the ones whose mothers indulge them. Letting them cry and not giving in to their every demand is better for them and for you. They'll be much better-behaved young children.'

'OK,' I say, reluctantly.

I try to eat my scrambled egg quickly, shoving huge forkfuls into my mouth. Once again it's hard to sit comfortably with my stitches pulsing in pain and I want to get back to Frances, who continues to scream. I hear my phone ringing and rush to answer it, praying that it's Ian. Or if not Ian, at least the midwife arranging another visit. I have so many questions for her. I want her to weigh Frances to check she's not losing too much weight.

I pick it up breathlessly. 'Hello?'

'I hear congratulations are in order.' For a moment I'm thrown, and then I realise it's Melissa.

'Thanks,' I say, hovering above Frances's baby chair, unable to focus while she screams.

'Mum told me yesterday. She said to give you a little bit of time to settle in before I called you. I hope that was the right thing to do?'

'Ummm… yes.'

I pick Frances up and hold her to me, ignoring Paula's frown.

'Are they both OK?' I can hardly hear Melissa over Frances's wails. I carry Frances to the living room, planning to try and feed her while I'm on the phone.

'Are they OK?' Melissa repeats more urgently. 'There's a lot of noise. I can call back later if it's not a good time.'

'It's fine,' I say as I manoeuvre myself onto the sofa and Frances onto my breast. I want to stay on the phone so I have a reason to be out of the room, so I can try and feed Frances, away from Paula.

'They scream a lot at this age,' I say to Melissa reassuringly, although I'm not entirely sure it's true. I need to check with the midwife that Frances's behaviour is normal.

'Sounds like you're taking it in your stride,' Melissa says, and I stop myself from laughing at just how wrong she is, as I try and get Frances to latch.

'Ow,' I say, but Melissa doesn't hear me.

'Is Ian helping out?'

My chest tightens at the mention of his name and I think I might cry. I can't tell Melissa the truth, can't tell her how much trouble I could be in. I feel so ashamed. I take a deep breath. I should tell her. I'll need help.

'Ummm… well…'

Melissa laughs. 'They never help out as much as you expect, do they?'

'It's not that,' I say, but my voice catches in my throat and Frances pulls away from me and starts screaming again.

'They're all the same,' Melissa says, warming to the theme. 'I bet he's still working all hours, isn't he?'

'Well, yes. Actually…'

'Sorry? I can't really hear you.'

'Never mind,' I say quietly.

'Well, at least he's around some of the time, I suppose. Mum said you were finding it a bit difficult. Just getting used to things.'

'Yeah.'

'She said you didn't want to see her when she came round yesterday. She was a bit upset.'

I feel a rush of guilt. I've texted Mum to apologise, but I know I should have phoned. I just couldn't face it. I don't know how to explain the way I treated her. Then I think about what Amy said. It's normal to feel out of control when you have a baby. 'I was a bit stressed,' I say. 'I didn't mean to upset her.'

Melissa doesn't read between the lines. 'Well, Mum only wants to help. And meet her grandchildren. When can we both come and meet the twins?'

I feel chastised. And guilty. 'How about Saturday?' I say.

'Great. See you then.'

After I hang up, I feel irritated. I didn't get the chance to explain to Melissa how difficult things are. Sometimes I feel like I'm on a totally different wavelength to her and Mum.

I don't want to finish my breakfast; it will be cold by now. Instead I pace the hallway, trying to calm Frances. There's no noise from Alice. I don't want to go into the kitchen and face Paula's criticisms for picking up Frances, so I wander into the musty dining room, to the piano. I'm drawn to it. I just want to sit down and play and play, forget all my worries about Ian, all my anxieties about looking after the twins, the tension between me and my family. Above me, I can see where water has dripped through the ceiling from the leaking bedroom, forming a light brown stain.

I sit on the stool cuddling Frances and close my eyes. Holding her across my chest with one hand, I start to play with the other. Even though the piano is out of tune, I become lost in the music and Frances's screams start to quieten.

I begin to relax.

'It's such a beautiful piano.' I turn to see Paula behind me. I didn't hear her come in. 'It must have been precious to someone once,' she says.

'I know. It needs some love to get it back into service.' I rest my fingers on the keys, calming as I feel the familiar smoothness.

'Then we could use it to entertain the twins. They'd be so lucky.' Paula smiles.

'I can put my time at music college to use.' I laugh lightly, but I feel regretful and I think of Mum and how much she'd wanted me to succeed. I'm not even doing gigs at pubs anymore. I stopped when I got pregnant. I look down at Frances and think of all my hopes for her future. I want everything in the world for her. I wonder if this is how Mum felt about me. For the first time, I feel like I might have let her down.

'We should get it tuned up,' Paula says. 'Then it will sound even better.'

I'd like that, but I don't reply. Paula won't be staying much longer. The more time passes, the more convinced I am that Ian isn't coming back. And then she'll have to leave. And so will I.

*

At lunchtime, the midwife still hasn't phoned and I keep ringing her, but I just get the answerphone.

'What's the matter?' Paula asks. 'You seem stressed today.'

'The midwife hasn't got back to me and I'm worried about Frances.'

Paula smiles at me reassuringly. 'It's only natural to worry. But I've worked with dozens of mothers and babies and I can see she's fine.'

'Thanks.' But as much as I value Paula's opinion, I'd still like to check with the midwife.

'It's hard at the beginning, but you're doing a great job.'

'Thank you. It doesn't feel like it.'

'You are, I promise. Who was that on the phone earlier?'

'My sister.'

'Did she have any words of wisdom?'

'No... Speaking to her always stresses me out.'

'Families can be difficult.'

'Yeah. I've never really had a close relationship with her or Mum.'

'What about your father?'

'He died when I was six,' I say, swallowing the lump in my throat and fighting the unexpected rush of emotion.

'I'm sorry.'

'I can't really remember it properly. Mum doesn't talk about him much. Sometimes it feels like he's been forgotten.'

'You were so young when it happened.'

'Yeah. I spent my whole childhood missing him. I felt like he was the missing piece of me, that he'd have helped me make sense of who I am. I imagined that if he'd been alive, that we'd just get each other somehow, in a way Mum didn't get me.'

'Your mother's not the most supportive person. She was so determined to barge her way in here yesterday against your wishes.'

'Melissa thinks I've been unfair to her. I've been feeling guilty about sending her away.'

'You have to stick up for yourself, otherwise she'll walk all over you.'

'Thanks,' I say. 'I just wish I had a better relationship with my family. I wish my father was alive. I wish Ian was here.'

'I'm sure Ian will be back soon.'

I nod. 'Are you married?' I ask. I'm hoping that she says yes, that she's had a long, happy marriage. Then she can tell me her secret.

But she says wistfully, 'I was once. I was too young. Young and naïve. He was penniless. He didn't leave me anything in the divorce apart from his name.'

'You didn't have children?'

'No. There was a time when I wanted them, but I've gone past the point where it's possible anymore.'

'I'm sorry,' I say.

'Don't be. I came to terms with it a long time ago.'

I appreciate how candid she's being and wonder if I should tell her how Ian hasn't contacted me. I scratch nervously at the scar on my arm. 'I haven't had any update from Ian,' I admit, my stomach knotting. 'I wanted my twins to have a good relationship with him, to have the relationship I missed out on with my own father after he died. But that's not looking likely.' I wipe the tears from my eyes.

'I'm sure he's on his way back. He must have found a flight by now.'

I'm about to tell Paula the truth when she wraps me in a hug and the words die on my lips. 'You're doing a good job in difficult circumstances,' she says. 'Don't let anyone tell you otherwise.'

'Thanks. Sometimes I'm not so sure.'

'It's because your family undermines you. You're so used to your mother's criticisms that you've internalised them. She makes you feel like you're not good enough and you believe it.'

I nod. She's right.

'I didn't have a happy childhood either,' she continues. 'That kind of thing affects you for life.'

'I'm so glad you understand.' I smile weakly but I feel a bit faint.

'I lost my own father recently. It's affected me greatly, even at my age.'

'I'm so sorry.' I reach out to touch her arm. 'I didn't know. When did you lose him?'

'Last year. It's weird, there's so much you forget about your childhood, but when you lose a parent, suddenly the memories start flooding back.'

I nod. I can't remember much of my childhood. I just have flashes of memories. Holding my father's hand. Playing the piano with my mother. Messing around with Melissa.

My mother and sister have had to fill in the gaps. Mum's shown me the photos. Family picnics, birthdays, Christmases. They should be happy memories, but they feel static and unreal, from another life. And underneath it all there's something just below the surface, something darker and unknown. I push down the thoughts, not wanting to remember.

CHAPTER EIGHTEEN

Frances has been screaming next to my breast for over an hour, latching and then sucking and then coming off again. Paula comes in and takes her from me. 'I'll give her the bottle,' she says.

'I could keep trying…'

'You've been so worried about her weight. You need to let her have the bottle. You can't have her screaming when the midwife comes round. She'll think you're not coping.'

'I really wanted to breastfeed. I'm succeeding with Alice.'

'Frances and Alice are different. They have different personalities. Think how different the births were. Alice's was textbook, whereas Frances tore you apart from the inside, while the hospital pumped you both full of drugs. You can't expect her to be the same as her sister after that. She's been more difficult from the beginning.'

'I just want to treat them both the same.' I blink back tears.

'What time is your mother coming round?' Paula asks.

'Two o'clock.' It's the time that fits in best with the routine that Paula has got the twins into. Feed. Nappy change. Sleep. Repeat. She's pasted up a timetable on the fridge and we try to stick to it. It makes everything go smoother.

I'm dreading seeing Mum. I don't know what to tell her about Ian. I never even told her he'd gone to Thailand. She'll judge me if she knows he hasn't seen his children yet. But if he's left me then I'm going to have to swallow my pride and ask for her help.

After the babies have fed and had their nappies changed, we put them down for their nap. They scream at first and then fall fast asleep, Alice's tiny hand reaching out to find Frances's and gripping it tight.

I smile at Paula, my heart brimming with love for my girls. 'Peace and quiet.'

'You see,' she says. 'A routine works. It makes everyone happier.'

I'm cleaning the living room and struggling to stay awake myself when the midwife arrives and bustles into the room. She has an iPad, and as she asks me how I'm coping she ticks boxes off on her electronic list. She asks me about how much support I get from my partner, and I can't bring myself to confess Ian's not been here. I hear myself lying yet again, saying that Ian helps where he can, but is out at work a lot and is just 'getting the hang of things'.

'I see.' She raises an eyebrow. 'And what other support do you have? Do you have family nearby?'

'I have a private doula helping me out.' She smirks, and I know she has already taken in the huge house and the expensive decor. The doula is the final confirmation that I have more money than sense.

'You know we offer you all the support you need through the NHS. You get an allocated health visitor, and then there's support in the community: breastfeeding clinics, mums' groups, baby-weighing clinics.'

I nod.

'But I suppose if you've got a private doula you don't need any of that.' I can see her mentally ticking me off her list as someone who doesn't need any help.

'Actually, I've been worried about Frances. I think she's losing weight.'

Paula appears in the doorway.

'I'm Paula,' she says, holding out her hand to the midwife. 'Katie's doula.'

'Sheila,' the midwife says curtly. 'Let me have a look at Frances first, then. We don't normally weigh babies again this early on. It's quite normal for them to lose weight in the first few days.'

She picks Frances up and examines her and then Alice. 'They both look fine. Perfectly healthy.'

'Frances hasn't been eating properly. She seems to hate breast-feeding.'

'Don't worry too much. She looks OK to me, and breastfeeding can take a while for you both to get the hang of. But I can arrange for the feeding consultant to come and visit if you like.'

'I've been helping her,' Paula says.

'It's still early days,' says Sheila.

'Exactly.'

'Right,' the midwife says. 'If that's it, then I'll head off. Or is there anything else you're worried about?'

'My stitches are very painful. It's very difficult to sit down.'

'I'm afraid that's normal at this stage. It will get better.'

I think about asking her to have a look at them, but she's already packing up her bag to go. And besides, Mum and Melissa will be round in a minute.

When Mum and Melissa arrive, the babies have been fed once more, washed and dressed in clean clothes.

'Hi,' I say, smiling as I open the door.

'Katie!' Mum beams. 'I'm so glad to see you looking so well. I was worried about you last time I came round.'

'I'm fine, Mum, honestly. Sorry to worry you.'

Paula walks out from the kitchen and Mum's face falls. She opens her mouth and then closes it again. She looks at Melissa, who gives a little shake of her head, enough to persuade Mum not to ask me why Paula's still here.

'I'm glad you're OK,' she says instead. 'I can't wait to meet the babies properly.'

'Me too,' Melissa says, slipping her shoes off.

'They're just in the living room.'

We go through and I pass Alice to Mum. 'This is Alice,' I say, as Mum coos over her. I see my sister swallow.

'So how was the birth?' Mum asks.

I wince as I remember how terrifying it was, how I had to go through all that without Ian beside me.

'It was OK,' I say. I don't want a lecture on how I was silly not to accept pain relief. She'd never understand why I wanted a natural birth.

'Birth is always horrible,' she says, and I realise she's seen through me. 'Quite frankly, I found mine traumatic. I wish I'd been knocked out completely when I gave birth to you.' I nod, not wanting to admit that, with hindsight, I wish I could have been knocked out for Frances's birth too.

'Birth is a natural thing,' Paula says, frowning.

Mum passes Alice to Melissa, who holds her in her arms stiffly, as if she's afraid that even the slightest movement might break her. I see tears forming in her eyes and realise how difficult this moment must be for her.

'Hello Frances,' Mum whispers, as she picks her up. Melissa winces at the name. We haven't discussed the twins' names since our falling-out. Whenever I tried to speak to her about it she just changed the subject.

'Frances is a lot lighter than Alice, isn't she?' Mum says.

'I know,' I say defensively.

'I wish I could have helped at the birth,' Mum says. 'I hate to think I wasn't there for you.'

I bite my tongue, thinking of all the other times she hasn't been there for me. But then I feel guilty. She'd only wanted to help me, and I shut her out.

'Don't worry. Paula helped me out. She's trained in caring for women during birth,' I say pointedly.

'Well, I'm glad you had someone with you.'

'So, where's Ian today?' my sister asks, sensing the tension and changing the subject.

'He's at work,' I answer quickly, meeting Paula's eye and praying she won't tell them the truth. There's a small chance Melissa might be sympathetic, but I can't bear the thought of Mum's judgement.

'I'm sure he'll have plenty to keep him busy when he gets back. I expect work's a rest for him, compared to looking after two babies.'

I manage a forced laugh.

'Is he good at changing nappies?' my sister asks with a smile.

'He's OK.'

The conversation continues and I can't help but lie. They ask how Ian's coping with the babies crying in the night, whether we're getting any sleep, who's cooking the meals. Once I start telling them how much Ian is helping, I can't seem to stop. And I don't dare look at Paula, as I lie and lie and lie.

That night, lying in bed under the crumbling ceiling I can't afford to fix and listening to the creaking house, I come to a decision. I'm going to ask Paula to leave. I have to. I can't keep thinking that Ian will come back, jumping every time the doorbell goes, praying it will be him. He might not ever be coming back. If I'm going to be able to cope as a single mother, then I need to learn to cope without Paula. The visit from Mum and Melissa brought it home to me: I can't just keep burying my head in the sand and relying on her.

'Thanks so much for all your help with everything,' I say to her in the kitchen.

'You're doing really well,' Paula says encouragingly, as she picks up the dry plates from the draining board.

'I don't think I'd have got through the birth without you.' I shudder at the thought of going through that on my own. 'And it's been great to have your help over the last week.' I take a deep breath and spit it out. 'But I think I can manage on my own now.'

Paula puts the plates away noisily in the cupboard. 'You haven't got the hang of breastfeeding yet.'

'No, but the babies are in a routine now. That helps. I need to try and cope on my own.'

Paula stops what she's doing and slams the cupboard door shut so hard that the crockery rattles. She turns round suddenly, her eyes sparking with anger.

'Are you asking me to leave?' she says, her voice heavy with rage.

9

'Who was that man, Mummy?' I whisper as Mum prepares the tea. Dad's upstairs, out of sight, but only just out of earshot.

'What man?' Her body has frozen into place as she dishes up our vegetables.

'The one who came round today.'

'Oh,' she says. 'Oh – he's a friend of your father's.' She struggles to lift the plates from the kitchen worktop, her arms shaking, and I wonder what Dad has done to her.

My sister looks at her, confused. 'But Dad doesn't have friends.'

Dad's thunderous voice bellows from the doorway. 'What are you telling them?' He strides up to Mum, pushes his face next to hers. She quivers. 'I told you not to tell them.'

'Don't you think they should know?' Mum asks. I glance at my sister, terrified. She never stands up to him. And what is it we should know?

'It's nothing to do with them. It's between me and him.'

He leans over the table, puts his face next to mine.

'Are you asking questions, you nosy little brat? Well, you need to stay out of my business.' He slams his fist into the table and the plate of food in front of me bounces skyward and then lands on the floor.

'Look at the mess you made!' he screams at me.

He turns to Mum. 'You see what I mean? Your stupid children. Can't even sit up at a table and eat their dinner without getting it all over the floor.'

He looks directly at me and I shrink away from him.

'Are you afraid of me?' he sneers.

Before I can reply, his hand thwacks me round the back of the head, and I collapse against the table.

CHAPTER NINETEEN

'You're asking me to leave?' Paula glares at me, her cheeks flushed, furious. She takes a knife from the draining board and starts to dry it, running the blade back and forth inside the tea towel.

I step back, surprised at her anger. 'Well, I suppose I am asking you to leave, in a way,' I say, smiling nervously. 'You've done a brilliant job, but now it's time for me to look after the girls on my own. I can give you a great reference.'

Paula sighs heavily. 'Is that what this was to you? A business transaction?'

'No. It's not that.' I scratch at my scar nervously, thinking of everything Paula's done for me.

I see she has tears in her eyes. 'Sometimes I think I get over-involved with my clients. I care too much. I really care about you, Katie. I suppose I wasn't expecting you to ask me to go, not yet.'

I think of how kind she's been to me, how she's listened to me talk about my worries about Frances, about my difficult relationship with Mum, about the loss of my father.

'I'm sorry – you don't understand. It's nothing to do with you,' I say. 'It's Ian. I don't think he's coming back. And if he's not coming back, then I can't afford to pay you. So I have to let you go.' I break down, sobbing.

Paula's face changes, and I see her anger subside. 'Of course he's coming back,' she says, putting her arm around me. 'Don't be silly. He'll be desperate to see his daughters.'

'I thought so too… but really, I think I've been kidding myself.' I glance at her, wondering if I can admit that he hasn't contacted me. I'm so ashamed.

'We haven't even spoken since I gave birth,' I confess, through tears. Paula wraps me in a hug, holding me. I shake with sobs. 'I think he's left me.' I stumble over the words.

'It will be OK,' Paula says. 'Even if Ian doesn't come back, you'll cope. You're a great mother. And I can stay a little longer if you need me.'

'Really, it's alright,' I say through tears.

'If it's money that's a problem…'

'I know Ian can afford it. He said he was happy to pay. But he hasn't sent anything through yet.'

'Look, let me stay a few more days, help you transition to life as a mother. It can be free of charge if you like.'

But I don't want it to be free. I want to pay my way. 'No, Paula. I can't let you do that, it's too much. I haven't even paid you for the work you've already done.' I look at the floor, embarrassed.

'Don't worry about that,' she says. 'Listen, you're providing bed and board, aren't you?'

'I suppose so,' I say.

'Well, I don't need the money. And I want to help you, Katie. I don't want to see you alone like this. So why don't I stay? In return for bed and board? That way, we both win. It would be so hard for me to leave now, I've become attached to you and the twins.'

I stare at the floor. The offer sounds too good to refuse. I'd feel so much happier if Paula could stay just a little bit longer. I can learn everything from her while she's here, and then when she goes I'll be confident enough to look after the girls on my own. Or, if Ian comes back, with his help.

'OK,' I say. 'If you're sure.'

*

'I'm taking you out,' Paula says the next day. 'You need to get out of the house. Stop thinking about Ian.'

'Where are we going?'

'It's a surprise. You'll see when you get there.'

'Paula, I really can't afford much.'

'It's not anything expensive,' she says with a smile, expertly changing Alice 's nappy while I fiddle with Frances's.

We get the bus together and I wheel the pram into the dedicated space. As I tap my contactless card on the reader, I feel sick. I'm not sure if there's enough money in my account to even pay for this journey.

When we get off the bus, we walk past the shops. There are so many things I need to buy. More nappies. Food. Baby clothes. But I can't afford any of them. I think of seeing Mum the other day. Am I going to end up asking her to bail me out? I can't let my babies go without nappies.

Paula looks at her watch. 'It's just round the corner.'

'What is?'

'The registry office. That's the surprise. I've booked you an appointment to register the twins.'

I frown. 'I don't think I'm ready for this.'

'You know it's not worth waiting for Ian,' Paula says. 'You need to start taking back control. So you can cope on your own, with or without him. It will make you feel better, instead of just moping around the house hoping he'll come back.'

I nod. Of course she's right. He still isn't answering his phone. At night, every possible explanation goes through my head. Could he have been in some horrific accident? And no one thought to tell me? Or perhaps he's gone missing and no one's reported him?

But in my heart I know the most plausible explanation is that he's left me.

My stomach knots as I sit in the waiting room, watching the couples that fill the other seats, their tiny babies in their arms. I stare at the fathers enviously as they coo at their babies.

When we're finally called into the office, we sit down opposite the registrar and she fills in details for each twin. When she asks for the name of their father, I give them Ian's name.

'Are you married?' she asks.

'No.'

'I'm afraid, for unmarried couples, we can only register the father if he's present at this meeting.'

I look at Paula. 'He's abroad at the moment.'

'It's up to you if he's on the birth certificate. But if you want him on it, then you'll have to book another appointment and come in with him.'

'You can always add him on later,' Paula says.

'OK,' I say, feeling unsure. 'Let's leave it blank for now. I'll speak to him about it when he gets back and he can come in then.' Paula and the registrar look at me, and I realise I haven't escaped the pitying expressions. Even the registrar has come to the conclusion that he's not coming home. I feel a flush of heat. Frances whimpers in the pram, and I use that as an excuse to pick her up and hold her close, trying to hide my tears.

By the time we get back it's dark, the day already starting to close in on us. Paula starts tidying up, dusting the shelves in the living room.

'You really don't have to do that,' I say.

I pick up Frances from her mat and give her a cuddle. Her eyes follow Paula round the room.

'I'm just trying to brighten the place up a bit,' Paula says. 'Now it's my home too.'

I frown. I know she's only working for bed and board, but I hadn't really thought of this as her home.

She takes an envelope of photos out of her handbag. 'I got some photos printed. Of the twins. I thought they'd look nice.'

'Oh,' I say. 'That's a good idea.' I've hardly remembered to take any photos myself. There's always so much to do. I look round the room now and notice how bare it is. No pictures on the walls. No photographs. If it wasn't for the twins' toys, a changing mat and some nappies piled neatly in the corner by Paula, you wouldn't know who lived here.

'Can I see the pictures?' I ask.

Paula hands me them. They are mainly of the twins. On their play mat, in their buggy, asleep in their cribs. There are a couple where Paula is holding them and has managed to position the phone for a selfie. She's got one of me, at the hospital with them when they were first born. There's a photo of Paula and the twins at the hospital too. Whereas I look pensive and unsure, she's smiling confidently into the camera.

'Do you have any frames?' she asks.

I only have a few and they already contain old pictures of my family and friends. I should really replace them with my twins. I feel guilty that I haven't even thought about it. I hurry upstairs and dig the frames out of an unpacked suitcase, remove the photos and then take them down to Paula.

She slides the new pictures inside and puts them up on the shelves.

'What do you think?' she asks. 'It makes the place look more homely, doesn't it?'

I swallow. 'It does.'

'Great,' she says with a smile, picking up a dirty mug and taking it from the room.

She's right, it does look better with the babies on display. But I wish there were photos up with me and Ian and the girls. That's what I'd hoped for, what I'd imagined. A family life. As it is there are more photos of Paula with my babies than there are of me with them. You would think Paula's closer to them than I am. I frown for a moment, unexpected tears welling up in my eyes. A part of me knows that's probably true.

That evening, Frances is sick on her babygrow. As I put her on the changing table to take it off, I glance out of the window. The huge hedge almost entirely blocks my view of the street outside, but I catch sight of movement on the driveway, a shadow in the dark. I shiver. I'm glad Paula's still in the house with me. I remember how my neighbour appeared suddenly behind me when I was emptying the bin. How he made me jump.

As I start to change Frances's clothes, I hear a rattling and then a knock on the door. I freeze. It's too late for visitors.

Then I hear a key turning in the lock.

I make out Paula's footsteps in the hallway. My heart is in my throat.

There's a muffled conversation.

I need to know what's going on. I pull my twins into my arms and hug them close.

On my way down the stairs, I suddenly recollect Amy toppling down them. My heart beats faster and I grip my twins tighter, looking down at every stair as I take each step.

And then I see him.

Framed by the doorway and lit up by the porch light.

Ian.

CHAPTER TWENTY

'Hi,' I say, shocked. Relief floods through me. He's back. I'm not going to have to bring the twins up on my own.

Paula takes a step away from the door. 'I'll leave you to it,' she says, glaring at Ian before she retreats into the house.

'Katie – I can't believe it. You've had the twins. I missed it.' Ian looks flustered and confused as he stares at the two babies in my arms and I make my way down to the bottom of the stairs.

I'm overcome by emotion and my relief is starting to turn to fury. How can he just turn up like this, out of the blue?

'Why didn't you fly back earlier?' I ask, still hardly able to believe he's here, standing in front of me. I stare at him, waiting for an explanation.

'What do you mean? When did you have them? I think there's been a problem with my texts. I flew back as soon as I got your messages yesterday.'

'Ian,' I say, rage building inside me. 'What do you mean, you only got my messages yesterday? I sent them as soon as the twins were born. And anyway, what about my calls? I rang and rang. How could you ignore me? How could you ignore your babies?'

'I didn't get any calls,' Ian says, doing a convincing impression of bewilderment. He takes his phone out of his pocket and stares at it as if he's never seen it before.

'What do you mean?'

'I didn't get your calls. My phone can't have been working properly in Thailand. I just got all your messages yesterday. They came through all in one go. And then I booked the next flight and flew back.'

'I don't believe you,' I say, although I really, really want to believe him. Could this all have been just a miscommunication?

'You can't have got my messages either,' he says. 'I sent you a couple to check how you were, but I didn't get any reply. I assumed you were busy.' He pulls out his phone and holds it out to me. 'Look – you can see all the messages here.'

He shows me the screen and I see a line of texts from me, telling him I'd given birth to the twins and asking why he hadn't got in contact. His phone says he received them all yesterday.

'Why didn't you call Amy or my mother if you couldn't get hold of me? Or our landline?'

'I didn't have any of those numbers programmed in.'

I sigh. 'I had the twins a week ago.'

'A week ago?' His face falls. 'Just after I went away…'

'Yes.'

'I can't believe I missed it. I thought, when I went away… I thought you wouldn't have them for ages. You weren't due yet.'

'They came early.'

'I'm so sorry. Oh god, Katie, did you have to give birth on your own? I really wanted to be there for you.'

'No, Paula was with me.' I can see him trying to place her name. 'The woman who let you in. My doula,' I clarify.

'That's a relief.' He reaches over the threshold and touches me. 'I'm so sorry, Katie. I don't know how to make it up to you.'

'I've had to do everything without you. Getting them settled. Learning to look after them. Feeding them, changing nappies, comforting them. You've missed it all.'

'It's only been a week…'

It already feels like a lifetime.

'The most important week. You have no idea how stressful it's been without you. I had no idea whether you were even coming back. I thought you'd left me. You didn't reply to my messages. I thought you didn't even want to meet our babies.' I'm crying now and my tears are a mixture of anger and relief. I'm angry he didn't try harder to contact me while he was away, but I'm relieved he's finally back. Not so much for me, but for the twins. They have a father who does want to be in their lives. He hasn't abandoned them.

He reaches out to touch my arm, and leans in close to the babies.

'Which one is this?' he asks, stroking Alice's face. I feel suddenly protective of my children. He needs to earn his place in their lives.

'It's Alice,' I hear Paula say from behind me. 'And it's time to change her nappy and then feed her.' I let Paula take her from my arms and into the living room.

'This must be Frances,' Ian says.

'Yes.'

Paula returns. 'And she needs her feed too. It's getting late,' she says pointedly.

I look at Ian. 'She's right. It's too late for this now.'

'Why don't you leave?' Paula says, her gaze flicking towards the door, where Ian's suitcase still sits on the mat. 'You can't expect to just walk back in here. Katie's been so worried.'

I nod. 'She's right, Ian. We can talk in the morning.'

'It's my house,' Ian protests. 'And I had no idea you'd had the twins until yesterday, I promise, Katie, please believe me.'

I can't get my head round it all now. 'I need to feed the girls,' I say, not knowing what to think. 'Come back in the morning.'

I toss and turn all night, unable to sleep. Paula comes in with the twins regularly so I can feed them, and each time I feel a sense of relief. I want to hold them as close to me as possible, to feel their skin on mine. As much as I've wanted Ian to come back, I feel unsettled by his return. I've got used to coping without him. I want to believe he didn't get my messages, but my trust in him has been shaken. I can't let him back into our lives if he's just going to disrupt the finely balanced routines we've established and then leave again.

The next morning, he arrives early. He must have been shopping after he left last night because he presents me with a beautiful wooden baby walker for the girls. I feel myself soften towards him just a little, as I lead him into the living room where the twins sit with Paula, one in each arm.

She stands, carefully balancing them. 'You've returned,' she says, her eyebrows raised.

'Paula.' Ian greets her with a smile. 'I think we got off on the wrong foot last night. The first thing I should have done was thank you for helping Katie out with the babies.'

'Katie needed someone. You were away.'

Ian looks taken aback. 'I've explained to Katie. I didn't get her messages.' He leans towards the babies. 'So these are my girls. Can I hold them, Katie?'

I nod and he takes them in his arms one at a time.

'They're beautiful.'

'They change so much in the first few days,' Paula says. 'They already look different. They're growing up so fast.'

'Wow,' Ian says. 'I can't believe I missed it all.' He turns to Paula. 'I'm so grateful you were here to help.'

'Paula's done so much for me,' I say, aware that Paula's still angry on my behalf because he missed the births. 'She's been living with me, helping me settle the babies. I don't know what I'd have done without her.'

'Well, thank you Paula. But I don't think we'll need your help now I'm back.'

I give Ian a warning frown, remembering how Paula reacted the last time I suggested she leave.

My phone beeps and I see a text message.

Ten minutes away. Amy. I frown. I'd completely forgotten she was coming round today.

'Katie!' Amy greets me with a huge hug and then hobbles into the house, on crutches.

'Ian's back,' I whisper.

'What?' Amy's eyes widen in surprise. 'When?'

'Last night.'

'Are you pleased?'

'I think so.' I nod. 'I'll take your coat,' I say, louder, for Ian and Paula's benefit.

'Thanks.'

'He's just in the living room with the girls.'

'Actually Katie, I need some help paying for the taxi. I'm out of credit again.' She smiles apologetically.

'Right. Ummm… I'll ask Ian.'

When I ask, Ian reaches his hand into his pocket for his wallet and hands a couple of twenty pound notes over to Amy.

'Thank you so much,' Amy says to Ian, when she comes back in with his change. 'I don't know what I'd have done without you. I'll pay you back, of course.'

'Don't worry about it,' Ian says with a dismissive wave. 'How's your leg?' he asks, eyeing her cast.

'Oh, not that great,' Amy says vaguely. She's already distracted by the babies. Ian is holding Alice, while Frances is lying on the play mat.

Amy sits down on the floor awkwardly and then picks Frances up and holds her high in the air, breathing her in. 'Oh my goodness, Katie. You've produced two such adorable children.'

Ian laughs. 'I think I had something to do with it too.'

'How was Thailand, Ian?' Amy asks, and I realise I haven't even thought to ask him yet.

'Actually it went really well. I think we're about to sign a new multimillion-pound deal to be involved in the building of new hotels over there.'

'Worth missing the birth of your children for, then?' Paula says.

Ian looks flustered for a second. 'Of course not. If I'd known they'd been born I would have rushed back immediately. I'd have been on the first flight as soon as I knew Katie was in labour. But my phone wasn't working properly. I didn't know.'

Amy looks at me and raises her eyebrows, as if to ask whether I believe him. I frown. I have to trust him if we're going to bring up a family together. But I still have an uneasy feeling in my gut. What if he's lying to me?

Ian looks down at Alice in his arms and tickles her under her chin. 'I'd never have missed your entry into the world if I could have avoided it, would I?' he says to her, beaming.

'I suppose the deal means you'll need to spend more time abroad?' Paula says.

'Well,' Ian sits up straighter on the sofa. 'They'll need me there to lead things. But I'm trying to limit my input as much as possible. I'm hoping I can get away with just the occasional trip over. I want to be here with my girls.'

'You're going to need to keep going back?' I ask incredulously. He hadn't mentioned this when he first told me about the trip. I'm angry that after all he's put me through, he's even considering leaving again.

'Well, I'm trying to get out of it. But I might need to go back once or twice. It will be worth it, though. The deal is worth a fortune.'

'I don't care about the deal,' I say. 'I need you here to look after the girls with me.'

Ian turns to me and smiles. 'Katie, I'm so glad you've said that. I was devastated last night when you turned me away. I know you're angry with me, and understandably. But I want to make things work. Can I move back in? I really want to make a proper go of things. As a family.'

I hesitate. In my head alarm bells are ringing. After everything that's happened it's hard to trust him. But despite it all, I love Ian so intensely it hurts. I want the twins to have a father around so badly. And I need the help. I can't look after the twins on my own. I take a deep breath. It's worth giving it a go. For my daughters' sakes. 'OK, then. But I need you around to help me. Not in the office all hours.'

'I'll do as much as I can, honestly. These two girls are the most important people in my life. I know we've got off to a bad start, but I want us all to be a proper family.'

10

We're waiting for the man to come round, watching for him from the huge stained-glass window that overlooks the driveway. He comes round every week at around 4 p.m., bag slung over his shoulder. Sometimes he arrives a little bit before, sometimes a little bit later, but he's always there.

We know he's not a policeman now. He doesn't look like a policeman at all. He always wears shiny clothes. I think it might be a football strip. It must be his favourite team because he wears it all the time. And he can't be a policeman, because if he was a policeman he'd want to punish Dad. But he seems to like him. We hear their laughter echoing up the stairs, before he goes out into the garden and Dad puts him to work.

He never takes a break when he's in the garden and my sister and I watch, fascinated, as he becomes red-faced and sweaty and covered in mud. It's almost as if he doesn't care about getting dirty, as if he enjoys it. The boys at school are like that too. Dad would kill us if we ever let ourselves get that dirty.

The garden looks better after his hours of labour. But nothing else changes. I wonder if Dad pays him for the work. He's never paid anyone to do any work around the house before. He says it's lazy to pay for work you could do yourself. But he's happy to make our mother do it.

My sister nudges me and my eyes are drawn to the driveway. Out of the window, we see him approaching the house as usual. For a second, he looks up and I think he might have seen us. I wave tentatively. He tilts his head back, staring up at the window. My face splits into a smile and I wave harder. But he's looking away now and we hear the front door open and close as he comes into the house.

There's only a brief murmur of conversation before we hear the back door open and we scoot across the hallway to our room to watch him in the garden.

We don't hear Dad coming up the stairs. We don't hear him open the door to our room. But I scream when I see him grab my sister and lift her up, clamping his hand over her mouth to muffle her scream of surprise.

'I'll be back for you!' he calls. I hear him clambering down the stairs.

I sit on the floor, shaking. In horror films children often hide under beds. But in horror films they're always found, dragged out by whichever angry man or monster wants to hurt them.

I wait, and he returns. When he lifts me up, I don't wriggle or protest like my sister. I let him carry me down the stairs. And then he opens a door. The door to the basement.

My sister screams from the darkness below. I'm thrown down at the top of the cold stone stairs that lead down into the black. The door shuts behind me and I hear the bolt move across.

CHAPTER TWENTY-ONE

That evening Ian opens a bottle of wine at the kitchen table and pours a glass for each of us. It's an expensive one he's brought back from duty-free. I know he means it as a peace offering, but I really don't feel like drinking and I tip mine into his and pour myself a glass of water. We can hear Paula pottering about upstairs, putting the twins to bed. Their wails echo around the house, as they always do at bedtime. My whole body is tense as I listen to them.

Ian turns to me and whispers. 'Shouldn't we see what's wrong with them?'

'No. Paula's sleep-training them.' Their screams reverberate inside me and I feel a primal urge to go to them, but Paula says it's essential to get them into a routine.

Ian takes a gulp of wine. 'Why's she still here?'

'She's helping me out, getting them settled.'

He nods. 'Well, she can go now. I'm sure she's been great, but you don't need her anymore.'

'Ian, I can't just get rid of her because you suddenly reappear out of the blue.'

'Why not? Surely a doula is a short-term role? I'm here now. I can help out.'

'Help out, Ian? You're their father. I'll need you to do just as much as me. Or else we keep Paula.'

'How much is this costing?'

I frown. I haven't paid her anything yet.

'Well, nothing at the moment. When I didn't hear from you, she offered to help out in exchange for bed and board. But now you're back, I want to pay her properly for all her work and the help at the hospital.'

Ian gets out his wallet, counts out twenty-pound notes and hands them to me.

'This should be more than enough for what she's already done. Why don't you thank her for helping you and ask her to leave?'

He doesn't understand. I can't just hand Paula some money and tell her to go. Ian has no idea what Paula's meant to me, how much she's helped me.

'She's very reliable. I need her.'

'But what about me? I want to be there for the girls.'

'You haven't been reliable, have you? You missed the births and you missed the beginning of their lives. I need to know I can trust you, Ian. And at the moment, I'm just not sure.'

Ian flinches and takes another sip of wine. 'I'll do anything I can to prove myself to you.'

'I'm going to bed,' I say. 'I'm tired.'

'Stay up a bit longer,' he says. 'Let's talk things through. I know I made a mistake. I should have tried harder to contact you from Thailand. I love you, Katie.'

I sigh. 'I'm too tired for this, Ian.'

'OK, I'll bring my glass up to bed, we can talk there.'

But I don't want to talk. I can't bear to confront everything. Ian missed the birth of our twins. He hasn't been there for the first days of their lives. And now he's waltzed back in and wants us to continue as before. The idea of him in bed beside me, talking at me, seems too much. We have so much to discuss, but right now I just want a bit of peace.

When we get upstairs, he turns left towards the main bedroom, and I grab his arm and pull him back.

'Don't. Paula's in there.'

'She's sleeping in our bedroom?'

'She had to. There was a leak in the spare bedroom and the other rooms haven't been done up.'

'Well, where have you been sleeping?'

'In the spare room.' I push open the door to my mouldy, damp bedroom and Ian crinkles his nose in disgust.

'This is crazy, Katie. How can this room not be good enough for her, but good enough for you? It stinks of damp.'

He looks round. 'And where are the girls?'

'They're with Paula,' I say, blushing. 'She helps them in the night.'

'Katie, this is ridiculous. We can't live like this.'

'I know,' I say. 'But I could hardly make Paula sleep here, could I?'

It takes a while, but I manage to convince Ian not to march straight into Paula's room and instead come to bed with me in the spare room.

'I can't believe you've been sleeping in here,' Ian says as he strips down for bed.

'I didn't have any choice. I desperately needed Paula's help. And I couldn't afford to fix the leak without you.'

'I'll take a look at that tomorrow. See if I can do some repair work. Then Paula can sleep back in here.'

'OK,' I murmur. 'Thanks.'

He runs his hands over the wallpaper peeling away next to the bed's headboard. 'I can fix this too. What are these marks behind it?'

'They're drawings, I think. They look like they were done by a child.'

'Oh,' Ian says absent-mindedly. 'I hadn't thought any children lived here.'

'I know. There's no evidence that a family lived here, is there? No old play equipment in the garden or anything like that. I'd have thought the drawings are years old.'

'Probably,' Ian says, as he climbs into bed beside me. He wraps his arms round me, pushes his torso up next to mine. 'I've missed you,' he says.

'I've missed you too,' I mumble sleepily, grateful for his warmth embracing me in the bed. I feel safe again as the house creaks and groans around us and the roof sags above us.

'I love you.'

'You too,' I say truthfully. Despite everything, I still love him.

I wake to the sound of the babies screaming and check the time once more: 1 a.m. I sit up in bed and start adjusting my nightdress, exposing my breast. Ian stirs in his sleep.

Then Paula pushes the door open, flicks on the light switch and brings the girls into the room.

Ian jerks up in bed at the sudden invasion of light and noise.

He stares at Paula, eyes wide. 'What are you doing here?'

'I'm bringing the girls in for their feed,' she says reasonably.

She places Alice on one breast and Frances on the other and sits on the bed next to me. As usual Alice immediately starts sucking vigorously, while Frances makes a half-hearted attempt and then pulls away. Paula pushes her back on, while Ian watches.

'Is there anything I can do to help?' he asks.

'No,' I say, concentrating on Frances.

When the feed is over, Paula leaves and Ian turns to me.

'Is this what you want?' he asks. 'Paula bringing the babies in in the middle of the night?'

'Not really,' I admit. 'I'd like them to be right beside me, to be able to just look over into their cots. But this room's far too damp.'

'I knew this couldn't be working for you. You're their mother. You need to be with them.'

I feel the familiar sense of longing for my children and tears prick my eyes. I roll away from Ian so he can't see my face.

I toss and turn, listening to Ian's deep, peaceful breathing. Time blurs, expanding and contracting as I fall in and out of sleep, waking frequently and suddenly as if alarms are going off. But each time I stir the air is thick with the silence of the cavernous house.

Until now. This time I've woken up to faint cries. I sit up in bed, listening intently. I can definitely hear them, but they sound far away. They can't be my twins. But my instincts won't let me go back to sleep.

After five minutes, I pad down the hallway to Paula's room, just to put my mind at rest. There's no sound coming from the room. Just silence. They must be fine. Asleep. Safe.

I stand stock-still and listen once more. I can definitely hear babies crying somewhere, in the distance. It must be someone else's children. Perhaps someone has their bedroom window open.

But something's not right. I'm sure of it. I can feel the tension in every muscle of my body telling me something's wrong. It's the sound of the cries that unnerves me. I can hear a slightly stronger cry, like Alice, alongside a weaker mewling, like Frances.

I'm so sure it's my girls and yet I know I must be imagining it. I stand outside Paula's room, listening. Nothing from behind the door. I think about going in just to alleviate my anxiety and then imagine trying to justify myself. Paula has the twins in a strict routine. I wouldn't be able to explain why I'd woken everyone up.

Giving up, I go back to our room.

'Where have you been?' Ian asks.

'Can you hear that?' I say.

'What?'

'The crying.'

He looks at me quizzically. 'I can't hear anything.'

'I was sure it was the girls, but there's no sound from Paula's room.'

He rolls over and wraps his arm around me. 'You must have been imagining it. It's because you're separated from them. It's making you paranoid. You need to be with them. You're their mother and they need you.'

CHAPTER TWENTY-TWO

The next morning, I go downstairs to feed the babies while Ian gets started on fixing the ceiling in our bedroom. After a few hours, he comes back downstairs triumphantly. 'I've been out onto the flat roof and fixed the source of the leak. And I've done a patch repair on the plaster. I just need to wait for it to dry and then cover it with a coat of white paint.'

'That's great,' I say, beaming. Soon I'll be back in our bedroom, sleeping next to my babies where I belong.

He puts his arms around me. 'Why don't we get out of the house? Maybe go for a pub lunch with the twins?'

'I'm not sure that will work,' I say. 'They tend to cry a lot.'

Ian smiles. 'We can't stop having fun. It must have been relentless for you since they were born. You need a break. And I've looked up a family-friendly pub, so we won't disturb other people. Besides, it's perfect weather to sit in a beer garden.'

I raise my eyebrows. Ian likes to eat at Michelin-starred restaurants, not family pubs.

'We'll have to go soon,' I say. 'Mum's coming round in the afternoon, with Melissa.'

'OK, let's have an early lunch. We'll make sure we're back in time.'

When we go downstairs, Paula is in the kitchen. 'I'm just making some lunch,' she says.

'I'm so sorry, Paula, but we're going out,' Ian replies graciously. 'I hope you haven't gone to too much trouble. Perhaps we could have it for dinner tonight.'

'I suppose so,' she says. 'Well, I can look after the twins for you then, give you some time to yourselves.'

'We're taking the twins with us,' I tell her.

She gives me a look I can't read.

'I'll go and get them ready,' Ian says. 'Why don't you sit down, Paula? Relax for once. Do you want me to make you a drink?'

'No, I'm OK,' she replies. 'I think I'll take the opportunity to go out myself.'

A few minutes later, Ian and I hear the door bang shut behind her.

'Do you think we should have invited her?' I whisper.

'She's your doula, not your friend,' Ian says. 'And she's always around. Either in the room or hovering at the edges. I feel like we can't have a private conversation.'

I nod. It would be nice to have some time with Ian alone. Even last night in our bedroom, I thought Paula might hear us through the walls.

We wander to the high street, Ian pushing the buggy, and go to a family-friendly gastropub. I feel relaxed and happy for the first time since I gave birth. Maybe this is the first of many family afternoons with Ian and the twins. I feel hopeful for our future together.

'I think we're taking advantage of Paula,' Ian says, over his Caesar salad. We're sitting outside at the pub, sipping ice-cold drinks and eating lunch in the sunshine. 'She does so much…'

'I know. I don't ask her to. She just seems to do it. I kind of wish she'd stop. It makes me feel a bit guilty.'

'I know she's been helpful to you while I've been away…'

'I couldn't have managed without her.'

'I can see that. She really knows her stuff. But I wonder if we should think about how much longer we need her for?'

'A bit longer,' I say, unsure if we'll be able to cope on our own with two tiny babies. Ian will probably still be working long hours and it will be just me on my own most of the time. I'll need Paula, at least to start with.

'I don't know what her motivation is for being so kind,' says Ian.

I frown. 'Can't you accept that she's just a nice person? She was willing to help me for free when we weren't sure if you were coming back.'

'We need to make sure we pay her properly. I think we should have a proper contract, make everything above board. We don't want to owe her. I've asked for her references too, just to be on the safe side.'

'Why?' I say. 'She'll think we don't trust her.' I don't want to offend Paula. I want her to stick around.

'She creeps me out a bit. The photos she put in the living room – there are more of her than of you. And she's always there, watching. You must admit, she's a bit strange. And I don't like the way she behaves with the twins. Sometimes she acts like she's their mother.'

'I know, but I don't want to let her go just yet. I think we need her to stay and help a bit longer. Just while we get settled.' He might be right, but while he's been away Paula has been my crutch, the one person I could turn to.

'Don't worry,' he says, reaching out across the table and taking my hand. 'She's given me four different references, so I'm sure they'll check out. And now the ceiling's fixed in the spare room, she can move in there and we can move back to the main bedroom. That way you'll be right next to the girls. Paula won't need to bring them to you to feed them in the night. And then we can both get used to being with them, and eventually Paula can leave.'

I imagine being beside my twins at night and immediately feel better. 'We can move her into the spare bedroom tonight, after Mum and Melissa have left.'

'That sounds like a good idea. It will give me time to put a quick lick of paint over the repair when we get back to the house. It should be dry by the evening.'

*

'How are you feeling?' Mum asks, in an exaggerated sing-song voice as she walks through the door. Then she pauses and her face falls.

'Hello, Paula.'

When Paula goes to get the drinks, Mum whispers to me, 'Why's she still here?'

'I needed her to help out. It's hard with twins. But she's leaving soon. Ian and I are starting to get things under control.' I smile. It's such a relief not to be lying about our relationship anymore.

'Yes, Cynthia's daughter had twins and she had terrible trouble. If one wasn't screaming, then the other was.'

'Paula's got them into a routine, which has really helped.'

'You know I could have helped. I could help now, with the girls.'

'I don't want to put you out.' But it's not that; it's all the terms and conditions the help comes with. I'd have to do everything the way she thinks is best.

'If you and Ian ever need me to take the twins for a couple of hours at the weekend and give you both a break, it's no trouble at all.'

'We're OK, Mum,' I say, touching her arm. 'But thanks.'

'If you're sure…' she says.

'Yes. We're going to manage without Paula soon too. We can do it on our own now. We *are* adults, after all.' I laugh lightly, but it's only partly a joke. Mum still treats me like a child.

'I think that's wise. Paula's here more often than Ian is.' I grit my teeth. They still don't know that Ian missed the first week of his children's lives.

My sister picks up a photo from the mantelpiece absent-mindedly. 'And what's with these photos? They are so many of Paula. But none of Ian.'

My cheeks flush with embarrassment. It's the second time the photos have been mentioned today.

'That is rather unusual.' Mum raises her eyebrows.

I sense Mum's jealousy, her displacement by Paula, a woman close to her own age, muscling in on her grandchildren.

'Let's take a photo of you and Melissa with the twins today,' I say. 'Then I can put it up on display with the others.'

Paula comes back in with the drinks and Mum nods, but I can see she's not satisfied.

We talk for a while and I start to feel more relaxed, as Mum talks about her friends and my sister sticks to the safe topic of her work.

Before they leave, Frances wakes up and Mum insists on picking her up and giving her a cuddle.

'She's still small, isn't she?' she says, frowning critically at my baby.

'Yes, Mum, I know,' I say, annoyed.

'Have you taken her to the doctor?'

'The midwife told me she's fine. She'll catch up with growth when she's ready.'

'You need to speak to the doctor. She's skin and bone.' She holds Frances up and we can both see her ribs poking through her tiny chest.

'Mum, I've asked the professionals. I don't know what more I can do.'

'You need to listen to your instincts. Don't let yourself be fobbed off. Don't take no for an answer. Doctors can be lazy. I should know, I've worked with enough. You have to keep going to the GP, keep bugging them.'

'OK, Mum.'

'You and Melissa were never this skinny.'

'She's a different child, Mum. Different genes.'

'It must be hard breastfeeding too. You need more milk for two babies. Have you thought about that, that you might not have enough milk for both of them?'

'It can't be that. Paula's topping Frances up with formula.'

Paula nods. 'That's the best thing for them. Katie can't produce enough.'

'Well, that might be a good idea.' She turns to me. 'You don't want to get too stressed about breastfeeding. If you're stressed the babies will be too.'

Mum passes Frances to my sister. 'What do you think?' My mother asks her. 'Does she seem too small to you?'

'What do I know about babies, Mum?'

My mother glances at my sister and then back at me. 'There must be something going on. I can come with you if you like, to the doctor.'

'There's no need,' Paula says. 'The babies are fine.'

I feel a headache coming on, caught in the middle of this battle.

Later, when Paula is out buying nappies, I go upstairs to feed the twins and find Ian in the main bedroom. He's stripping the sheets off the bed. Paula's meagre possessions are piled on a chair: her nightdress, her book, her reading glasses, changes of clothes, perfume. Her toiletries have been replaced on the bedside table by his collection of moisturisers and aftershaves.

'Ian?'

'I'm just getting the room ready for us to move back into.' He opens the window. 'It needs a bit of airing.'

Alice starts to moan and I pick her up.

'Ian, I think you're jumping the gun a bit,' I say as I rock Alice back and forth. 'I haven't had time to mention moving to the other room to Paula yet.' Although I can't wait to be back in the main bedroom next to the twins, I'm nervous about telling Paula about the move, particularly after the way she reacted last time.

'Well, perhaps you can do it soon.'

'Now seems like as good a time as any.' The voice comes from the door.

We both turn to see Paula standing in the doorway, hands on her hips.

'Paula,' Ian says, going over to her and reaching out to touch her shoulder. She pulls away from him.

I pick Frances up instinctively and hold my twins close to my body.

'You've come into my room without asking. And you've moved my personal belongings.' She glares at Ian.

'Paula,' he says. 'I'm afraid we want our room back. Katie was going to talk to you.'

'Was she now?' She looks at me.

'I've fixed up the spare room,' Ian says. 'It's perfect for you.'

But Paula ignores his words, her face flushed with anger.

'Don't come in here again,' she says.

She shoos us out and then slams the door behind us. In my arms, Alice starts to scream, almost drowning out the other sound. On the other side of the door, I hear a key turning in the lock.

Ian and I look at each other. Where on earth has Paula got a key from?

11

The basement is freezing cold, and it takes a while for my eyes to adjust. When they do, I see a dark shape curled up in the corner. It's my sister, lying on an old mattress, shivering. I slide down the steps on my bottom and go over to her.

'Are you OK?' I ask.

'What do you think? Of course I'm not.'

'What did he do to you?'

She starts to sniffle. 'The same as he did to you. He carried me in here and dropped me on the floor, that's all.' I reach out to hold her hand but she pulls it away.

'Will you have bruises?' I ask.

'I don't think I fell hard enough.'

I nod, dejected. When Dad was out, we saw a bit on the news where a child had unexplained bruises. It turned out her father was hurting her and she was taken away from her parents. Mum quickly turned the TV off, but my sister and I understood the message. If we want someone to believe us, if we want to escape, then we need evidence. We need bruises. Not the kind on your knees from falling over in the playground. Bigger ones.

But we don't have anything like that. Dad always hits us round the head where no one can see.

'Maybe the bruises will come up later,' I say.

Neither of us have heard anything from Miss Kingdom. She's been on playground duty, but she hasn't said anything to us. I'm not sure she believed us.

I sit down on the mattress and put my arms around my sister. She gets up and hobbles to the other side of the basement.

'This is your fault!' she says angrily through her tears.

'What?'

'Why did you wave at that man? You must have known it would make Dad angry.'

'I didn't think he'd find out.'

'Then you must be stupid.'

'I'm sorry.'

I go over to her. The only way we can get through this is if we look out for each other. Despite everything, we've always had each other. We've always needed each other.

I reach over to touch her shoulder. But she pushes me away.

CHAPTER TWENTY-THREE

Ian and I look at each other in shock, staring at the door Paula's just locked. 'Where did she get a key?' Ian asks me.

'I have no idea. I didn't give her one. I didn't even know the door locked.'

'She has to go, Katie. She can't lock herself in a room in our house.'

My temples throb with the beginnings of a headache. He's right. Seeing Mum earlier brought it home to me. Paula has taken over, putting up photos of herself around the house, taking control of the twins' routine and overwhelming me with a constant stream of advice. She's closer to my twins than I am. I needed her before, but now she's embedded herself completely into my life and my babies' lives. It's too much. This was only ever meant to be a short-term arrangement, but now she's acting as if the house is hers.

'It's time for us to be a family on our own, Katie,' Ian says gently.

I nod. As useful as Paula was, and as grateful as I was for her help, she was never going to stay forever. And now I've become too dependent on her. I need that to change.

I pass the twins to Ian and knock on the door. 'Paula?'

No answer.

'Paula? We need to talk.'

The twins start screaming. A chorus of demands: milk, nappy changes, cuddles. For a second, I feel sick. How will we cope on our own?

Ian rocks the twins as he takes them away down the corridor to our bedroom to change their nappies, leaving me to deal with Paula.

'Paula?' I call again.

I hear the key twist in the lock and the door opens.

'What was that about?' she says angrily as she opens the door.

'Ian fixed the ceiling in the spare room for you. We were going to ask you to move in there.'

'I see.'

'But actually, Paula, I'm not sure this is working anymore.'

'You mean with Ian? I told you, you should never have let him back in.'

'No, I mean, I don't think we need your help anymore. You've been completely invaluable to me, but now I think it's time for Ian and I to stand on our own feet.'

'You and Ian?' She laughs. 'You don't know the first thing about looking after your own children.'

Her words are like a punch and I recoil in shock. She's always been so supportive. But now she's throwing my own worries about my skills as a mother back in my face.

'I've got the hang of it now,' I say, cheeks reddening at the half-truth. 'And Ian seems to have picked it up quite quickly.'

'Hmm… that's all very well while he's here. So it doesn't concern you that he didn't contact you for a week after the twins were born?'

I flush, wishing I hadn't confided in her when Ian was away. 'No, not at all,' I say. 'He's explained.' I've put those thoughts to the back of my mind, instead focusing on how kind and attentive he's been since he got back. But now I feel a flash of uncertainty.

'And what was his explanation?'

'My messages didn't come through.'

'And you believe him?'

'Yes. Now Ian's back and we've settled in, we need to start our lives with the twins properly. On our own.'

'I see.' She turns away from me and I can see she's upset.

'We really appreciate everything you've done for us, honestly. I really couldn't have got through it on my own.'

She looks at me sternly. 'I know that. You were all over the place after the twins were born.'

'I'm so grateful. I don't know what I'd have done without you.'

'And yet it doesn't seem that way, does it? It doesn't seem like you're grateful at all.' She pauses and looks me right in the eye. 'So when do you want me to leave?'

'Ummm…' I'd assumed she'd leave immediately. 'We feel we could manage by ourselves now. Obviously we'll pay you for all the work you've done. And a bit extra too, to say thank you.'

'So, tomorrow? Or even today? You know, if I had a proper contract, then you'd have to give me notice to terminate. But we haven't got a contract, because I've done this as a favour to you. As a *friend*.'

'I can give you notice,' I say quickly. 'What notice would you need?'

'It's usually a month,' Paula says. 'But don't worry about it. It's clear you want me to go now.'

'It's not that we want you to go, Paula. It's that we want to try doing it on our own. And we can't do that with another person in the house. We need to find our feet as a family.'

'I understand that. But really, it's the babies I care about, the babies I'm worried about. I love your twins, I truly do. And I'd be worried about them if you and Ian were to look after them on your own. You've hardly proved yourself so far. You're completely dependent on me to do most of the nappy changes, cleaning, washing, comforting, bathing.'

'It was you who insisted on doing all that.' Why is she twisting everything?

'Because I could see you couldn't. I've had so many clients, Katie. But all of them could have coped on their own by now. Except for you.'

I feel creeping self-doubt. Perhaps she's right. 'I can learn,' I say. 'I can change.' I want to be a proper mother to my twins.

'Good luck.' Paula spits out the words.

'We can stay in touch,' I say, desperately trying to placate her. 'You can come round any time you want to visit if you miss the twins.'

'I'll have other clients,' Paula says gruffly.

'It's up to you.'

'This whole idea doesn't sound like you, Katie. Did Ian put you up to this?'

'No, it's what I want too.'

'OK, then,' she says, her voice calm, but her eyes dark. 'If that's what you want, then I'll start packing. But you're making a big mistake. I'm worried about you. You're burying your head in the sand when it comes to Ian. You know you can't trust him.'

I leave Paula to pack up her things and go downstairs. I need some air, and some time on my own. I bundle the twins into the buggy and leave the house. As we walk through the suburban streets, people stop to peer down at the girls, to tell me how tiny and beautiful the twins are. They share stories about their own children at that age. I realise that I rarely have time, just the three of us. Paula normally takes them on walks. I've been afraid of looking after them on my own, afraid I wasn't up to it, but now I feel excitement alongside the fear.

CHAPTER TWENTY-FOUR

When I return to the house, Paula's packed case is by the door. I can hear her rummaging around upstairs.

'Hello?' I shout. There's no answer. Paula's clearly not speaking to me and Ian messaged me a while ago to say he was going out to pick up some bits from the shops.

In the living room, there's a mess of muslins and baby toys and I start to tidy them up. I catch sight of Paula's photo on the mantelpiece, beaming as she stands over the twins at the hospital. She looks so happy. I feel a twinge of sadness. I'll miss her. Perhaps I'll keep the photo there to remind me.

I shove the baby toys in a cupboard and hear footsteps on the stairs.

Paula.

I go to the bottom of the stairs.

'Hi,' I say uncertainly.

'I'm sorry,' she says. 'I thought I'd be gone before you got back. I don't want to disturb you further.'

'I don't want you to leave on bad terms,' I say. 'Honestly, I've loved having you here. You've been a godsend. I hope you'll always know how much I've appreciated you. And how much the girls love you.'

She comes down the stairs without smiling and squeezes by my outstretched arms.

'Have you seen my reading glasses?' she asks brusquely. 'Once I find them, then I'll go.'

'Umm… Where did you have them last?'

'In the kitchen, I think.'

I go into the kitchen and scan all the surfaces, but I can't see them.

But I spot something else. A pile of bills. Ian must have been going through them.

I'm about to ignore them and continue looking for the glasses, when something catches my eye. The bill on top is from the water company with 'overdue' stamped across it in red. I quickly flick through the others. Gas, electricity, broadband. None of them have been paid.

And then there's one from the bank. I pull the letter out of the envelope. The mortgage is in arrears.

I feel sick. This doesn't make any sense. Ian's company owns the house. Surely Ian would have made sure they were paying the bills?

I remember how his credit card was declined when I tried to buy the buggy. I'd assumed I'd spent too much on baby clothes and maxed out his card. But what if his company is in trouble? Is that why he needed the deal in Thailand so much? I pace down the corridor and into the living room. Paula stands by the mantelpiece, the photograph of her and the twins in her hand. 'I'll take this,' she says. 'To remember them.'

But then she notices my pale face. Her cold, blue eyes turn from angry to concerned in less than a second. 'What's the matter?' she asks, kindly.

'I think you might have been right about Ian,' I say.

She frowns. 'What is it?'

'I've found something. I can't trust him.'

She smiles gently and puts her arms around me. 'Do you want to talk about it?'

There's nothing more I want to do than confide in Paula, but I hesitate for a moment. She was about to leave. I *wanted* her to leave. But now everything's changed.

Then I find myself nodding. 'I think I do need to talk about it. I'm so sorry about earlier, Paula. I really didn't mean to upset you.'

'Look, you made a mistake. But it's fine. I can easily stay a bit longer if you need me to. Sit down. I'll make you a cup of tea. Tell me what's happened.'

When Ian returns, he sees my wet eyes and immediately wraps his arms around me. I pull away.

'Has she gone?' he asks. 'I know it must be hard for you, but she needed to go. We need to get started on being a proper family.'

'It's not that.'

But he's not listening. Instead he's holding up a bag that smells delicious. 'I bought food from that new Italian restaurant up the road to celebrate. So we don't have to cook tonight.'

'How did you pay for it?' I ask bitterly.

'Sorry?' Ian says, as he places the takeaway cartons on the kitchen island.

'I said, how did you pay for it?'

He looks up, confused, then notices the pile of bills on the kitchen table. The blood drains from his face as he picks them up. 'Where did these come from?'

'Where do you think, Ian? The electricity company, the gas, the water. You haven't been paying any of them.'

He frowns. 'I'm so sorry, Katie.' He reaches over to kiss my forehead. 'What with the big trip to Thailand and all the preparations before that, and then getting back to see the twins afterwards, I must have completely forgotten.'

'Ian—'

'And don't worry, they wouldn't cut us off. Not yet. They'd need to go through proper procedures.' He continues to set the table, then glances up and sees my face.

'There's no need to look at me like that. It's really nothing to worry about. You're used to renting. When you own the house it's quite different.'

'What about the money you owe the bank?'

'What?'

'The mortgage.'

At this point he pauses and is completely still, a rabbit caught in the headlights. I can see his brain ticking over and I wait.

'This house is a big project. The company's taken out a mortgage to pay for the building work. It's called gearing. The more money you borrow, the bigger your percentage profit.'

'And wouldn't it be normal to pay the mortgage?'

'Of course... The company will have been paying. There must be some mistake.'

'There's no mistake, Ian.' I thrust a letter into his hands from the bank. 'Look, that's our address right there. We're thousands of pounds in debt.'

Ian comes closer and tries to put his arms around me. 'It's OK, Katie.'

I shrug away from him. 'No, Ian, it's not OK. I've tried to forgive you for missing the twins' births, tried to be understanding. But this is the last straw. You've been lying to me.'

'It's just a misunderstanding,' he tells me. 'I thought the company were paying the mortgage and the bills. They must have thought I was.'

'Another misunderstanding? Just like you thought the house would be done up ready for us to move in, but then it wasn't?' I say angrily. 'The people at your company sound incompetent, if that's the case. Why didn't you check the bills were being paid?'

'I should have, Katie, but I didn't. I'm sorry.'

I laugh, sick of his apologies. 'Just like you're sorry for missing the birth of our girls. Because your phone wasn't working.

Another piece of bad luck, Ian. These things keep happening to you,' I spit.

'Katie, that's the truth – I didn't get your messages.'

'You must think I'm stupid. Just a stupid girl working in a coffee shop. Someone who'll fall for all your lies.'

'Of course I don't think that. I love you.'

The words cut through me like a knife. They used to mean so much, but now I know they're empty.

'You need to leave. Right now. Get away from me. Get out of our lives.' I'm holding back tears.

'But Katie—'

'It's your house?' I interrupt. 'Is that what you were going to say?'

'No—'

I push him towards the door, and eventually he relents. 'We need to talk about this,' he says. 'Maybe when you've calmed down.'

'I'm not going to calm down.' I undo the latch. 'Get out. You're not welcome back.'

'But Katie – when will I be able to see the twins?'

I shut the door and burst into tears.

12

My sister won't play with me in the playground anymore. She's playing with other girls and I watch them jumping over the skipping rope and laughing. I tried to join in, but my sister told the others they couldn't play with me.

She hasn't spoken to me for two weeks. I try to start conversations as we walk to school together, but she insists on walking faster and faster until she is running away from me. I try to speak to her before we go to bed each night, to tell her that I love her, but she turns away.

She hasn't forgiven me for waving at the man. We were kept in the basement the entire time he was there. At one point we weren't sure if we'd ever be let out. But we were. But then the following week, Dad locked us in the basement before the man even arrived.

I have to do something. Today Miss Kingdom is on playground duty again. It's down to me to fix things for us, to make things better. I approach the teacher slowly, shaking. It's all up to me.

'Miss?'

'Yes?'

I can feel the colour rising in my face, going bright red. I feel sick. I have to get this right.

'Spit it out, dear.'

'We... we told you about our father.'

'Sorry?'

'Our father... he hurts us.'

'Oh, yes… your little game. I rang him and he told me all about it. You girls need to learn the difference between play and reality. Luckily I spoke to him before I reported him.' She strokes my hair affectionately.

'It's not a game…'

Miss Kingdom crouches down next to me and smiles. 'You've got a vivid imagination. That's a good thing sometimes. But it's not good to make up lies about your father.'

CHAPTER TWENTY-FIVE

I watch from the upstairs window as Ian retreats from the house. Then I go into the kitchen and sit at the table, shaking. I can't trust him at all.

I feel a gentle hand on my shoulder and I jump.

Paula.

'He's gone?' she asks.

'Yeah.'

'It's for the best.'

'I hope so.' The reality of what I've just done strikes me like a blow to the chest. I've chucked out the father of my daughters. Without him I won't have a roof over my head for much longer. Without him I'm a single parent of baby twins. I don't know how I'm going to cope.

'I've unpacked my stuff back into the bedroom. I can stay as long as you need me to.'

'I won't be able to pay you without Ian,' I say miserably. I won't be able to pay for anything without Ian.

'Don't worry about that,' she says, reaching out and stroking my hair.

'Thanks.' For a second, I think about asking her to move into the spare room, but then I think better of it. I need her around, and if she's doing me a favour I feel too bad to ask her to sleep in there. 'It shouldn't be too long. I think I'll have to move out. There's no way I can afford to pay the bills.'

'I wouldn't be too rash. You don't have anywhere to go. And if you move out, you'll lose any claim you have on the house.'

'I don't have any claim on it. Ian owns it.'

'But you're living here, Katie. With two vulnerable children. You've spent more nights in this house than Ian has. If you don't move out then Ian will have to kick you out. And I don't think he'll get very far kicking two tiny babies out of their home.'

The first few days after Ian and I split up are a blur, and Paula sweeps in like an efficient angel and looks after the twins and me. She runs me warm baths and lets me cry into my tea. I can't stop thinking about Ian. I miss him, miss the idea of our future together. I wish that none of this had happened, that we were still together. But when he rings me, again and again, I reject the calls because I can't bear to hear his excuses. I cry every day. Paula sits with me and listens. She helps me come up with a plan to get through the next few months. I'll find work that I can do while Paula looks after the twins. Whenever Ian has the girls I'll take the opportunity to try and get extra shifts. The coffee shop in central London is too long a commute, so I'm going to take my CV round all the local ones, and hope I can pick up a job.

On my first day looking for work I realise that none of my smart clothes fit me properly anymore. I pair a smock maternity dress with a baggy cardigan and scrape my hair back into a ponytail. I apply a bit of make-up and put on heels for the first time in months.

'You're bound to get something,' Paula says encouragingly. 'With your experience.'

'Thanks,' I say. I can't believe I'm looking for work so soon after having the twins. My body still aches all over, my stitches sting and I feel like I have permanent period pains. I'm not even sure I'll be able to stand on my feet all day.

'Do I look OK?' I ask, wanting reassurance.

'You look fine.' Paula reaches forward and tucks a stray hair behind my ear. 'But is this what you want to do? Go back to serving coffee? Is it what you really enjoy?' I sigh. She sounds just like Mum.

'Yes,' I say defensively. It's not like I can do much else.

'What about your music?'

'What about it?'

'You play the piano beautifully. Have you thought about teaching?'

'No…' I say. I never considered teaching before as we didn't have a piano in the flat. But now my mind suddenly races, imagining myself sitting on the piano stool all day, helping others to learn. 'But the piano's a bit out of tune. It doesn't sound right.'

'We could tune it.'

'We could,' I say, as I think it through, smiling. It does sound like a good idea.

'And I could make up some flyers and we could post them through letterboxes in the local area.'

'You don't have to do that.'

'I'd like to. It would be lovely to see you happy, doing something you love. After all the stress you've gone through with Ian.'

I nod, my mind wandering as I imagine a completely new life. A bubble of excitement rises in my chest. I feel hopeful for the first time since Ian left.

But in the meantime, I need to find work that I can start as soon as possible. I begin my search with the coffee shop across the road. I don't hold out much hope. Whenever I've been in it's always been the same wizened old lady serving the coffees, working morning until evening. I think she's the owner, and she never seems to take a day off. I can't imagine the shop makes enough money to afford a second member of staff. It hardly has any customers. But it's still worth a try. I'd only have to cross the road to get to work, and I could pop back and see the twins in my break.

I hover at the counter and wait for the owner to finish serving two builders sitting at the corner table. When she comes back to the till, she looks me up and down, taking in my ironed smock and heels.

'How can I help you?'

'I'm looking for a job,' I say. 'I've worked in coffee shops as a barista for the last ten years. I'd love to work here.'

'A barista?' she says, her eyebrows raised. I realise 'waitress' might have been a better word to use here. 'Why do you want to work here in particular?' she asks.

'I've moved into the house opposite. I have twin girls and, to be honest, working here would be very convenient.'

She narrows her eyes at me. 'Oh, yes. I think I recognise you. You've got the double buggy.'

I smile. 'Yes, that'll be me. And I've been in here before. When I was pregnant.'

'Well, I don't think we've ever had anyone living on this road asking for a job here.' She laughs. 'It's minimum wage, you know.'

'That would be fine,' I say, sensing an opportunity. 'I just want to be close to home.'

She peers at me again, studying my face. 'Are you the woman who moved into the house directly across?'

I nod and smile. 'Yes.'

'A strange choice for someone with young children.'

'Yes, well, we've done it up now.'

'It looks a lot better. But then again, it couldn't have looked much worse. I'm a bit superstitious about houses.'

'What do you mean?'

'I think that they can hold onto things. The emotions of the previous occupants can get under the skin of the house somehow, seep into the cracks between the bricks, become part of the fabric.'

'Oh,' I say. I remember the creepy feeling I had when I first moved in, the feeling of being watched.

She stares across the road. 'I've worked in this coffee shop since I was a teenager. My parents owned it before they died. And I don't think anyone was ever happy in that house. Not the adults. Not the children. No one.'

'Right,' I say, shifting my weight uncomfortably from foot to foot on my unfamiliar heels. 'Do you think you'll have any shifts for me?'

'Well, I'm the only employee here. But I do occasionally need a few hours off for hospital appointments and the like. But you'd need to get on with our regular customers.'

'I can do that,' I say, smiling.

'They tend to like to linger. And we don't move them along here. We're a friendly place. We let them stay as long as they like. We used to have a woman who came in every day, for hours. I would have said she was our best customer, but she only ever bought one drink when she was here. She used to like to sit by the window, staring out at the street.'

'What happened to her?'

'I was going to ask you that. That's another reason I recognise you. I've seen you with her. Out on the street and in here too, once. A while ago. Before she stopped coming back in.'

I search my brain for who she might be talking about. 'You mean Paula?' I ask.

'Paula?' The woman takes a step back and stares at me intently. I feel uncomfortable and the sleeve of my dress rubs against the scar on my arm, making it itch. 'Come to think of it, I'm not sure I ever knew her name. We exchanged pleasantries, but never introduced ourselves…' She trails off.

'Paula's my doula. She's moved in with me.'

'A doula?'

'Kind of like a nanny, or a nurse. To help with childcare.'

'Oh, right. That explains it, then.' For a moment she looks like she's about to say more, but she stops herself. 'Send her my regards,' she says. 'And leave your phone number with me. I can call you when I need temporary cover for the shop.' She pauses. 'I'll give you mine too. I'm only across the road. That way you can call me if you need anything.'

She hands me a business card with the phone number of the café on and I scribble my name and number on the back of one of the flyers displayed by the till. 'I'll pass on your regards to Paula,' I say, hoping she'll say more, tell me whatever it is she was about to say a moment ago.

But she doesn't. Instead she just smiles.

As I'm heading out the door, she says something so quietly that I can't be sure I've heard it right.

'Take care in that house,' she whispers.

CHAPTER TWENTY-SIX

Frances screams and Paula goes to pick her up.

'Don't worry, I'll get her,' I say quickly, but Paula has already scooped her into her arms and is rocking her. When Alice whimpers she picks her up too, and stands opposite me, one twin in each arm like a doting relative.

'Let me comfort them,' I say.

'No need. Isn't Melissa coming round soon? You should get ready.'

I frown. 'I am ready,' I say. Well, at least I'm showered and dressed. I wish Paula would lay off a bit. Since Ian's left, I feel like she's taken over. But I don't want to get on the wrong side of her. I need her. And I remember how angry she was when Ian and I asked her to leave.

'Are you going to tell Melissa that Ian's left you?' she asks.

I blink rapidly. I'm not sure I can face telling her. It will just be another thing I've failed at. 'Probably not. Not yet.'

I quickly dash around the house, checking there's no evidence that Ian's left. I notice that now the invasive aroma of fresh paint has faded, the house is starting to smell again, as if it's rotting from within.

I realise that Ian's hardly taken anything with him. His toothbrush is still in the bathroom, his deodorant by the bed. But it shocks me how small a footprint he's left in the house. He hasn't come back round to pick up his stuff because he didn't have much stuff here in the first place. I was too busy with the twins to notice, but he'd never got round to moving all his things in before he went to Thailand. I wonder where his real life is, where his things are, where he is now. He could be staying in a hotel or at one of his own properties. Or the home he was living in before he moved here. Not that he ever invited me there.

I come back into the living room. 'Can I give them a cuddle?' I ask Paula, and then get irritated with myself for feeling the need to ask. They're *my* twins.

Paula hands them over. 'I'm going out,' she says. 'Remember their routine. Nap in half an hour, milk in another three hours.'

'Sure,' I say. But while Paula's out I want to relax a bit more. I'm not going to put them down for their nap as soon as Melissa gets here. She'll want to see them.

When Melissa rings the doorbell, I'm excited to see her. Lately when I look at my baby girls I remember how close Melissa and I were as children. I want that back. I answer the door with one twin under each arm, both screaming their heads off. Their nap is ten minutes overdue, and I wonder if Paula was right about routine or if this is just bad luck.

My sister takes Frances from me and she immediately calms. I smile at her. 'She's really taken to you,' I say.

'Thanks.'

I put Alice down to make Melissa a drink and we go to sit in the living room.

I watch Melissa smiling and laughing with Frances. Frances is so much lighter than her sister, so much more docile. I wonder if it's just a personality thing, if she's just more laid back, or if it's more than that. Is the fact that she eats so little making her tired? But I don't know what more I can do. Frances never seems interested in feeding.

Both the twins were small when they were born, because they're twins and they were early, but whereas Alice is rapidly catching up with other babies her age, Frances still lags behind, her weight staying stubbornly beneath the line of the graph that the health visitor maps it against.

'Do you think Frances seems unwell?' I ask. 'She still doesn't eat. And Mum said she was worried.' Although I dismissed Mum's concerns at the time, they've been niggling away at me. Despite the health visitor saying that Frances is fine, I can't help worrying that I'm doing something wrong, neglecting her in some way. And I still can't forget what Paula said about me not being a capable mother.

'I wouldn't listen to Mum,' Melissa says. 'You're doing all you can to care for them.'

'Thanks. It's bloody hard sometimes, though.' I immediately take it back. 'I'm sorry. I didn't mean to say that. I know I'm lucky to have them.'

'It does look hard, though,' my sister replies, and laughs.

'I'm sure it will happen for you and Graham eventually,' I say, but my words sound empty. We both know the statistics. After five rounds of IVF and aged over forty, it's highly unlikely.

She sighs deeply. 'I'm not sure we can afford any more cycles. And we've been trying for ten years now. We're saving for one more round, but I think Graham... Well, I think he might have had enough. He wants me to accept that we won't have any children, plan our future together without them.'

'And what do you think?'

She looks at her feet. 'I'm not sure I can accept it, really. I had my whole life planned out. And when I pictured my life with Graham, I always pictured us with two kids. I've always imagined that was where we were heading. It's always been part of the plan.'

We both look down at the twins. It seems so unfair.

'You've always had a plan,' I say to her. 'I wish I was like you.'

'It doesn't get you anywhere,' she replies sadly. 'Isn't it ironic, that you're the one with the long-term partner and two kids?'

'Yeah,' I say. 'I suppose it is.'

'Where is Ian, anyway?'

'He's out,' I answer quickly.

'Mum thinks he's avoiding us. Whenever we come round he's never here.'

'He's—' I didn't want to tell Melissa what's happened, but suddenly I feel tired of it all, tired of Ian's lies, tired of pretending everything's OK. 'He's left me,' I say.

'Oh.' Melissa's mouth drops open. 'I'm so sorry.' She reaches her arm around me. 'How could he do that to you, when the twins are so tiny?'

'I asked him to leave.'

'Why?'

'Because he's in lots of debt. He hasn't been paying the bills. I just found out – he was hiding it all from me.'

'Oh my gosh.'

Maybe Melissa can help me. She is a lawyer, after all. And she's always been far more level-headed than me. 'What should I do? Should I leave?'

'No,' she says. 'Don't go. You need to stay put. You're the mother of his children. The twins live here. You have rights.'

'That's what Paula said.'

'Well, she's right about that.'

'I've found some work in a local café. To pay the bills. He's not been paying the mortgage either.'

'Well, don't pay his mortgage for him. He owns the house. It would be like giving him money.'

'OK…' I say, feeling daunted.

My sister gives me a half-smile. 'Neither of us are having an easy time of it lately, are we? Why don't we go out for lunch? My treat.'

We each clutch a glass of lemonade at a small Italian restaurant round the corner. I've come here before with Ian and I know the food's good. I dig into my steak while Melissa picks at her salad. The babies sleep peacefully in the buggy beside us.

'I can't believe he's done this to you,' Melissa says.

'I know.'

I run Melissa through my tentative plans for financial independence. Statutory maternity pay. Child benefit. Maintenance from Ian if I can get him to pay it. Shifts at local coffee shops. Piano teaching. To my surprise, she's supportive.

'I'm glad you're going to teach music,' she says. 'Mum would be really pleased for you.'

'Because it's better than working in a coffee shop?'

'No, I didn't mean that. It's just that being a barista never seemed to be what you really wanted.'

'True, I fell into it to pay the bills.'

'You were always so talented at the piano. Mum really hoped you'd follow in her footsteps. She really wanted to keep it up herself, but she couldn't after she injured her hand. Even with physio, it was never the same.'

'I kept going with my music until I got pregnant,' I say. 'Gigs in pubs and things like that. I still write songs. But I was never going to earn enough to cover my rent.'

It's got to the point where I hardly talk about my music anymore. My pub gigs started to feel embarrassing compared to the success of some of my friends from college, and to the high hopes my mother had for me.

'So the piano teaching's something positive that's come from all this then, isn't it?' my sister says.

'Yes, I suppose so.'

'And if you teach at weekends, I can always come and look after the twins for you. Or Mum could.'

'I'd love that,' I say, and then hesitate. I'm not sure what Paula would think of the idea. 'But Paula's very keen on keeping them in their routine.'

She raises her eyebrows. 'Paula's still there? Surely you can't afford her now?'

'She's looking after the twins in exchange for a place to live. That way I can start earning again.'

'Doesn't she already have her own place?'

'I suppose she must,' I say, although I haven't really thought about it. She'd said she was local. How could she just leave her previous home so quickly? Surely she'd need to pay bills there.

'Well, it sounds like a very good deal to me,' my sister says, tipping back her lemonade. 'Free childcare. It does seem like you always land on your feet somehow.'

'I suppose I'll have to move out of the house eventually,' I say.

'Yes, but not until you've come to some kind of financial agreement with Ian. He needs to support his daughters.'

I nod. 'Don't worry. I'll make sure of it. I won't leave until I know I'm secure.'

'I admire you, you know. I didn't realise you'd kept going with the gigs at pubs. You've never given up.'

'You're the one who's the high-flying lawyer. You're a thousand times more successful than me.'

'Thanks,' she says. She fiddles with the napkin, uncharacteristically nervous. 'I'm not sure it was ever what I wanted, though. I was just competitive. I wanted the best-paid job with the highest status. But I'm not sure I ever really liked it. To be honest, I'm not sure I ever really liked Graham. He just fitted in with the plan. Handsome and successful, a good potential father.'

I smile sympathetically, but I'm surprised at her words. I had no idea. This is the first time we've talked properly in years, and I'm glad she's confiding in me.

'You don't have to stick to the plan, you know. Not if it doesn't make you happy anymore.'

'I think it would have been OK if we'd had kids. But I can't picture a life with Graham without them. When I imagine that it makes me feel scared. Without us trying for kids together, I'm not sure what there's left between us – if there's anything at all.'

'What do you mean?'

'I'm not sure I love him, Katie.'

I put my hand on her shoulder. 'You don't have to stay with him. You could cut loose, start again.'

'We're saving for another round of IVF,' Melissa says miserably. 'It's our final shot.'

'And if it doesn't work?'

'Then I don't know what I'll do.'

'You could get divorced.'

She laughs. 'It's funny, isn't it? I feel that should be an option, but I'm not sure it is for me. I'd be letting everyone down.'

'Letting who down? It's only you and Graham.'

'Letting myself down, I suppose. Letting Mum down. I've always had to do everything exactly right, get things perfect. And it's kind of expected of me now. Getting divorced just doesn't fit into that.'

I stare at her, surprised. I never realised she felt under so much pressure. 'You don't have to fit into what everyone else wants.'

She laughs. 'I think you're describing yourself. You've never had to fit anyone else's expectations. You've always been such a free spirit.'

'Maybe we both need to make some changes,' I say.

By the time we've finished our meal, we're both in better moods. I have a plan for how to tackle Ian, and Melissa is going to take action and talk to Graham about their marriage.

'We should do this more often,' I say.

'We really should,' my sister replies.

'It's nice, just the two of us. Sometimes Mum can be a bit much.' I laugh, but my sister frowns.

'She tries her best,' she says, and I suddenly feel guilty.

'Please don't tell Mum that Ian's left. I don't want her to think any less of me.'

'Katie, I'll have to tell her. She'll only want to help.'

'But that's exactly what I don't want.'

She sighs. 'We're all adults now. I just wish we could be a bit more honest with each other. No more secrets.'

'What secrets?' I ask. 'Is it about her headaches? Is she alright?'

She looks up suddenly, startled, as she realises what she's just said. 'Oh no, it's not that. She's fine. They don't think the headaches are anything serious.'

'What is it, then?'

'Nothing for you to worry about. Sorry, I shouldn't have said anything. It doesn't matter anymore. It's all so long ago now.'

I frown. I thought we were being completely open with each other, but there are still things that she and Mum won't tell me. Even now we're all adults. 'Just tell me, Melissa.'

'I can't. It's not for me to say. You need to ask Mum. Maybe you can ask her when you tell her about Ian.'

My stomach knots. I'm dreading having a heart to heart with Mum about Ian. I can't face her judgement.

'OK,' I say. 'Just let me be the one to tell Mum that Ian's left me. Keep it to yourself until then.'

She frowns at me and then nods. 'OK. I suppose I can manage that. For you.'

After we've paid the bill, I get up to go to the toilet. It's only a short walk home but my pelvic floor is yet to recover from giving birth. As I exit the toilets, I catch sight of a dark green coat just like Ian's, held out by a waiter to a man with his back to me. I feel a pang of disappointment at the thought of Ian. If only he had been the man I thought he was.

The man shrugs his arms into the coat as he talks to the woman with him, in a bright red coat and heels. She's in her late fifties, neat ash-blonde hair cut into a bob. She looks slightly familiar and

I wonder if I've seen her around locally. She's impeccably dressed with perfectly done make-up. Unlike me. I've got no make-up on and I'm dressed in unflattering maternity clothes, which I suspect have a smattering of baby sick on them somewhere.

The man turns slightly and I see him in profile, as he pushes the door to the restaurant open to leave. I see the familiar features; deep-set eyes, a chiselled jawline and a slightly crooked nose from a childhood accident. It *is* Ian. My heart sinks. I know I should say something, but I freeze. I watch as he holds the door, letting the woman go through first. Who is she? I still can't place her.

I can't take my eyes off them as they leave the restaurant; can't rid myself of that sense of loss for the family life Ian and I could have had. I watch them, transfixed, as Ian walks confidently through the double doors, looking like a man without a care in the world. When they reach the street, they turn towards each other. Ian wraps his arms around the woman and gives her a passionate kiss.

13

'Your mother's gone out. I'm going to help you with your homework.'

My sister and I look at each other in surprise. I see my fear reflected in her eyes, her frown the mirror of my own. Where has Mum gone? Has she left us?

'OK,' I say warily. My sister fetches our books from our school bags and brings them to the table. We've got vocabulary homework this week. A list of ten words to learn, that we'll be tested on at the end of the week.

'Words and their meanings,' Dad reads from the piece of paper slowly.

He laughs, suddenly. 'Look at this one here. "Mistake!" Do you know what that means?'

My sister and I look at each other, confused by his smile and the laughter in his voice.

'It's when you do something wrong,' my sister says cautiously.

'Yes,' he says. 'Quite right. It's an error. Something that should never have happened. Can you think of any examples of mistakes?'

I squeeze my eyes shut and concentrate as hard as I can, hoping to come up with an answer. When he hits us, I'm sure that's wrong. But it isn't a mistake.

I think of something else. 'When I drew a line instead of a circle and had to rub it out,' I say triumphantly.

He looks at me. 'Yes, you would do something stupid like that, wouldn't you? You're a stupid little girl.'

I stare at my feet.

'What about when Mum didn't wash the dishes properly?' my sister says.

I look at her, confused. Why's she bringing Mum into this? He shouted at Mum for hours after that. I don't know why she wants to remind him.

'Yes!' he says. 'Well done.' He tussles my sister's hair aggressively. She recoils, but luckily he doesn't notice. Instead he whisks her up and out of the chair and spins her round. I see the fear in her eyes. She thinks he might throw her across the room.

But he doesn't. He puts her down gently. She's shaking.

'Your mother does make a lot of mistakes. Every day. Simple things you'd think she'd know how to do by now. The dishes. The washing. The ironing. She can't get anything right. What would she do without me to put her right? I spend my whole life trying to control that stupid woman.'

I want to stick up for Mum. To tell him that if he thinks she's so awful, he should just leave. I open my mouth and my sister kicks me under the table. Hard.

'But do you know what your mother's biggest mistake was?' He's on a roll now, loving the sound of his own voice.

'No,' my sister says. 'What was it?'

'It was having you two, of course.' Dad laughs uproariously.

I glare at him. Mum always said we were her little miracles, not mistakes. She said we were a lovely surprise, a gift from God.

'We wanted a son,' he continues. 'But instead we got two daughters. Life's not fair, is it?'

CHAPTER TWENTY-SEVEN

I stare, trying to process what I'm seeing. Ian. Kissing another woman.

'Are you OK, miss?' a waiter asks, as he manoeuvres past me to reach for a customer's coat.

'I'm fine.'

Outside, the kiss ends, but Ian and the woman stay caught in their embrace, his arms wrapped tightly around her.

'The toilets are upstairs.'

'Thanks,' I say absently, as I watch Ian and the woman pull apart. They say a few words to each other and then he puts his arm round her waist and they walk away together, his hand resting on her hip in exactly the same way it rests on mine when he's with me. They go to a car parked a few doors down, get in and drive away. I feel sick.

When I return to our table, my sister is already standing, her bag in her hand. We part company outside the restaurant, promising we'll meet more frequently. But I hardly absorb her words. My brain is flooded with the image of Ian's lips meeting the woman's, his hand on her hip, the scene repeating again and again in slow motion in my mind. He's been cheating on me. Or else he's met someone else already.

I hurry home with the buggy, barely even aware of my own children's screams.

When I get back, Paula is already there. For once I'm grateful when she whisks the twins away from me, berating me for not feeding them when we were out and telling me that we're now completely off her schedule.

I sit down on the sofa and try to make sense of what I saw at the restaurant. I'm devastated by his betrayal. Finding the unpaid bills was bad enough, but now this. How could he let me down so completely? How could he be so uncaring? And how long has he been cheating on me?

I close my eyes, tears stinging them, and the kiss replays again in my head. I don't want to see it; don't want to remember. Our relationship is definitely over. There's nowhere left to go with it.

I get out my phone and google Ian. I don't know why I expect Google to give me an answer when the truth's been staring me in the face. Ian's clearly never cared about me at all. I never went to his house, never met any of his friends. He kept everything separate and compartmentalised. How could I not have seen it? How could I be so stupid? I've never been the suspicious type in relationships. I've always just taken people as they come, but now I wonder if I've been naive. I've only googled Ian once before. It was after our third date and I'd just found out his surname. I hadn't seen anything that alarmed me that time, but then again, I hadn't been expecting to. I'd just been curious. He was only supposed to be a fling at the beginning. I never expected us to end up here.

This time I'm more thorough. I scan through pages and pages of results. In the background, I hear the twins screaming and Paula trying to calm them down. At first her voice is soothing, but then it gets higher and more irritable. I've only heard her like that once before. When I asked her to move out.

I blink, focusing on the sound. She's angry with them.

I turn away from my search as I hear Paula's voice grow louder. 'You little brat,' she says. 'Take your medicine.'

What medicine? They don't take any, except Calpol.

Frances's screams have stopped now. As I race up the stairs, I hear Alice's cries fall silent too.

I meet Paula at the top of the stairs.

'Don't worry,' she says. 'They're asleep.'

'What medicine were you giving them?'

'Just Calpol. I think they've caught a bit of a chill. How many blankets did you put over them when you took them out earlier?'

'Blankets? They were wearing jumpers.' Although the oppressive heat of the summer has faded now, it's still warm.

'You see, they must have caught something. Next time you need to put blankets over them in the buggy.'

'OK, right,' I say, feeling a stab of guilt. 'I'm just going to check on them.'

'They've just dropped off. You might wake them.'

'I'll go in anyway.' I push open the door to the room softly, with Paula standing over me.

I can see from the doorway that they are both fast asleep. I go over to the cots and watch the rise and fall of their tiny chests, feeling myself calm. Paula's right. They're fine.

'Satisfied?' Paula asks, smiling.

'I'm sorry. I just worry sometimes. Particularly about Frances.'

'You're a first-time mother. It's perfectly normal to worry. But I've seen it all before.'

I return downstairs and back to my phone. I need to find out more about Ian: where he lives, who his friends are, his history. It's crazy that I've been with him for so long without knowing any of this. I've had his children without knowing who he really is. I feel so foolish.

Most of all, I want to know who the woman he was kissing is. I want to know where he's gone; if he's staying with her. I search for Ian Ainsworth along with Wimbledon, as he'd told me he lived near there. There are pages and pages of results for Ian Ainsworths, but no connection with Wimbledon that I can see.

But what really surprises me is that there seem to be no records of anyone with his name operating as a director in a property business. Surely if he'd set up a successful property company, then there'd be some record of that online?

I frown. There must be another way of finding out where he's gone. I wonder if he still has the house where he was living before he moved in with me, if he's gone back there. I search 192.com for his address, but can't find it. He must be ex-directory. And then I think of his credit card that I still have in my wallet. The one that was declined. I go to my wallet, pick up the card and turn it over in my hands. Credit cards are always linked to addresses. I wonder if I phone up the bank, could I get his address? But they'd never give it to me. His address would be on his Amazon account or his eBay account. But I don't have access to those. Then I remember: he put his credit card details into my phone once when we ordered takeaway online on a romantic weekend away in Ireland. He'd have had to put in the address his credit card was registered to.

I rack my brains and remember the name of the takeaway. When I log into my account on their website, his credit card details are still there. Alongside an address in Morden where it's registered. I smile to myself, momentarily forgetting that I've made a complete mess of my life, and instead being pleased with my detective work. This is where Ian was living when he first met me. I wonder if he's there now.

I make a note of the address in my phone. I deserve to know who Ian really is. Tomorrow I'll go over there. I'll confront him. I'll find out who the woman is. For the sake of my daughters.

I feel so lonely at night, without my twins, without Ian. I'm devastated. I love Ian. But it wasn't enough. I wasn't enough for him. The ceiling that Ian fixed has started to leak again and the water drips down the walls. I sniff, trying to hold back tears. Behind the peeling wallpaper I can see pencil drawings of the family. More paper has come away now, and I see there is another picture underneath. This time it is just a family of three. A mother, father and a little girl. I pick at the wallpaper and see more markings. Two children lie at the feet of the family. Whereas the other people are delicately drawn, these two children are scribbled out, with big, thick pencil marks scoured through them.

I feel unnerved, even though I know the drawings are years old. I wish Ian was beside me, just for the comfort of another person breathing in the room. Another body to share this journey. At night thoughts circle in my head, an endless loop of worry.

In the stillness, I think I hear the faint sound of a baby crying. I strain my ears and I'm sure it sounds like Frances's faint whimpers. My heart tugs in recognition.

I get up, throw on a nightdress over my sweaty body and walk down the corridor to Paula's room, stepping over a cuddly toy that's been dropped near the top of the stairs.

I hear a scuttling sound over the wooden floor and flick on the light to see a huge rat, its tail swishing behind it before it disappears through a gap in the skirting board.

I stifle a scream. Goosebumps spread over my skin. Trying to rid myself of the image, I listen at Paula's door for the twins, but there's no sound at all. I know I should feel relieved, but I don't. I just want my babies beside me, to see them breathing, to feel them in my arms. Sometimes I get so jealous of Paula sleeping next to them, smelling their soft baby scent, seeing their chests rising up and down, hearing their gentle breaths. She's there to pick them up when they cry, to comfort them. I want that for me. I'm their mother.

But for now, I just need to see them, to know they're safe.

I knock on the door. No answer.

'Paula?' I call through the door, knocking once more.

She must be fast asleep. How would she hear the twins wake if she can't even hear my loud knocks? I think how she has brought the twins in less often for their night feeds lately, telling me they're almost sleeping through the night. Is that true, or is it Paula that's sleeping straight through, while my twins cry out?

I push open the door.

The room is empty.

No Paula.

No babies in the cots.

'Paula?' I whisper, unable to believe what I'm seeing.

I leave the room quickly, going back out to the corridor.

'Paula?' I shout.

The house is completely silent.

I check the bathroom, then run downstairs, my feet thumping down the wooden steps.

I run from room to room, but there's no sign of them.

CHAPTER TWENTY-EIGHT

Where have they gone?

They aren't in the house. I've searched everywhere, downstairs and upstairs.

And yet, when I stand still in the silence, I can hear the faint sound of a baby screaming. I'm sure it's Frances. I'd know her weak mewling anywhere. But where is she?

Paula must have taken the twins out. But where would she have taken them at 3 a.m.? And why?

A thought crosses my mind. Has she stolen them? Did she want them for herself? Often she seems closer to them than I am; a better parent to them than I am. But that's just because she knows what she's doing. Her job is to care for children. She's a professional.

I wonder if I should call the police. But to say what? My nanny has taken the kids out? Or that Paula and the children are missing? It doesn't make any sense.

For a second, I think about calling Mum. But I can't bear her judgement. She can't stand Paula. She'll tell me that Paula has kidnapped them, that I clearly can't trust her.

But I have to do something.

I grab my keys and go outside the house. I look both ways but there is no sign of my babies or Paula.

'Paula!' I shout, my voice carrying on the still night air. 'Paula!'

A curtain twitches across the road. The flat above the coffee shop. The owner is watching me. It twitches closed again.

I go back inside the house, heart hammering. I have to phone the police now, just in case.

I run upstairs as fast as I can and grab my mobile.

And then I hear something from the bottom of the stairs.

I dash back out of the bedroom and look down, eyes wide.

Paula is in the hallway, rocking the babies in her arms, cooing at them.

She jumps when she sees me.

'Katie? What are you doing up?'

'I… I thought I heard Frances crying… and when I went to your room, you weren't in there. Neither were the girls.'

'The twins were unsettled. I took them for a walk to calm them down. They're better now. Look – Alice is fast asleep.'

I come down the stairs slowly, my mind racing.

I look at the twins in her arms. She's right. Alice is in a contented sleep, but Frances looks anxious still, sweat on her brow, her eyes darting from side to side.

'I'll feed Frances,' I say. 'She might be dehydrated.'

'She's fine. She just needs her sleep.'

I take Frances out of Paula's arms. She's cold and clammy and I feel a desperate need to protect her. I hold her close, feeling a flush of inadequacy. What's wrong with her? Why is she so tiny and weak? Did I make her worse by not putting blankets on her when I went out earlier? I take her to the living room and put her to my breast.

'Bring her up soon,' Paula calls into the living room, before she carries Alice upstairs to bed. 'You don't want to mess up her routine.'

But for once Frances is latching easily and sucking vigorously. And as I hold her close, I realise something. Paula said she'd taken the twins outside for a walk. But when I'd gone downstairs, the buggy had still been in the hallway. Where were they?

*

The next morning I feel a desperate need to be close to my babies. The fear from last night hasn't left me. I change their nappies, feed them and cuddle them. When Frances falls asleep in my arms I wonder if I really could do this all on my own, without Paula.

But I have to hand them over once more because I'm teaching my first piano lesson today. The flyers that Paula printed out have clearly worked, as I already have five students signed up. I whizz round the house spraying air freshener in the hall and the piano room, to try and disguise the festering smell that rises up through the floorboards. I haven't had time to do any preparation, aside from getting the piano tuned. I haven't been able to stop thinking about Ian kissing the other woman, replaying it in my mind over and over. As soon as the lesson finishes I'm going to go over to the address I discovered. I dread to think what I'll find.

Paula's agreed to take the twins out. I feel a bit uncomfortable about it because of what happened in the night, but there's no alternative if I want a silent house while I teach. And I can't afford to criticise her; I'll need her to babysit when I go to Ian's house later too.

The lesson goes well, and as I watch the ten-year-old boy walk away from the house, chatting excitedly to his father about the piano, I feel a sense of pride. I imagine a new life on my own with the twins, and a career teaching piano.

The address I have for Ian is on the other side of London and I take the train and then the Tube to get there. When I arrive, I'm taken aback. It's a tiny two-up, two-down mid-terrace. The kind I could only ever dream of affording, but that's surely far too small for someone like Ian. I check the address. It's the right house.

Anger rises in me. I rehearse in my head what I'm going to say to him, how I'm going to tell him exactly what I think of him.

I take a deep breath and knock on the door.

I open my mouth as I hear the latch unclicking, ready to say my piece.

But it's not Ian behind the door.

It's a woman. Ash-blonde hair. Piercing blue eyes. Ian's age.

There's no mistaking her. It's the woman from the restaurant. I take a step back, shocked.

'Hello?' she says, looking me up and down.

Without any make-up on, she looks different. Older, more weathered. She has a duster in her hand and behind her the hallway is clutter-free and sparkling clean.

'Hi,' I splutter.

'What do you want?' she says impatiently.

'It's about Ian,' I say quickly, before she can shut the door in my face.

'Ian?' Her expression's unchanged and for a second I worry that I've got this completely wrong.

'Is he alright?' she asks, shattering my illusion.

'Yes, he's fine. As far as I know.'

'Well, who are you, then?' She pauses. 'You're not another one of his girls?' She stares at me angrily. 'He said he'd stop... He promised.'

'I'm sorry?' *His girls?* I repeat in my head, stunned.

'Are you having an affair with him?'

'No. I'm not—' My mind races. 'We've been together a year.'

'A year? He's been seeing you for a year?'

'Yes,' I say, shocked. 'When did your relationship with him start?' I ask. 'Was it after we split up?' The questions burst out of me hopefully, but I have a sinking feeling.

She laughs. 'You think a year's a long time? Well, I'm afraid I trump you. We've been married twenty.'

I swallow, feeling the colour drain from my face. 'That can't be right. Ian was with me.' He's been married to her throughout our relationship? I feel sick.

'Where did he tell you he lived?'

'I thought he… I mean, he was living with his mother… and then he was living with me,' I say quietly. But I can see through it all now. He said he was living with his mother so I didn't ask questions. And I was stupid enough to fall for it.

'Where did you think he was half the time?' the woman says.

'He said he was working.'

'He told me he was working when he must have been with you. I wanted to believe him. I knew I shouldn't. You're one in a long line of girls, you know. Always younger.'

I feel sick. I'm not even special, just one of many. The reality of my situation hits me. How could I have been so blind? Ian hardly ever stayed over with me. His phone was so often switched off. I never met his friends or family. The signs were there, but I didn't want to see them. Once I knew I was pregnant and Ian was no longer a casual relationship, I couldn't afford to question his honesty. I needed him to be reliable. I needed him to be a good father to my children. So I believed what I wanted to believe.

'Do you have children?' I ask. I can't bear the thought that I might have been splitting up a family. Alice and Frances might have brothers or sisters. Ian might have done this all before: the pregnancy, looking after our young babies. Perhaps none of those moments were special for him, because he'd been through it all before with someone else.

'No,' she says quickly. 'We don't.'

I feel a rush of relief, despite everything.

'We have twins together,' I say, my voice wobbling.

Her face has turned pale. 'You have twins? With Ian?'

'Yes. Two girls.'

'How old are they?'

'A month.'

'Oh my god.' Her hand flies to her mouth. 'He's been pretending our marriage is fine, while you've been having his babies? We've been going to marriage counselling. You were probably giving birth while I was trying to mend my marriage. Was he there? Was he there when you gave birth?'

'No,' I say. 'It was when he was working in Thailand.'

'Thailand?'

And then it hits me. The week Ian was away in Thailand he'd been uncontactable. Surely he wouldn't lie to me about something as huge as that. He wouldn't have missed the girls' births because he was with this woman. Would he?

'Was he with you the first week of August?' I ask.

'Yes,' she says.

'And he didn't go abroad?'

'No.'

The truth hits me like a ton of bricks. 'I have to go,' I say, through tears. When she shuts the door, I collapse on her doorstep and sob.

14

We're in the basement again. We're locked down here more and more often now. Not just when the man comes round, but other times too. Whenever Dad thinks we've been naughty.

My sister hardly speaks to me anymore. She thinks it's my fault we're down here, that me waving to the man started all of this.

I've been trying to cheer her up by thinking of escape plans: climbing up to the tiny window near the ceiling and crawling out, finding a secret tunnel behind some old bricks, breaking down the door. Each idea is more unbelievable than the last, but at least I'm trying.

'Be quiet,' my sister says suddenly.

'What?'

'Listen.'

And then I hear it. It's very faint but I hear it.

The piano.

It's the lullaby Mum plays us every night before we go to bed.

She must be above us. In the music room.

'Do you think she's playing it for us?' I ask.

'Maybe. If she knows we're down here.'

I frown. She must *know we're down here. But I don't want to think about that. Why doesn't she rescue us?*

Instead I close my eyes and listen.

I imagine we are up there with her, that we're dancing to the music, our feet light on the floorboards. Unwelcome tears run down my face. I wipe them angrily away with my hand. It's no time for crying. Crying is for babies.

My sister's eyes snap open.

She stares at me, disgusted. 'What are you doing?' she asks.

'What?' I mutter, confused. I'm not doing anything.

'Stop crying.' She kicks my leg. It hardly hurts, but it makes me cry harder.

'You're such a cry-baby.'

'I'm not,' I say, desperately trying to stem my tears, which only seem to fall faster.

She kicks me again, harder this time, and then runs away to the other side of the room. She stands with her back to me, her face to the wall. I can see her body shaking, hear her sniffing. She's crying too.

CHAPTER TWENTY-NINE

I stumble back to the train station, my mind whirring. I can hardly believe what I've just been told. Ian's married. They've been together twenty years. I'm so angry I can't think straight.

I ring Ian. He's been trying to contact me ever since we split up, and he picks up immediately. Unlike when we were together and he was so difficult to get hold of.

'Katie – I'm so glad you've finally called me back. I've been worried about you. I've sorted out the bills now. It was all a big mistake. Somehow my bank card had got cancelled, so none of my direct debits came out. But it's fixed now. I'm desperate to make it up to you. Can I come over and take you out to dinner?'

I'm shocked by how easily the excuses tumble out of his mouth, and for a moment I'm speechless.

'What do you think?' he asks.

'I've just met your wife,' I finally say.

There's a silence. 'Sabrina?' He misses a single beat and then continues. 'Oh, god. I can explain everything. I've wanted to leave her for years. I don't love her. We're married in name only.' He speaks quickly, as if he doesn't want to give me any space in the conversation to question him.

'So why didn't you leave her then?'

'She's fragile. She has some emotional…difficulties.'

'I don't believe you.' For the first time I can see clearly. He'll say whatever's necessary to convince me that his being married isn't a big deal.

'She gave you the impression we were still in a physical relationship, didn't she?'

'She said you were married and living together as a couple.'

Ian sighs. 'She's done this before.'

'Has she now? She's told your other numerous flings that she's been married to you for twenty years?'

'Katie, you're overreacting. And I can understand why. It must have been quite a shock. And Sabrina can be very convincing in her delusions. She's still in love with me, you see. But we're not together anymore, no matter what she'd like to believe.'

'She said you went to marriage counselling.'

'We did. I did it for her. And it just confirmed what I already knew. That there wasn't a future for us.'

'But you've been living there.'

'Well, yes, I lived with her before I moved in with you. But only out of convenience. And I had to move in there when you chucked me out. I had nowhere else to go.'

'What about your other properties?'

'They're all occupied, otherwise I'd have gone to one of those.'

'Business is booming, then?'

I hear him sigh with relief. He thinks he's out of the woods. 'Yes, we're doing well.'

'What happened to the opportunity in Thailand, Ian? Have you got the contract?' I give him one last opportunity to redeem himself, to admit the truth.

'It's looking promising. You wouldn't believe the hotel, Katie. The plans look amazing.'

I go in for the kill. 'I know you weren't in Thailand, Ian. When our twins were born, you were on the other side of London. With your wife.'

'Katie – I'm sorry – I—'

'It's over, Ian. Forever.'

*

As soon as I get on the train, I can't stop crying. All my dreams of a future with Ian are completely shattered. Our relationship has been a lie from the beginning, our future a fairy tale that would never come true.

I'm angry. Why didn't he come clean when I was pregnant? Why didn't he let me have a fresh start without him? I could have moved on, found my own place, psyched myself up for being a single mother, got support. But instead he pretended he was going to be involved, pretended we were going to have a proper relationship, all the time still seeing his wife. And then he missed the births. If something's unforgivable, it's that.

When I finally arrive home, I hear the sound of piano music as I come through the door, and for a moment I'm transported back to my own childhood. When my mother was around there was always music in the house. Before she hurt her hand, she'd practise at home for concerts, and after her injury she'd play for her own pleasure.

I go through into the dining room and see Paula sitting on the piano stool, eyes closed, lost in the music. It's a simple piece but she plays it well. The twins are on their mats across the room, gazing up at her.

'Hi,' I say.

She doesn't pause. I go over and tap her on the shoulder.

Her fingers clamp down on the keys and she jumps off the stool as if she's been hit.

'I'm sorry—' I say quickly.

'Oh, it's OK. I didn't realise it was you.'

I frown. Who did she think it was?

'The girls have been fine,' she says quickly. Then she looks at me more closely, and strokes my hair off my face. 'You've been crying.'

I nod. 'It's Ian. He's married.'

'Oh my god. I'm so sorry.'

Paula puts the girls to bed and then we sit down in the kitchen. 'How did you find out?' she asks.

'I saw them kissing. Then I found out where Ian lived. I went to see him today. She was there.'

'You didn't know where he lived?'

'No, he told me he lived with his mother before she was moved into a home, that she had dementia and would have been confused by strangers in the house. Our relationship wasn't that serious back then. And after I got pregnant, I was just so pleased that Ian was sticking with me and had found us somewhere to live. I didn't think to question anything.'

'You poor thing. He's really had you fooled.'

'I know. I can't believe I didn't see through him. I've been so stupid.'

'It's not your fault. Ian's charming. I can see exactly why you trusted him.'

'He didn't fool you though, did he?' I remember how suspicious Paula had been of Ian.

'I never liked him. But I've had years of experience of nasty men. I knew something about Ian wasn't right as soon as I met him.'

'Why didn't you say anything?'

'I didn't know you that well back then. And when Ian didn't return from Thailand, well, I was hoping he wasn't coming back at all, to be honest. I didn't trust him.'

'I found out that he was never in Thailand.'

'What?'

'He made it up. He was with his wife.'

'I thought it seemed suspicious. Odd to go so near to your due date. And to take so long to get back.'

'I know. But even if he was with her, surely he would have come back when the twins were born?' It still doesn't make any sense, even now. Ian's admitted to lying about Thailand, admitted he was with his wife. But if he was just on the other side of London, why didn't he come back when the twins were born? Why did he lie about his phone not working?

CHAPTER THIRTY

The next day, Melissa's coming round after a client lunch in the local area. I've opened all the windows in the house to try and get rid of the musty smell, but it still persists, lingering in every room.

Melissa's late, and I'm beginning to think she's not coming when she rolls in at seven after Paula's put the twins to bed. 'Hello,' she slurs as she wraps her arms around me. 'It's so good to see you. I've had such a great day.'

I smile cautiously. Melissa hasn't drunk alcohol for years, but she's clearly the worse for wear today. 'Come in. The twins have just gone to bed.'

'Oh, that's a shame, I really wanted to see them. But I wanted to see you even more. I've brought champagne to celebrate my good news.'

'What good news?' I ask cautiously, as I take the bottle from her and put it in the fridge. She can't be pregnant. She wouldn't have brought the champagne if it was that.

She follows me into the kitchen and I pour her a glass of water and hand it to her. She gulps it down and wipes her mouth with the back of her hand.

'I just got a heap of new business from my client. Three million pounds. Can you believe it?'

'Of course I can. You're brilliant at your job. That's why they made you a partner.'

'Thanks. At least you're supportive. Graham never congratulates me when I succeed. I think I'm going to leave him.'

I take her water glass and top her up. 'Let's go into the living room and sit down.'

'Aren't we going to open the champagne?'

I frown. Melissa really needs to sober up.

'I'm breastfeeding, so I probably shouldn't,' I say.

But Melissa has opened the fridge and is popping the cork off the bottle.

'Where are your champagne glasses?'

I sigh. 'Top right cupboard.'

She hands a small glass to me and we both go through into the living room.

'You're moving fast, leaving Graham.' I'm shocked that she's seriously thinking of going through with it.

'Yeah, I've thought about what you said when we met. You inspired me, chucking Ian out. Well done.' She raises her glass to clink mine. I feel guilty about suggesting divorce so casually in our last conversation. I never thought she'd do it.

'I'm so glad I split up with Ian.' I take a deep breath. 'It turns out he's married.'

'Married?' Melissa laughs drunkenly. 'Seriously?'

'Yeah. Twenty years.'

'What?' She turns to me, her eyes wide, and drapes her arm around me. 'I'm so sorry. You don't deserve this. I never would have thought it of Ian. Did you have any idea?'

I frown, feeling embarrassed and stupid. The signs were there. I just chose to ignore them because I wanted our relationship to work. 'He wasn't around much,' I admit. 'He even missed the first days of the twins' lives because he was with his wife.' As I say the words the depth of his betrayal hits me once more and tears well up in my eyes.

'What? I'll kill him.' I see the unadulterated rage in Melissa's unfocused eyes. 'Unless Mum gets there first. Have you told her that you've split up yet?'

'Of course not. She's going to be furious with me for being so stupid. I can't face it.'

'Don't worry.' Melissa pats me on the back. 'We can speak to her together. I'll tell her I'm leaving Graham and you can tell her Ian's married.' She slurs her words. 'She can be angry with us both at the same time. We can share the pain.'

I smile. I'm not sure she'll remember anything I said in the morning, but I'm glad I confided in her.

'Ian makes Graham look like an angel,' I say.

'Well, I suppose he's not that bad. I just don't love him.'

'I do feel a bit sorry for him,' I admit. 'He's a nice guy.'

'I think that's the problem. I chose him because he was a nice guy. And had a good job. Not for any other reason. I don't think I ever truly loved him. I just didn't want to marry someone like our father.'

'What?' I ask, confused. 'Why would you say that?'

'You don't remember what he was like.'

'I remember bits,' I say, not wanting to admit I don't remember much at all.

'I was older. I remember it all.'

'But you wanted to name your baby after him. So he can't have been that bad,' I say. She's drunk and talking rubbish. Maybe I should just put her to bed, let her sleep it off. It's a pity, I wanted to talk more to her about Ian, but that can wait until another day.

'I'd never name my child after him! I didn't even want you to.'

'But Mum said—'

'What did Mum say?' Melissa is usually so calm and collected. But now her face is flushed and she looks furious.

'She said I couldn't call my baby Frances because you'd reserved the name for your baby.' I frown.

'Really? Well, that's the joke of the year.' But Melissa's not laughing.

'Didn't you want to call your child Frances?'

'No. I didn't want you to call your daughter that because Dad wasn't the kind of person you'd want to name your child after. He wasn't a nice man. But Mum doesn't want you to know that. She'd prefer it if you kept an idealised image of our father forever.'

'But he was a good guy. He used to take me to the playground, push me on the swing, walk me to school. He understood me.'

'Where did you get that idea from?'

'I just remember—'

'I wouldn't trust your memories.'

'What do you mean?'

'You remember what Mum wants you to remember. She's shown you photos over the years, photos of you and him smiling, him walking you to school on the one day that happened, you two playing the piano together. But it's all an illusion.'

'But the photos are real. Those things happened.'

'They did. But not often. You were too young to remember what he was really like. Mum rewrote history for you. She thought it would be better if you remembered him as a good father, so she only ever talked about the good times. But I was too old for that to work on me. I knew the truth.'

'I don't believe you.'

Melissa sighs and looks down at her empty glass, suddenly regretful. She seems calmer now, as if the conversation has started to sober her up. 'I was never meant to tell you. Mum always told me not to. Which made sense when you were six. Less so now. But she still wants to protect you.'

I feel a bit sick. I always thought Mum and Melissa didn't understand me, but that my father did. Now Melissa's telling me I've got it all wrong.

'What was he like then?' I ask.

'Nasty and drunk half the time,' she slurs.

'I don't believe you. He might not have been perfect. But he was a good man. Mum always said so.'

Melissa laughs. 'Did she? But she still suffers now, years after he died. She still has the headaches.'

My eyes widen. 'What have they got to do with Dad?'

'She got her head injury when she was with him. I never knew exactly what happened. But when they went out he was in a bad mood, angry with her over some little thing. They didn't come back that night. She went to hospital with concussion. I remember because I had to make our dinner while they were at the hospital. Later, the police came to question him. They thought she'd hit her head when Dad pushed her into a wall, but they must have been satisfied with what he told them as they never took it any further. Ever since, she's had the headaches and the dizzy spells. It was his fault.'

'But it could have just been an accident. Accidents happen all the time.'

'Maybe,' Melissa says. 'Look, I'm sorry. I shouldn't have told you what he was really like. I know how much your memories of him mean to you. Let's just forget it.'

'I don't understand. If Dad was so awful, why does Mum tell people how wonderful he was? Even now, she still says she misses him.'

'She wants people to think they had a good marriage. She tells everyone that the love of her life died. How she had to put everything back together afterwards. She thinks it impresses them. It sounds far better than the truth.'

When Melissa finally leaves, I'm still reeling. I'm not sure how much of what she said was true. She was so drunk. I sigh and pour myself a glass of water. Could it be that everything I thought I knew about my father was a lie? I scratch at the scar on my arm, racking my brain for memories. But all my memories of my father are just snapshots. Like photographs. Perhaps Melissa was right.

Paula comes in and sits beside me.

'It's late,' she says. 'Is everything alright?'

'Yeah,' I reply.

'I heard Melissa. I tried to stay out of your way, give you two the chance to catch up.'

'Thanks.'

'You've been crying.'

'She just upset me a bit, that's all.'

'I could hear her from upstairs. She woke the twins up.'

'I'm sorry.'

'It's alright. What happened?'

'It's about our father. She claims he was a drunk. She thinks he once gave our mother concussion. That he caused the headaches she still has today.'

'Really?'

I tell her what Melissa said. I analyse every word, trying to work out what she meant, why she never told me before.

'Who knows why she said all those things,' Paula says. 'Maybe she wants to hurt you.'

'But why would she want that?' If anything, Melissa and I have been getting on better lately.

'She's jealous, isn't she? Of your babies.'

'I suppose so.'

'Families are tough,' Paula says. 'I didn't have a good relationship with my sister either. She was vindictive, like Melissa.'

'Melissa isn't a bad person,' I say. 'We were really close when we were little.'

'Your relationship is all one-way. She's so busy working that she hardly sees you and then, when she does, she drops something like this on you.'

I feel hot. Paula's right.

'It's hard thinking about the past. I grew up around here,' Paula continues. 'Every corner triggers a memory.'

I notice her use of the word 'triggers', as if the memories are uncomfortable for her, as if they hurt.

'That must be difficult.'

I think of how she used to sit in the coffee shop every day, staring out at the street. I wonder if it's something about the area that drew her here, something she can't let go of.

'It's hard to move on from the things that hurt us in childhood.'

I look at Paula, surprised. She's only a bit younger than my mother. Can it really be true that difficult childhoods will haunt us forever?

I think about what Melissa said. 'I just wish my family would be honest with me. Everyone must have lied to me for years, pretending my father was a nice guy. It sounded like in reality my sister detested him.'

'You can't always trust sisters. I hated mine.'

'Why?'

'I suppose we were always competing for our parents' attention, like there was only really room for one of us. We looked so similar on the surface. But we weren't, of course. Not in personality. My sister was a manipulative bitch.'

'Oh,' I say, shocked. As much as Melissa annoyed me, I'd never refer to her like that.

'But she was good at hiding who she really was, pretending. My parents always preferred my sister to me.'

'Mum always seemed to prefer Melissa. She did everything right. Did well at school, then got married and became a lawyer. I never feel good enough in comparison.'

'They try to make you feel like that. They try to hurt you. But deep inside I knew my sister wasn't better than me.'

'Do you see her now?' I ask.

'She died,' Paula says, matter-of-factly.

'Oh. I'm so sorry to hear that.'

'Don't be sorry. She wasn't a nice person, Katie.'

'What did she do?'

'What didn't she do? She hurt me.'

'How?' I ask, not sure I want to hear this.

'When I was little she tortured me.'

'Didn't your parents stop her?'

Paula laughs. 'No, she got away with it all. It's part of the reason I became a doula. I suppose I wanted to help young families, stop them turning out like mine. I wanted to protect the children.'

'Your relationship never improved, not even as adults?' I think about how my relationship with Melissa had started to get better.

'We didn't have the chance. She died when we were still children.'

I feel a lump in my throat. 'That must have been awful for you to cope with.'

Paula looks at me, her expression completely unreadable. 'Of course, a part of me was sad. She was my sister, after all. But another part of me was happy. I was free of her.'

15

The days are getting hotter. At school there's the hum of a lawnmower outside the window and the smell of freshly cut grass. We do all our PE outside now on the school field, running, jumping and throwing balls.

Everyone else is excited about the end of term, but we're not. The summer looms ahead of us. The other children at school talk excitedly of summer holidays, beaches, trips on planes. But my sister and I know that without the safety of school, the summer holidays can only mean one thing. More time with Dad.

As usual, my sister doesn't wait for me after school. She walks home as fast as she can, almost as if she's running away from something. Running away from me.

I dawdle, kicking at stones on the pavement, watching them bounce into the path of oncoming traffic.

When I get back home, my sister is in the living room on the sofa, next to Dad, watching a wildlife documentary. They stare at the television in silence as a lion tears apart a gazelle. Dad takes a gulp of his beer. I hover in the doorway, unsure whether to go in.

'See,' Dad says to my sister. 'It's survival of the fittest out there. That's the way it's supposed to be, the way we were designed.'

'Yes, Dad,' my sister nods.

'Humanity is overdeveloped. Take medicine, for example. It's a great thing, but it keeps people alive when they shouldn't be. Elderly people, babies, very ill people. So many of them would have died without medicine. So many of them should *have died. Hospitals interfere with natural selection.'*

I want to say something, to tell him he's being stupid, but my sister is already agreeing with him. 'You're right, Dad.'

'Take you two, for example.' He looks up suddenly from the TV and points at me in the doorway, and I can't help but jump. 'Without medical care, only one of you would have survived.' He stares at me intently. 'Maybe that's the way it should have been.'

CHAPTER THIRTY-ONE

The next day, I'm still getting my head around everything my sister said about my father when I hear a knock on the door. It's insistent and loud. I look at my watch. Perhaps my piano student is early. I finish changing Alice's nappy and then strap her into her chair.

The knocking gets louder.

'I'm coming,' I shout.

I open the door to see Ian's wife.

'I thought so,' she says. 'You're living in his house.'

I nod. 'We moved in here together. I'm not leaving.'

'When you came to my house the other day I knew I recognised you from somewhere. It just took me a while to remember. It was here, outside this house. When you were pregnant.'

'Sorry?' Then I have a vague recollection. A woman standing outside the coffee shop, ash-blonde hair, staring at the house. It must have been Sabrina. Why was she here?

'He told me you were a tenant.'

'I'm not a tenant,' I say, shocked. Is that what he'd let Sabrina believe? 'I'm living here as Ian's partner.'

'Are you even paying him anything to live here?'

'No,' I say, angrily. 'I could never afford to.' I think about how I moved out of my flatshare. Where I was happy. I'd always paid my own way until I got pregnant.

'So you think you're entitled to live in his house for free, do you? I expect you'll be asking for maintenance next. You just want to take him for everything he's got.'

'I don't! I love him.'

She laughs bitterly. 'No wonder he's in so much debt. We couldn't afford to do the house up unless we got a tenant in for a bit to make money first. And to cover the mortgage and the loan repayments. He said he'd sorted it. Instead he let you live in the house for free.'

My mind's spinning.

'What's it got to do with you?' I ask, irritated. 'It's his house.'

'He was going to have to sell the house to pay the inheritance tax before I stepped in. He had to take out a mortgage to cover the tax, but they wouldn't lend him enough money. His credit rating's not good enough. So I took out a loan to help him.'

'The inheritance tax? You mean, he inherited the house?' I ask, reeling from shock. 'It's not from his property business?'

She laughs. 'What property business? Is that what he's saying now?'

'So he doesn't own a load of houses across London?' My eyes widen in disbelief. I can hardly take in her words.

'Of course not.' Sabrina snorts.

'What does he do then?' I ask, as I dig my nails into the palms of my hands, trying to control my emotions.

'His latest job is as a security guard. At least that's what he's told me. When he said he was on the night shift he must have been with you. He never keeps a job for long. He loses them as quickly as he charms his way into them. He won't cooperate with the bosses, or he tries to steal from them. Most of the time his lifestyle is funded by me.'

My heart beats faster. I can hardly believe what she's saying. Ian isn't the person I thought he was at all. Everything he ever said has been a lie. Our relationship was built on sand.

'So this house – whose was it?'

'His father's. He died nine months ago.'

'He never mentioned that.'

'He was estranged from his father. They were never close. He grew up nearby, but not in this house. He lived with his mother.'

I've learnt more about Ian in this five-minute conversation with his wife than in the whole year I've been dating him.

'Right,' I say. 'But what's all this got to do with me?'

'Well, as you're living here and there's no tenant, then there's no way Ian can afford to keep the house. You're going to have to start paying rent. Starting today.'

'But I can't afford to.' I feel sick. Am I going to be evicted from my home with my twins?

I hear footsteps behind me and Paula appears, Alice in her arms. 'Is there a problem here?' she asks.

Sabrina stares straight at Paula without speaking.

'This is Ian's wife,' I say to Paula.

The blood has drained from Sabrina's face. She stares at Paula. 'I—' she says. But she doesn't finish her sentence. Suddenly she collapses, her legs crumpling beneath her. Her head tips back and her body crashes onto the Victorian tiles of our doorstep, her head hitting the cold ground, bouncing up a few inches and then twisting to the side against the tiles.

Paula and I stand over her for a second, stunned.

'I hope she's OK,' I say, kneeling down beside her. 'Wake up,' I whisper, shaking her arm. 'Wake up.'

'I'll go and get an ice pack,' Paula says.

When Sabrina comes to, she's breathing fast.

She looks up at the house, her eyes darting from side to side.

She starts to stumble to her feet, and I reach down to help her up. Inside the house the twins start screaming.

'Are you OK?'

She puts her hand to her head and then winces. For a moment, she looks like she might faint again and she blinks rapidly, dizzy and disorientated.

Paula reappears with the ice pack.

'Do you want to come in and sit down?' I ask Sabrina, taking pity on her. I don't want her to go back out in this state.

'I'm fine,' she mumbles. 'I need to go.'

She moves clumsily away from us, down the drive.

I follow her and catch her up, grabbing her arm.

She jumps away from me and when I look into her eyes I can see pure terror. She must still be confused.

'I'm not going to hurt you.'

'I just need to go,' she says. 'Now.'

'Do you want me to take you to the hospital?'

'No, no, I'm fine.'

And with that, she hurries off into the dark.

When I go back inside the house, Paula is sitting with the twins in the living room.

'What did she want?' she asks.

'She wants me to pay rent.'

Paula laughs. 'Good job she fainted, then. It meant she left in a hurry.' Paula smiles to herself. 'I don't think she'll be back.'

CHAPTER THIRTY-TWO

Ian comes round the next day, insisting he wants to see the twins.

'Are you here to apologise for your wife?' I ask when I see him at the door.

'She mentioned she'd visited. I'm sorry if she disturbed you.'

'She asked me to pay rent,' I say angrily. 'I can't afford it. I've started teaching piano, but it only just about covers food. Anyway, you should be paying me maintenance for the twins, I shouldn't be paying you.'

Ian puts his hand on my shoulder. 'We've got a lot to discuss. Can I come in and see the girls?'

'No,' I say. He's been calling for days, but I can't face handing my children over to him. Not after everything he's done.

'When can I see them, Katie? I miss them.'

'It's not like you made any effort to see them in the first days of their lives, is it? When you told me you were in Thailand.'

'I didn't realise they'd been born. Honestly.'

Paula appears behind me at the door. 'I hope this is just a flying visit.'

'Paula,' he says. 'Still here, are you? We're trying to have a private discussion.'

'Anything you can say to Katie, you can say to me.'

I turn to her. I know she's only trying to help, but I'd prefer to have this conversation on my own. 'It's OK, Paula. Can you go to the twins?'

'Don't let him in,' Paula says. She looks me in the eyes. 'Promise me.'

'I won't.'

One of the babies starts to cry and Paula reluctantly retreats into the house.

'I can't believe she's still here,' Ian says.

'I need her to look after the twins while I work to pay for food.'

Ian runs his hand through his dark hair, looking regretful. 'I wish things hadn't turned out like this.'

'It's your fault, Ian.'

'Please let me see the girls. I miss them.'

'We can sort something out,' I say. Despite everything Ian's done, I still want him to have a relationship with his daughters. I missed out on my own father when I was growing up, and I don't want them to.

'Is there any chance I could see them now? Take them out for a bit?'

'Now's not a good time,' I say.

'I wish you could forgive me, Katie.'

'I wouldn't know where to start.' I laugh bitterly. 'Everything you've told me has been a lie. Sabrina told me that you don't have a business. That you inherited this house and you don't have any other properties.'

I can see Ian's mind racing as he tries to think of an explanation. 'The house was just the start. I was building up the business slowly.'

'Extremely slowly.'

'Well, yeah. It turns out that it's not going to work anyway. I came to tell you we're going to have to sell the house.'

'Because you can't afford it? Because you don't have a property empire, or any money at all to your name?'

'Sabrina wants to sell it. She put some money into it so I wouldn't have to sell it to pay the inheritance tax. And now she wants to sell up anyway. I'm devastated. It was my father's house. I used to visit as a kid, when my father lived here with his new wife. I always wanted to live here.' He looks round the hallway wistfully.

'Your dream came true in the end.' A tiny part of me is starting to soften, to feel a little bit sorry for him.

'Yeah. Once I realised I'd inherited the house, I felt vindicated. It was finally my turn. It was going to be the first property in my portfolio.'

'Why did you lie about having a property business?'

Ian shrugs. 'It always impresses people, having my own business.'

'But you didn't have your own business.'

'I would have done soon enough. I was going to do up the house. Make a fortune.'

'But then I needed somewhere to live with the twins,' I say. 'And that changed your plans.'

'Yeah. I didn't get the keys for ages. There was so much paperwork. By the time I actually got the keys, you were ready to move in.'

'And you didn't see it before?' This explains why the house was falling apart when I first saw it.

'Well, no. I thought it would be a bit dated, but I didn't think it would be in such a bad state. I hadn't realised my father had been in a care home for the final years of his life. I arranged for a waste removal company to clear any junk from the main rooms. But I only picked up the keys myself the day before you moved in. I had to give them to you that evening and I didn't have time to check the house first.' I remember how confusing it was when the house wasn't the one Amy and I saw on Rightmove. We had been completely convinced that was the one I was moving into. But Ian had inherited this house, so it wouldn't have been advertised online.

'You completely fooled me. I thought we had a future together.'

'I know, Katie. It's all gone wrong.' He says it as if he takes no responsibility for the way things have turned out. 'I'm so angry with Sabrina. Even if we just did the house up a little bit more, we'd make a huge profit. But now she's not up for that. She wants to sell it. And I can't keep it without her.'

'You seem more concerned about losing the house than losing me.' I try to keep my voice steady, but my lip quivers.

'You know I wanted to be with you,' Ian says. 'I've stayed with Sabrina because it's convenient for both of us, and because I was worried about how she'd cope if I left. But if we sell the house then we'll have enough money to separate. I think she's stable enough now to cope without me. You and I could get our own place together.'

I laugh bitterly. I don't believe a word he says. 'It's over between us. It was over as soon as I found out you'd lied to me about Thailand, that you were with your wife when our twins were born.'

He looks at his feet. 'I didn't intend to be with Sabrina that week, I intended to be with you. But I was being blackmailed.'

'What do you mean?'

'I got an anonymous email threatening to tell you that I wasn't who I said I was. They were going to tell you I was married and that the property business didn't exist. They said I had to stay away from you until I'd paid to keep them quiet.'

'You were being threatened?' I stare at him, surprised. There's so much he hasn't told me.

'They wanted £20,000. I didn't have it. I was planning to stay away until I'd negotiated some kind of deal with them or persuaded them not to tell you anything. I thought if I told you I was going abroad on business it would buy time. But I went back to Sabrina. I was planning to come back to you as soon as I'd sorted it out.'

A thought occurs to me. 'Are you sure it wasn't Sabrina who was blackmailing you?' I wouldn't put it past her. She said she hadn't known about me until I turned up on her doorstep, but perhaps that had been a lie. Perhaps she had wanted to keep Ian away from me when I needed him most. To have him back with her.

'I don't think so. It's not her style. She prefers face-to-face manipulation.'

'Did you pay up?'

'No. I didn't have the money. I explained that over and over and whoever it was eventually seemed to lose interest. The emails stopped. I was planning to come back to you when I got all your texts through to say the babies had been born.'

'I can't believe all that time you were only the other side of London. You could have rushed over when I was in labour. But you didn't see your babies for a week.'

Ian sighs. 'I know I've lied about a lot of things, but I told the truth about my phone not working properly. None of your messages came through until days later.'

'What about my calls?'

'I didn't receive any missed calls.'

I frown. 'None?' Surely if he was in the UK, he'd have received them.

'No. And your text messages came through all at once. As soon as I got them I came over. I would never have deliberately missed seeing my twins.'

My stomach twists. I feel so confused. Despite everything, I believe him.

'I need to move out,' I tell Paula miserably over lunch.

'Oh?' she says.

'Ian's selling the house.'

'Surely you should stay here as long as you can. Ian owes you that.'

I shake my head. 'It's too unstable. I don't know when he'll chuck me out for good. And anyway, it's time to move on, time for me to start our lives as a family of three, not living day-to-day all the time.'

Paula nods, but the atmosphere in the kitchen is tense. 'Where will you go?' she asks.

'A one-bed flat. At least an hour from the city. It's the closest I think I'll be able to afford.'

'What about the piano? Your lessons?'

'I'll have to leave that all behind. Maybe in a few years I'll be able to afford to start again. Buy a piano and teach. But not now. I need a stable life for the twins. A new life.'

Paula frowns. 'I understand,' she says. 'But I'll miss you.'

'I know,' I reply. 'I'll miss you too.'

'I can help you look for flats if you like. Ask around friends. Ring round some estate agents.'

I smile. 'That would be great.'

'In fact,' Paula says, smiling back at me, 'I have a friend who's about to move out of her one-bed flat in Enfield to go abroad. I could ask her if you could have a first look at the flat before it goes on the market. She really wants someone who'll look after it properly while she's away, so I'm sure she'd make sure the price was reasonable for the right person. Do you want me to ask her about it?'

'That would be brilliant. Thanks.' I smile at the thought of finding a new flat and putting Ian and this house behind me.

16

We're finishing dinner when Dad returns from the pub. We smell him before we see him, the stale smoke stuck to his clothes.

He's in a good mood, and when my mother rises from the dinner table to greet him, he wraps his arms around her and kisses her passionately. I glance at my sister, but she doesn't look back. I can smell his breath from here and I try not to cough.

He turns to my sister and kisses her on the cheek. I can tell she hates it, hates the bristles of his beard on her cheek, hates the sweaty, smoky smell that surrounds him. Sometimes I can feel exactly what she feels at the same time. It's like we're connected by an invisible cord, binding us together.

She doesn't pull away despite her discomfort. Instead she smiles at him. 'Hi, Dad.'

'I bought you a present.' He digs around in his jeans pocket and produces a beer mat, blue and green and soggy at the edges.

'Thank you,' she says, and this time I can see she means it. She has a whole collection in her room. She likes to show me them, to make me jealous.

This one looks interesting. I like the way the blue and the green merge into each other in the pattern, and the curly writing on the front.

'Can I have a look?' I ask.

'No,' my sister says, and pulls it away protectively.

'It's a present for your sister,' Dad says. 'Don't you understand that?' I look down at the floor.

'Didn't you get one for her?' Mum asks.

'Of course not. She doesn't deserve one.'

CHAPTER THIRTY-THREE

Mum and I wander round the local shops together. I'm hoping that this will be a chance to repair my relationship with her after I pushed her away when the twins were born. I've reluctantly let Ian take the twins out and shopping's a good distraction from their absence. Mum knows Ian's looking after the twins, she just doesn't know we've split up.

She seems in a good mood, spending money left, right and centre on the twins. Clothes, toys, new blankets. Everything she sees, she seems to want to buy. I'm so relieved. I can hardly afford to buy anything myself. My child benefit hasn't come through yet, and I haven't agreed maintenance with Ian. I don't want the twins to go without.

I can see the joy in Mum's face when she selects things, how much she loves taking on the grandmother role. Maybe I could let her have a bigger part in my twins' life. Just because she wasn't the perfect parent doesn't mean she can't help out with the twins. I can see how much she wants to get involved; how much she wants to be there for me and my family.

Mum leads me into yet another shop and we go to the womenswear section.

'I thought I could buy something for you too. A gift,' she says.

'Mum, you really don't need to.'

'Think of it as a "new mother" gift. As a congratulations for the birth, but a present for you instead of the twins.'

She starts pulling winter dresses off a rail. None of them are really my style, but I nod appreciatively anyway. She insists I try them on.

We start walking to the changing rooms, but on the way I freeze. Ahead of us is an ash-blonde woman pushing a double buggy. It can't be her.

But I recognise the buggy. My buggy.

I flush with anger. Just the other day, Ian was telling me that he and Sabrina were married in name only. And now she's here, looking after my twins. She's stolen my whole life.

Just at that moment, Ian appears beside her.

Luckily, Mum hasn't noticed him. She's looking through the dresses that are slung over her arm, going through the prices. But we're on a collision course with Sabrina and Ian, who've stopped to chat in front of us.

Just then, Ian looks up.

'Katie,' he says, running his hand through his hair as if for once he might be embarrassed. 'Hi.'

Mum's attention shifts. 'Oh, hi Ian. How are the twins doing? Great that you could take them out for the day. Katie and I are having a lovely time shopping.'

'No problem,' Ian says, looking from me to Mum and back again, weighing up the situation.

Sabrina has been inspecting a pair of trousers, but now she turns, one hand still on the buggy with my twins inside.

Blood rushes to my head, as she introduces herself to Mum. 'Hi,' she says, 'I'm Sabrina. You must be Katie's mother.' She looks at me.

Mum only misses a single beat. 'Yes,' she says. 'I'm Jackie.' She looks at Ian and then back at Sabrina, then into the buggy with the twins.

'Are you helping with the twins?' she asks.

'You could say that.' Sabrina smiles serenely. I want to scream at her, to shout at Ian. How could he let her look after my babies? I can't bear to see her with them, her hands gripped tightly around the buggy handle as if the twins belong to her. They're *my* daughters.

But as much as I want to grab them off her, to berate Ian, I need to get Mum away from them.

I loop my arm through Mum's. 'We'd better go. The queue to the changing room's getting longer by the second.'

'OK,' Mum says, looking up. 'Well, nice to meet you, Sabrina.'

As soon as we're out of earshot, she whispers, 'Who was that?'

'Oh, just Ian's sister,' I say quickly. 'She comes round sometimes to help.'

'You never let me or Melissa help.'

'Well, you should come round more often.'

Mum beams. 'I'd like that.' As we join the queue to try on clothes, I breathe a sigh of relief. I can see that she's so distracted by thoughts of being a doting grandmother, she isn't questioning who Sabrina really is.

Later, we have lunch, piles of shopping bags under our table. I need to ask Mum about what Melissa said about Dad, but I don't know how to broach the subject.

'Katie,' Mum says, when the starters come. 'You know I'll always be there for you, don't you?'

I nod, touched by how nice she's being.

'And you know that if you need help with anything – childcare, money, anything at all – you can always come to me?'

'Yes, Mum,' I say. 'Thanks.'

'OK, so now I'm going to say something that I think might upset you, but I'm afraid I have to say it.'

I take a deep breath. Is she about to tell me about Dad?

The starters are in front of us now, and I know she's deliberately chosen a time when she knows I can't escape.

'What, Mum?' I say, scratching the scar at the top of my arm anxiously.

'That woman – Sabrina. She wasn't Ian's sister, was she?'

'Oh,' I say, surprised. I flush and look down at my plate. There's nowhere to hide. 'No, she's not his sister.'

'I didn't think so. When you were in the changing room, I saw them together. They seemed a lot closer than brother and sister.'

I have a sinking feeling in my stomach. I can't hide things from her any longer. 'She's his wife,' I say, ashamed to even look at her.

'Oh, no,' Mum says. She reaches her hand across the table. 'I thought that might be it. Ian always seemed too good to be true.'

Too good to be true? She never said anything.

'When did you find out?' she asks. And then I see the thought cross her mind. 'Or did you always know he was married? From the beginning?'

'No, Mum. I just found out recently. You don't need to worry. I've chucked him out.'

'And he went back to her?'

'Yes.'

'I'm so sorry, Katie.'

I expect her to say it's all my fault, that I always make bad decisions, that I should have seen it coming.

But she says none of this, and just holds my hand while I cry.

When we're asked if we want dessert, I'm not hungry, but Mum insists.

'You shouldn't live in that house by yourself, you know.'

'I've got the twins. And Paula.' But I know I won't be able to stay there forever.

I see her bristle at Paula's name.

'You could always move in with me,' she says. 'I've got two spare rooms. You could have one and the twins could have the other.'

I look at her, surprised. I would never have thought she'd put up with the noise of the twins.

'I can't do that,' I say quickly.

'Think about it,' she replies. 'It doesn't have to be for long. Just until you get back on your feet.'

'I'll think about it,' I say.

She nods. 'And if you fancy getting away, Melissa and I are renting a cottage in the south of France at the end of the month. For a holiday. You could come with the twins. Get away from everything for a bit. I'd pay, of course. Graham's not coming, so it would just be the three of us and the twins.'

I imagine going on holiday with her and Melissa, having a break from the routine, from all this heartbreak. 'That would be lovely,' I say.

CHAPTER THIRTY-FOUR

It's two weeks before I manage to get a viewing of Paula's friend Caroline's flat. I feel a buzz of excitement as I get off the final bus after two hours of travelling. The flat sounds perfect. I can't wait to sign a contract for a new place to live, so I can get settled into my new life, just me and the girls. I haven't seen anything else that's suitable, so I have high hopes for this flat.

I've dressed in my smock dress, with navy high heels and matching earrings. Paula's told Caroline all about my situation, but I still want to make sure I come across well. So many landlords aren't keen to rent to me when I tell them I'm a single mother with baby twins.

I arrive at the address, take a deep breath and press the buzzer for the flat.

No answer. I wait a minute and look at my phone at the details Paula's texted me. It's definitely the right address.

I press the buzzer again.

No answer.

I ring the number I have for Caroline, but she doesn't pick up. I try Paula, but she doesn't answer either.

I hover around the doorway for ten minutes, but no one goes in or comes out. I try them both again. No answer.

I walk round the block a few more times, sussing out the local area. It feels safe and welcoming. Just the kind of place where I could bring up the twins. After ten minutes I come back and try the buzzer again. Perhaps it's broken.

I try ringing the flat next door, but they won't let me in without knowing who I am.

I look at my watch. If I don't leave now, I'll miss the twins' feed.

I try calling one final time, then kick at the ground and head back home.

By the time I get back home, I'm tired and frustrated, angry with the Tube delays, and that I've wasted a whole afternoon.

'Hi,' Paula says as I come through the door. 'How did it go?'

'Why didn't you pick up your phone?' I ask angrily. 'I've been trying to call you. Caroline wasn't even there.'

'I'm sorry. I was busy with the twins. They've been very fractious this afternoon. Did you ring Caroline?'

'She didn't answer,' I say accusingly. 'But why wasn't she at the flat? I thought you arranged the time with her.'

'Maybe she popped out,' Paula says vaguely.

'I travelled halfway across London to get there.'

'Well, that's not my fault. She said she'd be there. Are you sure you have the right phone number for her?' Paula goes into the kitchen and I follow her. She picks up a Post-it note from the island in the centre of the kitchen, a number written neatly on it. 'Here it is.'

I pick up the note and cross-check the number with my phone. The final digit is different.

I clench my fist in frustration. 'I can't believe it. I was ringing the wrong number. I'll never find somewhere to live.'

'You only think of yourself, Katie.'

'What do you mean?'

'I mean, I've done you a favour. And you've come home angry with me for not picking up my phone. When I was looking after your twins. For free.'

'I'm sorry—'

'I've found you a flat, I told Caroline you'd be a great tenant. You only had to go and meet her. But you couldn't even be bothered to note down her number right. And you come back blaming me for her not being there.'

'I am grateful, Paula… I'm sorry if it didn't seem that way. I was just disappointed not to see the flat. You know I've been going through a tough time.'

'I do know that. I know every single detail about that.'

'Oh, I—'

'You never ask about me. Never think about me. Never ask how I might be feeling.' She folds a dish towel over and over in her hands.

I realise she's right. I hardly know the first thing about her, her life or her background.

'I've been a bit self-obsessed lately. I'm sorry. What's wrong?'

'What do you think's wrong? You're moving out! I'm losing my job.'

'But Paula, I'm not even paying you. I've appreciated you staying with me, I've needed your help. But I can cope on my own now. And I'm moving out myself. I'll be in a tiny flat. There won't be any space…'

'You're taking away my home.'

I feel baffled. 'You want to stay here? You don't want to go home?'

For the first time, I wonder where she was living before. How bad it must have been for her to spend so much time hanging around at the coffee shop over the road.

'Yes, I wanted to stay here,' she says. 'I love this house. It's beautiful.'

'But it's being sold. We both have to move.'

'I don't think you realise the sacrifices I've made for you.' She sounds just like Mum used to when she talked about paying towards music college. Her voice is bitter.

'I do, Paula. You've done so much for me.'

'I gave up my home for you.'

'I'm sorry?'

'You heard me. I gave up my home. When I started working for bed and board, I couldn't afford to stay at my old place. So I gave it up. To look after you.'

'You did?' I don't understand. Why would she do that? She knew I wouldn't need her forever. And she was the one who suggested working in exchange for bed and board.

'Yes, I did. Because I cared about you, Katie. Because I wanted to help you. And now you throw it all back in my face. Make me homeless.'

'You don't have anywhere to go?'

'No. And I've seen the flats you've been looking at. They're all one-bedroom. You didn't even think of taking me with you, did you? And you have the audacity to ask me to help you look for a place. Well, I'm busy, you know. Looking for my own place. Because of you.'

'I'm so sorry, I had no idea.' But what she's saying makes no sense. Why would she have given up her own place to move here with me?

'You never have any idea. Because you never think of me. You just sprung it on me one day. Like you did before. When Ian came back. You just expect me to move out at a moment's notice. Whenever's convenient for you. Whenever you find a place to live. You don't care about me at all. All I am to you is a shoulder to cry on, a mother figure, because your own mother doesn't love you enough, because you're so supremely selfish. Look at you, Katie. Look at your life. Ian's left you. No one wants to help you. But I've stayed here. I've put up with all your selfishness, listened to you sniffling about your slightly less-than-perfect childhood. I've done everything for you. And this is how you repay me.'

I'm shaking when I get upstairs to my room. I pace up and down, scratching at the scar on my arm. I can't believe Paula doesn't have anywhere else to go. I realise I know nothing about her. I never asked for references. Never looked up her qualifications. I trusted her from day one. As soon as she helped me with labour there was a bond between us, like she was family. I thought she only wanted to help me, but now I'm not so sure. It feels like she wanted somewhere to live more than she wanted to help me out. And she's capitalised on my trust, made me feel like I owe her. I don't know how I'll ever get away from her.

I remember how distrustful Ian was of Paula when he got back. Maybe he was right. Mum never liked her either, but I just thought she was jealous. Maybe they could all see something I couldn't, because I was so indebted to Paula, so dependent on her, that I didn't want to see it.

I remember how Ian insisted on getting references from her once he returned to the house to live with me. I know he planned to follow them up, but I'm not sure he ever did. He wasn't at the house long enough. I found the unpaid bills so soon after he came back. The day I asked Paula to leave.

I stop stock-still, thinking back. Paula was living with us in return for bed and board. And she'd made it very clear she didn't want to leave. I'd told her she couldn't stay now Ian was back. I'd gone out, and when I got back the unpaid bills were sitting on the table, as if they were waiting for me. Would Ian really have left them out, knowing how angry I'd be? Or was it Paula who put the bills out for me to see? Did she engineer Ian leaving?

I ring Ian, heart thumping.

'Katie – good to hear from you.'

'Ian.'

'I hope it was OK that Sabrina helped me with the twins the other day?'

I'd almost forgotten about that. 'Of course it wasn't.'

'She insisted. She always wanted children of her own, but it never happened for her. She loves children.'

I frown. I know she hates me. I don't want her in charge of my children.

'I'd prefer you to look after them on your own.'

'Absolutely,' Ian says. 'I'll speak to her. But remember, she wants to charge you rent. At the moment I've persuaded her not to. But I wouldn't recommend getting on the wrong side of her. She can be vicious.'

'I guess you would know. You've cheated on her enough times to find out.'

Ian says nothing.

'Anyway, it doesn't matter. I'm looking for somewhere else to live. I didn't call you about that. It's over between us.'

'Then what did you call about?'

'I think you might have been right about Paula. I'm not sure if I can trust her.'

'There's always been something odd about her. I said that from the beginning.'

'I thought you just didn't like her.'

'She behaved so strangely, working for free, putting pictures of herself up around the house...'

'Yeah, I suppose so.' I ignored all the signs, too exhausted from looking after the twins and too distracted by Ian's lies to care about her odd behaviour.

'Did you ever call up her references?' I ask.

'No, I didn't get round to it before I left.'

'Can you give me their numbers?'

'Sure, I'll send them over to you. Are you going to ring them?'

'Yeah.'

'But why? Surely she's leaving now you're moving out?'

'She's supposed to be. But it's proving difficult.'

'Let me know if I can do anything to help. I can't stand her. I'd happily get rid of her for you.'

I ask him the question that's been bugging me.

'Ian, that day I chucked you out, when I found out you hadn't been paying the mortgage – did you leave the unpaid bills on the kitchen table?'

'No. I hadn't even really looked at them. I'd just shoved all the post to the house in a drawer. I knew I couldn't pay them. I was going to speak to Sabrina about them, ask her to pay. But I didn't want her to discover that I didn't have a tenant and that you were living there instead. I was still working out what to do.'

I imagine him thinking of Sabrina when we first moved in together, and I feel anger rising in me. But I swallow it. I need to get to the bottom of this. 'So you didn't leave them out?'

'No, of course not.'

'Do you think Paula could have planted them?'

'Umm… I didn't leave them there, so I suppose she could have,' Ian says slowly. 'But why?'

'She knew that if you stayed living there, she'd have to leave. And she didn't want to. Remember how badly she reacted when we asked her to move out? She locked herself in her room.'

'I remember. She was furious.'

'And now she's saying she can't move out because she hasn't got anywhere to go. That she's given up everything for me.'

'Doesn't she have her own place to go back to?'

'Apparently not. I think she planted those bills so you'd move out and she could stay.'

Ian pauses. 'I never trusted her.'

'I know you didn't. That's one thing you might have been right on.' I feel tense. For reasons I don't understand, Paula has completely embedded herself in my life, in my twins' lives. A shiver runs up my spine. I have to get away from her.

17

My sister is out with Dad. I don't know where or why, but I miss her terribly. We've always done everything together. From the moment we were born, we were inseparable. We didn't need anyone except each other. We knew we'd always be there for each other, always protect each other. But not anymore. My sister hates me now. Dad's turned her against me.

'Come with me,' Mum says gently. 'Let's listen to the piano. It always makes you feel better.' I follow her slowly, dragging my feet. When we get to the music room I sit on the rug on the floor, while she perches on the piano stool.

I sit miserably on the floor while my mother plays, her fingers dancing over the keys. Usually it would calm me, but today nothing can make me happy. I remember when we were down in the basement and she was up here, playing on her own. She must have known we were down there. We're down there more and more often these days. But she's never come down to get us. She lets Dad do whatever he likes to us. She can't love us. Not really.

I hear the front door open. Dad must be back. Mum doesn't even glance up, she's so lost in the music. Dad marches in, and I scoot into the corner away from him.

'What are you doing? Why isn't the dinner on?'

My mother looks up from her trance, just as he slams the lid of the piano on her fingers with all his might.

Mum screams and my eyes widen in horror.

But the most haunting sound isn't her agony. It's my sister's laughter.

CHAPTER THIRTY-FIVE

Ian sends the email with the references as soon as we get off the phone. When Paula goes upstairs to put the twins down for a nap, I go to the far side of the kitchen, out of earshot of the bedroom and go through them. There are four families listed, four telephone numbers. I ring the numbers one by one. None of them pick up. I leave messages asking them to call me back, and then put down my phone, feeling deflated.

I don't sleep that night. I feel uncomfortable with the twins sleeping in the same room as Paula. I should have confronted her about the bills she planted, told her to get out of my life. But I know in reality she won't leave. And making her angry will make things a thousand times worse. It's best to just try and stay out of her way.

Every hour I go and stand outside the door, wanting to be close to my girls, checking they aren't screaming. Paula's told me they sleep through the night now. She never brings them in to me to breastfeed until the morning. I'd thought I was lucky that my babies were exceptionally well-trained, sleeping through when they're so young, all thanks to Paula. But now I'm not so sure. I'm worried that she's giving something to them to make them sleep. I remember overhearing her giving them 'medicine', how they were both fast asleep straight after.

The next morning, I keep checking my phone, but none of the families that Paula gave as references have called me back. It's been less than fourteen hours since I called them, and I know I shouldn't feel anxious, but I can't help the nerves festering in the pit of my stomach. I tell myself that it won't be a priority for them to give me a reference. They'll have busy lives and better things to do. But I still can't shake my anxiety.

Melissa's coming round this afternoon, and I'm feeling apprehensive. I hope she'll apologise for everything she said about Dad when she was drunk, that she'll tell me she was exaggerating. I've tried to put what she said about him to the back of my mind, but it's been eating away at me.

We're supposed to be planning our holiday to France with Mum. I can't wait to get away with the twins, away from the house and away from Paula. The more I think about it, the more convinced I am that she planted the bills. I have no idea what she wants from me, or what she's got against Ian.

The doorbell rings and I jump. I make us drinks and then we sit in the living room together, Melissa cuddling Alice and me cradling Frances. Melissa seems nervous as she coos at Alice.

'How's Graham?' I ask.

'Just about coping,' she replies. 'He didn't see the split coming at all. I feel so guilty.'

'You've told him then?'

'Yeah. Yesterday. I told him I'm moving out when I get back from holiday.'

'Where to?'

'In with Mum.'

'Really?'

'Yeah. I've told her what's going on. I thought she'd be angry that I was throwing away my marriage, but she understands.' I nod. She was understanding about Ian too.

'She says she wishes she'd been brave enough to divorce Dad. Before he got so bad,' Melissa continues.

'I had no idea what he was like.' I'm still struggling to get my head round it.

'He was always heading for trouble, Katie. She'd have been better off out of it. So would you.'

'What do you mean?' I stare at her, eyes wide.

'Mum and I have been keeping secrets from you for so long. It's time you knew the truth.'

I swallow. 'The truth about what?' What she told me before about my father was bad enough. There can't be more.

'About how Dad died. About how you got that scar on your arm.'

I recoil, feeling sick. Whatever she's about to say, I don't think I want to hear it.

'I thought he died in a car accident on his way to work,' I say, my voice worried, praying she'll just confirm what I remember. I scan my memory, but I can't recall any more than that.

'That's not true. He died in a fight. At a pub. He was knocked out cold. Hit his head on a glass table and smashed through it, severed an artery in his neck. He bled to death before the ambulance arrived.'

'Oh, god. Really?' I imagine him bleeding out in the pub, no one able to save him. 'Why did the guy pick on him?' Why my father? Why not someone else in the pub?

'He didn't pick on him. Dad started the fight.'

'But why?' I'm holding my breath.

'It was because of you.'

'Me?' My heart beats faster. I feel guilty, but I don't know what for.

'Yes, you and Mum. Dad wanted revenge.'

'For what?' I whisper.

'The week before, he'd fought the same guy. You were there.'

'I was there? But I don't remember…'

'Dad was supposed to be looking after you, but he'd taken you to the pub and got drunk. You got caught up in one of his brawls.

You were only little. Someone threw a glass and it smashed over your arm. That's how you got that scar.'

I scratch at it. 'I thought I fell off my bike.'

'You didn't.'

'Mum was there when it happened. She'd realised that you were at the pub with him and had come to collect you. She jumped in the way of the glass. She managed to block your face, to stop the damage being any worse. The glass smashed on her hand, cut a tendon in her wrist.'

'That's why she stopped playing the piano professionally?'

'Yes. She was never able to play as well as she had before the fight. Instead she put all her hopes into you.'

'Oh.' Suddenly Mum's behaviour, pushing me with my music, makes more sense. 'What happened to the man who killed him?'

'He went to prison for a bit, but he was out years ago. I've no idea where he is now.'

I can hardly believe what Melissa's just told me. Dad died in a violent fight that he'd started himself. Trying to get revenge on my behalf. And Mum's career ended because she was protecting me. I know it wasn't my fault, but I can't help feeling guilty. This changes everything.

'I don't understand. Why did you both lie to me?' I ask. 'Why did you let me believe that Dad was a good guy?' I scratch at my arm anxiously.

'It wasn't me. It was Mum. I was a child too, remember.'

'But you're not a child now. You've lied to me for years.' No wonder I always felt left out. I was the only one who didn't know the truth.

'After he died you were so fragile that Mum just wanted to protect you. She started to rewrite history with you. She'd take us both through the memories, telling us about the happy times we'd had together. At the swings in the park. Dancing in the living room. And after a while you just forgot the unhappy times. You forgot the times he'd lost his temper. Mum had taken you through the happy photos enough times for you to think that was what our childhood had been like.'

'But why would you go along with it?'

'Mum made me pretend. I hated Dad. He'd always been drunk. But after he died I was never allowed to say anything against him. For a while I liked it – I felt like Mum and I were in league together, looking after you. I felt like an adult. But when I got older I questioned it. Why should I know the truth and not you? And I hated listening to you talk about our father. How great he was. How kind and caring. You even named your daughter after him. Everything you knew about him was a lie. But you believed it all. And I knew it would destroy you to be told otherwise.'

CHAPTER THIRTY-SIX

The next day, my mind is still spinning after everything my sister told me. Ian is looking after the twins, and Paula went out this morning saying she was going to search for somewhere to live. I'm relieved to have some time to myself to think. I've decided not to go on holiday with Mum and Melissa. I can't face pretending that I'm not angry with them both for lying to me about my father's death. I need some time away from them.

The 'For Sale' sign has gone up outside my house, but no one's called me to arrange any viewings yet. Ian has said I'm welcome to stay until it's sold and it's looking like that could be months away, but I'm desperate to get out of here and start afresh.

I want to get away from Paula as soon as I can. She told me that she got the day wrong for my viewing of Caroline's flat and now Caroline's found another tenant. I'm not even sure the flat was ever on the market. But why on earth would she send me there? Maybe she's been so angry with me about moving out that she made up the flat to rent to distract me and buy more time in the house. Even though she's been great looking after the babies, I just can't trust her.

I search through the top drawer of the dresser in the dining room for the documents I'll need if I finally find a flat to rent. Proof of income, my bank statements, proof of address and my passport. I think my passport must have fallen down the back, so I look in the drawer below, pulling out the sheets of paper on the top. I pause for a moment when I see what they are. They're an architect's drawings showing detailed plans for the house. Ian must have got them done when he was doing up the house while I was in the hotel. For a moment I feel sorry for him. He had such big plans for this place.

I study them. The first drawing shows an open-plan kitchen diner and living area. On the first floor, en suite bathrooms have been added to the double bedrooms and the box room has become a walk-in wardrobe for the master bedroom. And then there's an attic office. I flick through the sheets. There's another page. A basement flat is marked out. I blink, staring at the plans. This can't be right. The house doesn't have a basement.

But it must do. It's marked out neatly in the plans.

A shiver runs down my spine. There's a whole room in my house that I didn't even know was there.

I go into the hallway and walk all the way along it, feeling the walls. There's no shadow of a door to a basement, no sign of anything bricked over. There's a bookcase at one end of the hallway, filled with old books and paperwork that doesn't belong to me. It must be Ian's father's. Painstakingly, I take everything off the shelves. The bookcase is heavier than it looks. It scrapes across the dusty floorboards and wobbles precariously as I slowly push it aside. I expect there to be a doorway behind it, but there's nothing. Nothing at all.

I remember the understairs cupboard. I peer in using my phone torch to light it up. When the roof leaked and I had to turn the power back on at the mains, the cupboard was filled with stacks of newspapers and magazines. I remember squeezing past them. But now there's just one remaining box of newspapers and a hoover. Ian must have cleared out the rest before he left. With all the clutter gone, I can see a door at the back of the cupboard. It looks like it could just be another cupboard, but I wonder if it leads to the basement.

I take a deep breath and go over to it. I pull the rusty bolt across and turn the stiff handle tentatively. The door sticks a little as I pull it towards me. On the other side there's pure darkness. I'm filled with fear as I shine my phone torch onto the stone steps leading downwards, a sheer drop on either side of them. I scratch at my arm violently.

My heart pounds as I go through the door and start down the steps, shining my torch onto each step in turn to check for obstacles. I force myself to keep going, breathing in the dusty air. I hate to think what might be down here. I remember the rats that ran from the house on the first day I looked around. Had they come from the basement?

There is no handrail, nothing at all to hold onto. Blood rushes to my head and I feel off balance for a second. I steady myself and shine the torch down further into the dark space. I can make out a large grey shape in the corner on the floor, but otherwise there seems to be nothing there.

I wonder what this room was used for. A laundry room, maybe. Or storage. I hear a scuttle and something scurries beneath me, making me jump. But I press on.

At the bottom of the steps, I see there is space on both sides of me. I turn left and right, shining my torch up at the walls and ceiling. I can see water running down the wall at the back; more damp. There's a puddle in the corner, stagnant and brown. No wonder I can't get the festering smell out of the house.

I take a tentative step and feel my shoe tread into something mulchy. I nearly slip over and I scream, shining my torch down to see a small furry form. A squished, decaying rat.

Then something soft brushes against me and I jump, dropping my phone. I hear it clatter on the floor. It must have knocked against something because the torch goes out and the basement goes completely black and the only sound is my breathing, fast and frantic.

I need to find my phone. I don't want to feel around on the floor with my bare hands. But what else can I do? Without the phone I'm not sure if I can even locate the stairs to get back up into the house. There's no light at all, not even from the doorway, which only leads into the dark cupboard under the stairs.

I try to find the phone with my feet. I'm sure I dropped it to my right, so I inch along the floor. Eventually I bump into something solid. The stairs. I sigh with relief. If I could just manoeuvre myself back up them. But I remember the sheer drop on both sides. I'd have to crawl up.

Reaching out my hand, I run it along the stair until I feel it go down onto the next step. In the darkness, I start moving slowly towards the bottom of the staircase. I step on something hard.

My phone?

I reach down, shaking with nerves.

Touching the reassuring plastic, I lift the phone up and press the home button. It casts a feeble glow and I turn the torch back on.

As I shine it back around the room, I'm sure that something is crouched, ready to jump from the shadows and attack me.

But there's nothing.

I run the torch round the room a few more times to reassure myself and calm my racing heart.

In the corner at the far end of the basement the blurry shape has turned into an old, single mattress, patches of mould turning it from white to grey. On top of it there's a hairbrush, tangled with thick black hair.

Has someone been living down here?

I think of the noises I sometimes hear at night. My worries about squatters when I first moved in. The creaks and clunks of the house. The distant cries of the babies. They can't have been coming from here, can they?

I want to get out of here. Right now. I start towards the stairs when I hear a loud bang.

When I shine my torch up the stairs, heart thudding, I see the door has slammed shut, trapping me.

18

The long school summer holiday seems endless, trapped in the house with my father's temper. The man who works in the garden doesn't come round for ages, and then suddenly he's here again, working outside in the heat of the summer. We find ourselves back in the basement, lying beside each other on the mattress, waiting for the time to pass. I've tried to make it nicer down here, putting a pile of our books in the corner, sticking photos of us on the walls.

'I wish we could enjoy the summer like other kids,' I say, imagining myself outside in the open air, playing in our huge garden. I rub at the purple bruise on my leg. For any other child it would be a result of an exciting summer, from tumbling out of a tree, or falling off a bike. But not me. For me it's because I put my elbows on the table at dinner.

My sister sighs. 'If you were better behaved, perhaps we wouldn't be down here in the basement, perhaps we'd be outside playing.'

I stare at her. 'I don't do anything wrong, he just hates me.'

'You do. You answer back. You don't smile when he comes in. You're ungrateful for everything he does for us.'

'I'm not any worse behaved than you.' She just can't see it. She can't see that if it's both of us messing about it's me he picks on. If we both haven't tidied our room, it's me he punishes.

'You're just not nice to him. If you were nice to him, then maybe he'd be nice to you.'

'I don't think so.'

'Well, I'm nice to him and look what he got me.' She pulls a silver chain out from under the neckline of her dress, triumphantly. A tiny silver bird dangles from the end and she holds it out to show me.

'It's beautiful,' I whisper. I don't have any jewellery. Dad's always bringing back gifts for my sister but never for me.

'He might give you one too, if you're good.'

I shake my head.

She frowns. 'I'm trying to help you here. To help you change. To be a better person. To stop you dragging me down. Dad says you hold me back. That without you bringing me down I could go on to great things. Maybe even be an actress.'

Tears prick my eyes. I don't understand her anymore. I used to know what my sister was thinking before she even knew it herself. I used to be able to sense her emotions. But our bond has been severed. It doesn't even feel like we're twins anymore.

She's started to think she's actually better than me, to believe my father when he says that she's the good twin, and that I am rotten to the core.

CHAPTER THIRTY-SEVEN

I climb the basement stairs shakily. Has the door blown shut? Or has someone slammed it? What if I'm locked down here? No one will ever find me.

I look at the signal bars on my phone. No reception.

I keep going up the stairs, careful to maintain my balance. I remember the water running down the wall and worry that the stone steps could be wet too. I imagine slipping over, hitting my head and slowly sliding down the stairs, never to be found, my children left without a mother.

When I get to the top of the stairs, I push at the wooden door. It doesn't open.

'Paula?' I call out. 'Paula?' But then I remember she's gone out for the day. She won't be back until late this evening. And it's hours before Ian's due back with the twins.

I push the door harder still, but nothing happens. Gritting my teeth, I shoulder-barge the door, crying out in pain as my arm hits the solid wood. At last the catch gives way and the door shoots open. I fall through it, still clutching my phone.

I hit my head on the wooden floorboards of the cupboard, but I'm OK. I quickly crawl completely out of the basement and shut the door behind me, my breathing ragged. How could the door have blown shut in the still air of the cupboard? Was someone trying to shut me in?

My thoughts are all over the place. I tell myself it's just because I hit my head, that there must be a rational explanation for the mattress, for the hairbrush. But I can't stop shaking. Because the more I try and rationalise everything that's been happening, the more I think there really is something to be afraid of.

I crawl out of the cupboard and stand leaning against the wall, adrenaline pumping.

I shout into the house. 'Hello? Paula? Ian?' Nothing. 'Is anyone there?' I wonder if an estate agent might have come over to show round a viewer. They could have shut the basement door, not realising I was in there.

But the house is silent. There doesn't seem to be anyone here. I check each room just in case. No one.

Picking up my phone again, I catch my breath. I ring my friend Mick, the maintenance guy who used to work with me in the coffee shop. After I've updated him on the twins, I ask him if he can come round and fix a lock to the basement. The kind with a key, so that no one except me can get in. He agrees to come straight after work.

I'm waiting for him to arrive, and I've just put the twins down for a nap, when my phone rings. I'm shocked to see it's my mother calling. She's supposed to be in France with Melissa. I pick up the phone in a panic, worried that she's had an accident on holiday. I didn't even speak to her before she went away. I was too shocked by what Melissa had told me.

'Katie,' she says breathlessly. 'I need to talk to you.'

'Mum – what is it?' My mind spins with worry, images of tragic accidents flashing through it like a slide show.

'Melissa told me why you haven't come on holiday with us. She said she told you about your father.' Her words come out in a rush, as if she doesn't have time to pause for breath.

'Mum, I—' I'm relieved she hasn't had an accident, but a mix of anger and sadness bubbles up inside me. I need to talk to her about my childhood, but I don't even know how I feel about it myself.

'You have every right to be angry, Katie. I should have told you what your father was like years ago. But the more time I left it, the more the lies seemed real to me. I wanted to believe them myself. Wanted to believe I'd had a happy marriage before he died. I wanted to forget all the horrible memories.'

'You let me believe he was a kind man, that he looked after me.'

'He did care about you. He just wasn't around a lot of the time. He was always at the pub.'

'Why did you let me believe it? Do you know how it feels to realise all your childhood memories are false?' I feel like the ground beneath me has shifted, the very foundations of my identity rocked.

'You'd been through enough. Your father was dead. You had the horrible injury to your arm. I didn't want anything else to hurt you.'

'But I must have known at the time. You let me forget, over-wrote my memories with what you wanted me to believe.'

'I thought you were young enough to forget. And I felt so guilty. I should have left him. I should never have let him be involved in yours and Melissa's lives. When you hurt your arm at the pub, I blamed myself. I thought the one thing I could do for you was give you a stable upbringing and let you believe you'd had a happy childhood. When I became more interested in psychiatric care, I read a lot of self-help and psychology books. So much of it was about how an unhappy childhood messes you up as an adult. Patients I see now, they rehash things from their childhood again and again. I thought I could give you the benefits of a happy childhood just by telling you that was what it was like. It seemed like the least I could do for you.'

'I don't know what to think, Mum. You lied to me about so many things.'

I think about how she lied to me about her own injuries too; never let on that they were anything to do with Dad. She played down her headaches so I wouldn't worry about her. And then I think about how Mum stepped in front of the glass, letting it smash into her instead of me. She was trying to protect me then. Has she only been trying to protect me since?

'I hope you can forgive me, Katie. I had to ring you as soon as Melissa confessed that she'd told you. I know I've made a mistake.'

I wander into the bedroom and look down at my babies, asleep in their cots. I know I'm not perfect myself. I'm going to mess up sometimes. I hope when I'm older they'll forgive me too.

The doorbell rings, interrupting my thoughts.

'Mum, I have to go,' I say quickly. It will be Mick, and I rush down the stairs before he knocks on the door even harder and wakes up the girls.

When I let him in, he's still in his maintenance uniform. He looks around the house, fascinated by its nooks and crannies. 'It's a real beauty,' he says, inspecting the Victorian ceiling rose.

'So, what's so urgent you call me out of the blue?' he asks.

'Well, I found a basement.'

'You found a basement?' He raises his eyebrows. 'You mean you didn't know it was there before?'

I show him the cupboard under the stairs, shine my phone torch in and point to the door at the back.

'I've never seen one like this before,' he says. 'Mind if I have a look?'

'Of course not. I'd like you to, actually, I think someone's been living down there.'

'In your basement? Do you think you're in a horror film or something?' He laughs, but he quietens when he sees the expression on my face. 'Don't worry, I'll check it out for you, damsel in distress,' he teases. I slap him on the shoulder for winding me up, feeling relieved that the atmosphere in the house has lightened.

He opens the door and goes through, propping it open with his toolbox. His workman's boots stomp down the stairs confidently.

'Is it this mattress that makes you think someone's been living here?' he asks.

'Yeah,' I say.

From the top of the stairs I see him poke it with his hand. 'I reckon it's been down here a long time. Years and years, in fact. It's as mouldy as anything. I doubt anyone's slept on it recently.'

'Are you sure?'

'Well, you can never be completely sure, but I reckon they'd be better off sleeping on the streets than breaking into your house, going through your cupboard under the stairs and then coming down here to sleep. This mattress was just dumped down here. Probably years ago. You have to pay the council to take mattresses away, you know. It was most likely easier for the previous owners to just leave it down here and forget about it.'

The way Mick's put it, it seems ludicrous to think that anyone would be sleeping down there. I know I should feel relieved, but I can't seem to shake the uncomfortable feeling I have deep inside my stomach.

'I think these pictures have been here ages, as well,' he says. 'They do look old. Interesting, though.'

'Pictures?'

'Come and take a look.'

I ease myself onto the steps and then go down slowly, but I'm not shaking like I was earlier. With Mick's high-powered torch, I can see it's just a room.

He's standing by the wall, shining the torch on a couple of old photographs on the wall that I hadn't noticed before. The photos are faded and water-damaged but I can just about make them out.

One is of a family, a mother and father and two children. They are standing by a beach, scowling at the camera. The mother's sensibly dressed in a flowery smock, and the two little girls are dressed the same. Only one of the girls' faces is visible. The other's has been scratched out, perhaps by time and damage, but it looks more deliberate than that. It looks like she's been scratched out with fingernails.

The second picture shows just the two girls, holding hands. Sisters, identically dressed, their dark hair in pigtails. Again, one of their faces has been scratched out. This time there's no doubt it's deliberate. Whoever damaged the photo has scratched so hard that there's a hole in the middle of the girl's face.

'They're weird,' I say, shuddering.

'Yeah. But from a very long time ago. They must have been here for decades. Every house has a history.'

I peer more closely at the pictures. Whoever damaged the photo was clearly angry. Then I notice the pencil markings on the wall beside them.

More drawings, like upstairs. A family of three. A mother, a father and a little girl. All smiling.

I shiver. Where's the other girl? The one who's been scratched out in the photo? What happened to her?

He turns to go back up the stairs. 'Happy no one's living in your basement now?' he says, smiling.

'Yes,' I reply. 'Thanks.'

'I take it you don't want me to fit a lock? There wouldn't be much point, as someone would have to break into the house first to get to the basement.'

'You're right,' I say, feeling silly. But as I go up the stairs, I can't get the pictures of the family out of my head; the way the little girl's face had been scratched out so viciously that she'd disappeared entirely.

Mick leaves, and I'm left alone in the house. Just me and the twins. Paula's still out. I go up and wake the girls from their nap, feed them and then sit cuddling them on the sofa. I can't help but feel afraid. There's a whole part of the house I didn't know existed. A secret basement with a mattress and family pictures.

And the weird thing is that Ian must have known. He's included it on the architect's plans. Why did he never mention it to me?

I need to get out of the house. I bundle the twins into the pram and walk down the drive. My next-door neighbour is gardening, trimming his perfectly straight hedge.

'Hi,' he says.

'Hi,' I reply. I try to hurry away. I want to avoid his questions, but he's coming down the ladder.

'I've been trying to catch you. I see you've put the house on the market.'

'Yes,' I say, not sure what explanation to provide.

'It's a shame,' he says. 'I was pleased to have you as neighbours. Glad someone was doing up the house at last.'

'It was too big for us in the end.'

'Have you had many viewers?'

'No, none.'

'I guess people don't forget. It will be hard to sell. It's a pity the project's too big for you. You seemed like the right type of people to turn the house around. Overlook its past and make it a happy home.'

I laugh bitterly. 'It hasn't quite worked out like that. And what do you mean, overlook its past?'

'Oh,' he says. 'I assumed you knew. But I guess it was a very long time ago now. Over forty years. But people round here have long memories. That's why I doubt you'll have much interest. No one local would buy it.'

'What happened?' I ask, suddenly afraid. I think of the pictures in the basement, the girl with the scratched-out face.

'A child died there.'

'In my house?' I say, blood draining from my head.

'Yes. She fell down the stairs. They say she was pushed.'

'Pushed?'

'They thought the father did it, but they could never prove it.'

I feel sick. 'Which stairs? Where in the house?' But I already know what he's going to say.

'In the basement.'

CHAPTER THIRTY-EIGHT

I walk as quickly as I can with the double buggy, manoeuvring round trees and lamp posts at speed as I try to calm my racing thoughts. But no matter how fast I go, I can't shake the horror from my head. *A girl died in my house. In the basement.*

I think of the pencil drawings on the wall in the bedroom, the scratched-out girl in the photo in the basement. They must have been her. The girl who died.

A drop of rain lands on me and I turn back towards the house before it gets heavier. At home, I reach for my phone. I google my own address and 'suspicious death' but get no results. It was so long ago. Forty years. The records probably aren't online.

I go to the kitchen and pour myself half a glass of wine to calm myself down. Then I remember. The old newspapers I'd seen in the cupboard under the stairs. Most of them had been cleared, but one dusty box had been left in the corner.

I dash into the cupboard and pull out the old cardboard box of newspapers. The box disintegrates in my hands, but the newspapers remain intact. I flick through them. They're all local papers. Dated forty years ago. I hold my breath.

On page 3 of the first paper, I see the headline.

Devastating household accident leaves girl dead.

I scan the article quickly for information. It's definitely about the girl who died in this house. It mentions the road and a girl falling down the basement steps to her death.

Halfway down the article I see the words:

Her father has been arrested on suspicion of murder and her twin sister has been taken into care.

I gasp, hardly able to believe what I'm reading. The girl who died was a twin. They'd lived here, in this house, just like my twins.

I remember when I first told my neighbour I was expecting twins. He'd stepped back in shock. I thought he'd just been surprised, but now I realise he must have been shocked at the coincidence.

Underneath the paper there's a scientific journal. A psychiatric one. The kind of journal my mother used to keep in the magazine rack when she was retraining to be a psychiatric nurse. I frown, puzzled, and flick through the pages. A few pages in there's a study focused on a girl whose twin sister died. The girl isn't named because she's a minor, but it's clear it's the surviving twin. I read the details of the case. It's horrific.

Both twins had been hurt by their father. The twin who died had been a bully, helping her father to abuse her sister. The surviving twin reported a catalogue of abuse from name-calling, to punches and kicks, all at the hands of her sister. It only stopped when her sister died.

The remaining twin had been put into foster care immediately. There are pages of analysis of the impact the psychiatrists think the abuse had on the girl. I shiver. That poor girl. I can't imagine being used as a punching bag by a father, let alone a twin sister. She was so lucky to survive.

I put the journal down, and turn to the next newspaper.

'Local father protests innocence over death of daughter in basement', the headline says.

I feel light fingertips on my shoulder and I jump, letting out a scream.

'Are you OK?' Paula asks, but my twins, sensing my alarm, are already screaming hysterically.

'Sorry – I—' I turn to Paula and see the look of concern in her eyes. She picks Alice up and rocks her in her arms, calming her.

'What's wrong?'

'Paula – did you know there was a basement in the house?'

She looks at me and sighs, taking in the newspaper articles on the table. 'Yes,' she says simply. 'I grew up round here. I know what happened.'

'Why didn't you tell me?'

'What good would it have done? I was so shocked when you said you were having twins. It felt like history was repeating itself. And you seemed so scared of the house already. I was hardly going to tell you a girl died here. It would have made you feel awful. Much better that you didn't know. That you could have a fresh start without the burden of it all.'

I nod. 'It's all just so horrific. I can hardly get my head around it.'

'Maybe you should just forget about it,' Paula says. 'Try not to think about it, and don't go down to the basement.'

'Why not?'

'It might not be safe. The stairs could be slippery. You could fall.' Her voice is emotionless. I stare at her for a moment, goosebumps travelling up my arms.

'Do you want me to take the twins upstairs for their nap?' she asks.

'Yes,' I say gratefully, glad to hand them over so I can concentrate.

When she's gone, I turn back to the newspaper article.

A police source has reported that there is evidence to suggest that Luke Ainsworth had been violent to his twin daughters over a number of years.

I read it again. Luke Ainsworth.

The same surname as Ian's. He must be Ian's father.

I swallow. That means the girl who died was Ian's sister. And Ian never even mentioned it.

The next morning I give Paula £5 and ask her to get the twins some cheap nappies. She wants to take the girls with her, but I insist they stay with me.

Once she's gone, I go with the twins to her room. I know I shouldn't be looking through her stuff, but I can't help myself. She knew what happened in this house and she never told me. And so much about her is a mystery. Like why she has nowhere to go if she moves out. Why wouldn't she have her own place? What other secrets is she keeping? I go through her bedside drawer. Just underwear. She really doesn't have very much, and I feel embarrassed that I'm even looking. But then my hand closes over something plastic at the back of the drawer.

A phone.

Not Paula's Samsung phone. It's a first-generation smartphone and not particularly sophisticated. It must be an old phone. Maybe it will provide some clues to who she really is.

I press the power button and am surprised to find it's not locked.

I quickly flick through her contacts. She only has about twenty people listed. But then that makes sense. Since she's been living with me, she hasn't met up with any friends or family. She told me her parents and sister were dead and she doesn't have children. I wonder if she has any living relatives at all.

My number's in her contacts. There's also an entry for Ian. I open the contact. It's definitely Ian's number. Why does she have it? I frown. I've never even seen her using this phone.

The next contact, Hanna, has a German country code. I remember Paula telling me she worked for a German family as a nanny before she came back to England when her father became ill. Could this be the family?

None of the references Paula gave Ian have called me back, and I'm desperate to speak to someone who's employed Paula before. I make a note of the number and then take out my phone and call it. No answer. I leave a phone message explaining that Paula's helping look after my daughters and asking for Hanna to get back to me on my mobile or the landline. I know there's only the slimmest chance she will. I have to leave the message in English as I don't know any German. But it's worth a shot.

Returning to Paula's phone, I go to the messages. I'm shocked to find there are lots of text messages between her and Ian. My heart beats frantically as I open them. The latest one is from just after the twins were born.

I'm catching the next flight back. I love you.

I swallow. He loves her?
Then I read the next one.

I've tried to ring but can't get hold of you. Perhaps a bad line? Can't wait to meet the girls.

Just before those messages there's a whole string of texts from Paula to him.

Why aren't you answering my calls?
When are you coming back?
The girls can't wait to meet you. Ring me!!
Hope you get these messages soon! I'm shattered but it's all so exciting.
Keep trying to ring you but no answer.

There are pages of messages. They seem familiar. And as I scroll down, I realise why. They are all the texts I sent to Ian after I gave birth. And they've been sent from Paula's phone to Ian's in one big block. On the day before he came back to see me.

I stare at the phone in shock. Ian told me my messages came through all at once. He was telling the truth.

I look back at the texts and scroll up to the older messages. They started just before the twins were born, after he'd told me he was going to Thailand. The messages from Ian are clearly intended for me, asking how my bump was doing and updating me on his fake business dealings. But I never got the messages. Paula did.

I feel like I might throw up. Ian had told me he'd messaged me. We'd thought the texts hadn't gone through. But he'd been contacting Paula, thinking she was me. How could he have got Paula's number confused with mine? It doesn't make any sense. My stomach churns.

I go through the phone contacts and click on my own number, holding my breath, afraid of what I might find. There are loads of missed calls to Paula. All dated from the time I was in hospital with the twins. I hadn't called her from the hospital. She was with me. I'd thought I was calling Ian. I see the same stream of texts. The ones I thought were going to Ian. My pulse quickens and anger rises inside me. I can't believe she's done this. Ian was telling the truth about not receiving my texts or calls. Paula received them. She's intercepted them. She was the one who made sure Ian didn't know I'd given birth. She was the one who stopped him coming back to meet his babies.

19

The man is here again, in the garden. Dad can't have known he was coming because he's gone out with my sister. Mum let him in and he went straight outside. I thought Mum might come up to our room to take me down to the basement, but she didn't. I'll stay upstairs out of the way, just in case. I kneel on a chair by the window, watching him, waiting for the hours to pass. Hoping that Dad doesn't come back.

I've spent a lot of time in the summer holidays hiding in our room away from Dad. I've doodled on the wall behind the headboard of my bed, where Dad won't be able to see it. There's a picture of me and my sister, holding hands, smiles on our faces, happy the way we used to be. I've drawn our parents behind us, Dad towering over Mum.

The man's close to the house today, cutting the hedge just below my window. He's totally absorbed in what he's doing. I want to wave or knock on the window so he sees me, but I don't. I know what happened last time. When he finishes, he climbs down the ladder and looks up at his work. At first I think he's looking at me, but he hasn't even noticed me. He's gazing intently at the hedge.

From this angle I can see his face clearly. Spots litter his pale skin and his hair is slicked back with gel. He's young. Not a man at all. Like one of the big kids that go to the secondary school up the road.

A hand touches my shoulder and I jump, nearly falling off the chair. But it's only Mum. She strokes my hair back from my face.

'You were watching him,' she says.

I nod, unsure what she's trying to say. 'I'm sorry,' I say tentatively, remembering how angry Dad was when I'd waved.

'*You know who he is?*' *she says softly.*

'*No.*' *I stare up at her, see the tears threatening to fall from the corners of her eyes.*

'*He's your brother.*'

CHAPTER THIRTY-NINE

I throw Paula's phone down on the bed, furious. I don't understand why she'd intercept my calls to Ian. I pace back and forth across the room, my mind whirring and my anger building.

I hear a key in the door. Paula's back.

I grab the phone and run down the stairs, my heart thumping.

'I got the nappies,' she says when she sees me.

But then she catches my expression. The fury in my eyes. 'Katie? What's wrong?'

I hold up the phone. 'What's this?'

Her face goes white. 'I have two phones. One's for work and—'

I step closer to her, barely able to contain my anger. She recoils from me, as if she's afraid of me. Or afraid of being caught.

'Liar.' My voice is louder than I expect, the pent-up emotions of the last few weeks exploding out of me. Upstairs, the girls start to scream. 'I found messages, Paula. My messages. The ones I sent to Ian when I'd given birth. Except they didn't go to Ian. They went to you. You intercepted them. You made sure he didn't know his babies were born. You made him miss the birth. How could you?'

I expect her to deny it, to come up with some complicated explanation, but she doesn't. When she speaks, her voice is a whisper. 'I was trying to protect you.'

'What? Why did you think it was your place to protect me? And how did you do it? Did you redirect our calls and texts?'

'No. All I did was change the contact details in your phones. Just before he went away I changed the number you had listed as

Ian to my number, and the number he had listed as you to the same number. I switched them back as soon as he returned.'

I stare at her, shocked. 'You're not even sorry.'

'No, I'm not. I'm not sorry because I did the right thing.' My blood runs cold. Upstairs the twins' screams have quietened and I wonder if they've cried themselves to sleep.

'How can you possibly think a father missing the birth of his children is the right thing?' I'm on the verge of tears, remembering how she held my hand in labour, remembering how pleased I'd been that she was there when Ian couldn't be.

'Katie, I needed him to go away. And once he was away I needed him to stay away for good.'

'What do you mean, you needed him to go away?' My stomach turns as I remember the anonymous email Ian said he'd received, telling him to stay away from me or they'd tell me about his wife. 'Did you send Ian an email telling him to leave? Were you blackmailing him?'

'Yes. But it wasn't for the money. I knew he didn't have it. It was to get him away from you. It was for the best. If you knew what he was really like…'

I can't believe what I'm hearing.

'What do you mean? Do you mean the fact he was married? I know that's awful, but I didn't need you to punish him for me. You could just have told me what was going on.'

Paula sighs. 'It's not that. It's far worse than that. I needed to protect you.'

'Protect me from what?'

'From Ian.'

'What?' She's not making any sense.

'You read the newspaper articles about what happened to the girl in the basement, didn't you?'

I nod.

'Then you know Ian was the brother of the girl who died.'

'Yeah.' Paula had known that too? And never said anything?

'There were two girls living in this house. Twins, like yours. Twins run in Ian's family. When I found out you were having two babies, I thought your daughters would have the chance to be happy here. To rewrite history. As long as I didn't let Ian anywhere near them.'

'Why?' I ask. 'Why wouldn't you want Ian near them?'

'Because I know what really happened to his sister.'

My chest clenches and I can hardly breathe. I'm not sure I'm ready for what she's about to say. 'The newspapers said his father was arrested.'

'He was. Ian's father nearly went to jail because of it. A lot of people round here think he killed her. But other people, people who knew the family a bit better, think it wasn't him at all. They think it was Ian. He was jealous that she lived in this big house, while he lived a few streets away in a council flat with his mother.'

'What?' I ask, breathlessly. 'They think Ian murdered her?' My head's spinning.

'Yes. I had to keep him away from you. To protect you. And the twins.'

I can't make sense of it. Ian may be a liar, but he's never been violent. And back then he would only have been a child himself. 'Was he arrested?' I ask.

'No, the police couldn't quite prove it. But everyone who knew the family knew it was him.' She reaches out her hand and puts it on my shoulder. 'Including me. I've no doubt in my mind. Ian killed her.'

CHAPTER FORTY

I can't believe what Paula's just told me. Ian killed his sister. I feel sick as an image flashes through my mind. Ian pushing his sister down the stairs. Her small body crumpled at the bottom.

'Are you alright?' Paula asks. 'You've gone pale.'

I feel like I might faint and I sink down onto the cold tiles in the hallway. Paula brings me a glass of water and I sip it gratefully.

She places her hand on my shoulder. 'You see why I moved in with you now?' she asks gently. 'I had to.'

I nod, but I'm still trying to digest what she's said. I can't believe it.

'I think I need to go and lie down,' I say.

'You do that. You've had quite a shock. I'll look after the twins.'

Lying on my bed upstairs, I stare up at the dusty ceiling. Everyone has been lying to me. And now I'm scared. Ian's supposed to be coming round tomorrow to take the girls out. I can't possibly let him. I think about calling him, but then decide to text him instead to cancel. I don't want to listen to anymore lies from him. I need to digest what's happened.

My mind spins. I'm not sure I can handle this. I think of the call I had with Mum just a couple of days ago. She lied to me too. She lied about my whole childhood. But she said she did it to protect me. I believe her now. I forgive her. And now I need her help. I don't know what to do.

I pick up the phone and call her, but it goes straight to answerphone. I hang up and try again. Still no answer. I leave a garbled message, explaining about the basement, about what Paula's said about Ian. And then at the end of the message, I tell her I forgive her for my childhood, and for the lies she told.

The next day, I wake up in a sweat and check my phone. I haven't had a reply from Ian to the text message asking him not to come round this morning. He hasn't even asked why I don't want to see him.

My phone beeps as I'm breastfeeding Alice and Paula's giving Frances a bottle.

We need to talk. I'm still coming over.

I hold up my phone and show Paula the message.

'We won't let him in,' she says.

I stand by the stained-glass window on the landing overlooking the driveway, anxiously waiting. When I see his shadow crossing the driveway, my body tenses, on high alert. I hold Frances close to me as I watch him approach the door.

I hear the knocks. Quiet at first. And then louder. More insistent. He shouts out my name through the letterbox. 'Katie! Open the door.'

I stand stock-still, waiting for him to go away, heart beating fast.

'Katie!' he shouts again.

And then he takes out his key and lets himself in.

Paula can't have heard him. She's in the kitchen, sterilising baby bottles. I hurry down the stairs with Frances in my arms, stepping as carefully as I can.

'Oh,' Ian says at the bottom of the stairs. 'You *are* in.'

I stand there, staring at him, looking at him through new eyes. This is the man who killed his sister.

'I told you not to come round,' I say, my voice shaking. I just want him as far away from me as possible.

Ian looks perplexed. 'It's my house, Katie. And I wanted to take them out. I was going to take them to the lake, show them the ducks.'

'You can't have them today.' I wish Paula would hurry up and come through from the kitchen. I want to shout for her, but I don't want to alarm Ian.

'Why not? Are they ill?'

'I found the basement, Ian.' I look down at the floor, too afraid to look at him and see the guilt I know will be in his eyes.

'The basement? What's that got to do with anything?'

'Why didn't you tell me about it?' I whisper.

He reaches out to me and I pull away from him. 'When you first moved into the house, you seemed frightened enough of it already. You were here alone and it didn't seem worth mentioning. I've never even been down there myself. I don't know what it's like.'

'Ian, it's clear Katie doesn't want you here.' I jump. I hadn't heard Paula coming up behind me, but I'm so relieved she's here.

'Can't I just take the twins out? I miss them.'

'No,' Paula says firmly. 'You can't. You need to leave now. Katie's not feeling herself.'

He turns to me. 'Katie – are you alright?'

I look at Paula. 'No,' I say. 'I'm actually feeling quite sick.'

'Katie's under a lot of stress. What with you selling the house, and discovering all your lies. It's taken its toll on her. She just needs to rest. And to be close to her twins. They're all she has in the world.'

He looks at me. 'OK. I'm sorry you're stressed. I never meant to hurt you—'

'Just go,' I say.

When the door shuts behind him, Paula looks at me. 'We need to change the locks,' she says. An hour later, I hand over half of my emergency supply of cash from my piano teaching to an on-call locksmith, and we have new locks and new sets of keys.

After everything that's happened, Paula suggests I take a long bath to try and relax, while she takes the babies for a walk. I agree. Every muscle in my body feels permanently tense after the revelations about Ian and the girl in the basement. I feel like my mind is about to explode and I can't make sense of anything, can't piece it all together.

While I'm in the bath, my phone rings. I've left it on the sink beside the bath. I think for a moment that it might be Mum calling me back.

I wipe my hand on the towel and reach for my phone. But it's a number I don't recognise. I'm about to put the phone down, but then I think it might be one of Paula's references returning my call.

I pick it up.

'Are you on your own?' the voice says, and my body goes tense.

I sit up straighter in the bath. 'Who is this?'

'It's Sabrina.'

'Sabrina? Now's not a good time.' Why on earth is she ringing me?

'Is Paula with you?' she asks.

'No. What do you want?'

'Look, I know you sent Ian away this morning. I don't understand why, but this isn't about that.'

'What is it about, then?' I ask impatiently. I wonder if she knows about Ian's past.

'Ian told me not to mention this. He thinks I'm imagining things. But after he told me about this morning, how you and Paula chucked him out, well, I thought it was my duty to tell you.'

My blood runs cold. Is this about the girl in the basement?

'Tell me what?' I whisper.

'It's Paula. I know who she is. When I fainted at your house it was because I felt terrified. At first I couldn't work out why.

But then I saw Paula again when I regained consciousness and I recognised her.'

I listen intently, desperate to find out how Sabrina knows Paula.

'Ian thinks I'm wrong, but I'm sure I'm right. Years ago I had a horrible accident. I was pregnant...' Sabrina's voice breaks and she takes a moment to recollect herself. 'And I fell down an escalator. I lost the baby.'

'Oh,' I say, suddenly feeling sorry for her. Ian had told me how much she'd wanted children. And he'd told me she had emotional difficulties. Maybe the accident and the miscarriage were the root of her problems.

'Everyone thought I'd fallen, but I knew I was pushed. I remembered. But no one believed me. They thought it was my head injury making me delusional. But it wasn't. I knew someone had pushed me. I could see her face so clearly in my mind's eye. I tried to find out who it was. I even spoke to security at the shopping centre, but there was no CCTV by the escalator so I never got anywhere. When I first saw Paula and I fainted, I didn't know why I felt so scared. Then I saw her again and I knew it was her. She was the one who pushed me.'

20

We have a brother. My sister says she doesn't care, but I lie in bed at night and I can't stop thinking about it. Mum told me his name is Ian and he lives on the council estate up the road with his own mother. He's a bit older than us, old enough to stand up to Dad if he knew what Dad did to me, how he hurt me. I don't think he knows he has sisters. I think of him walking around town, completely unaware of our existence. Will he be as excited as I am when he finds out? I wonder if he likes the same books and TV as me, if we have similar taste.

I wrap my arms around the toy rabbit I've had since I was a child. It smells musty, of dribble and dirt, but the smell comforts me. It's always been there for me. As I cuddle it, I imagine my brother's arms around me. I imagine him comforting me when Dad hurts me, I imagine him standing up for me when Dad shouts at me, I imagine him standing in the way when Dad tries to hit me. I smile. If he was here, would everything be alright?

I have an idea. I'm going to have to be brave, but it will be worth it. I wait until our parents come upstairs to bed, flushing the toilet and cleaning their teeth and then finally quietening. I creep out of our bedroom. Outside our parents' room I listen for my father's heavy breathing before I scurry on to the study. Once I'm there, I take a sheet of notepaper from the pile at the edge of the desk. When I get back to our room, I flick on the nightlight and try and work out what to write.

'What are you doing?' my sister whispers.

'I'm writing our brother a note.'

She frowns. 'He might not even want to know us.'

'Maybe he could help us,' I say. 'Help us get away from Dad.'

'I don't want to get away from Dad.' She fiddles with the necklace that Dad bought her, pressing the tiny silver bird between her fingers. 'You know he'll be angry if he finds out,' she says.

I know she's right, but I can't bear to think about it. Anything's worth a try to get out of here.

I return to the blank piece of paper in front of me. No matter what she says, I think a part of her wants to escape too. She can't feel safe here. Because I know, deep down inside, that neither of us are safe.

CHAPTER FORTY-ONE

I gasp, shocked by what Sabrina's said, and the phone slips out of my hand and into the bathwater. When I pull it out the screen is mottled with blue and green dots. I press it urgently with wet fingers. No response. I get out of the bath, quickly wipe the phone with the hand towel and then try it again. Nothing. I put it next to the radiator to dry. Then I hear the front door opening and Paula coming in with the twins.

'Hello?' she calls out.

'Hi,' I call back, my voice shaking. I quickly dress and then rush downstairs. Pulling my twins out of the buggy and into my arms, I think about what Sabrina just said on the phone. Is she just crazy, or is there something in it?

'Are you alright?' Paula asks, looking worried. 'I can sort out the babies while you dry your hair.'

'I'm fine,' I say.

'Really?'

'Sabrina called.'

'Did she want to know why she couldn't see the girls today?'

'No. It wasn't that. It was about you.' I study Paula's face, looking for a sign, a flicker of worry, but there's nothing.

'Oh really? What about me?'

I take a deep breath. 'She thinks you pushed her down an escalator. A long time ago.'

Paula's eyes crinkle and she laughs. 'Is that the best she could come up with?'

I frown.

'You didn't believe her, did you?'

'I—'

'You're so naive, Katie.' She ruffles my wet hair. 'You'd believe anything.'

'She sounded convincing.' My voice falters.

'She just wants to see your twins, that's all. It's no coincidence she's telling you this just after you've told Ian to get out, is it?'

'I suppose not…' Now I'm talking to Paula about it, the whole thing sounds ridiculous.

'Think about it. She's married to Ian, who's lied to her for years. And she's stuck with him despite everything. She'd do anything for him. And now she sees me as someone who's stopping Ian from seeing his daughters. And stopping her from seeing them too. So she makes something up so you don't trust me.'

'She was just so convincing on the phone…' I say again, but already I'm doubting her. What Paula's saying makes sense. Sabrina just wants to discredit Paula. Paula's only been trying to protect me. Ian's the one who's lied to me again and again.

In the night, I startle awake.

I thought I heard piano music, but I must have dreamt it, because now the house is completely silent. When I venture downstairs, I see the piano sitting unoccupied in the dining room. But the haunting music still echoes round my head. I must be imagining it. The events of the last few days have unnerved me. I'm losing my grip on reality.

I pour myself a glass of water and then sit down to calm my nerves. The clock on the oven reads midnight.

When I walk through the hallway to go back to bed, I can just make out the music, the only sound penetrating the silence.

It's coming from the cupboard under the stairs. From the basement.

It can't be. I open the cupboard and peer inside. The music is louder now and I recognise it as a childhood lullaby. My eyes adjust to the dark, and at the back of the cupboard I see a gaping hole into nothing. The basement door is open.

I must be dreaming. Everything I've learnt about the girl who died in the basement must be filtering into my subconscious.

I feel a sense of unreality, that fearlessness I have in dreams, as I take a step closer to the entrance to the basement.

'Hello?' I shout down.

There's no sound except the music.

I peer into the darkness below, but I can't see much without my phone. I scan the basement as my eyes adjust to the pitch-black emptiness, going over the area methodically, until I'm convinced no one's down there.

There are shadows in the darkness, on the mattress. Small objects, not human shapes. I can't make out what they are.

As I lean forward to look further in, I'm aware that if someone came up behind me, it would only take a single push for me to go tumbling down the stairs. I scratch nervously at the scar on my arm.

Remembering the door slamming shut behind me last time, I look down for something to prop it open. But whoever came before me has already done that, propping it open with a heavy box of tiles.

I shiver. Where are they now?

I try to convince myself there's a reasonable explanation for the open door. Perhaps the house has finally had some viewers and the estate agent has opened the door to show them the basement and forgotten to shut it. But that doesn't explain the music.

I take a step inside and creep down the stairs. When I get close to the bottom, I can make out the belongings on the mattress.

An old tape player, broadcasting the lullaby, the sound slightly static.

Next to it sit Alice's caterpillar toy and Frances's elephant. I stare at them in horror.

Someone has brought my twins down here.

I reach out my hand to the wall to steady myself. But instead of the wall, I feel something shiny. The unexpected sensation makes me jump and I turn to look at what I'm touching. It's a photograph. A new picture sellotaped to the wall, in line with the other two. I can hardly make it out in the dim light, but when I get closer, I gasp. It's a picture of Frances and Alice. Frances's face has been scratched out, just like the girl's face in the old photo. The girl that I now know died down here, in this basement. I stifle my scream. What's the picture doing down here? And what does whoever put it here want with my girls?

I look at the other photos again. The family with the daughter scratched out. The two girls side by side in pigtails, scowling at the camera, one of their faces completely erased. I peer closer at the remaining girl's features. Thick, dark curly hair. Round face. Pronounced nose and defiant jaw. But it's the look in the girl's eyes I recognise. Pure anger. I've seen that look before. A shiver of recognition runs through me. I know who she is.

CHAPTER FORTY-TWO

I stare at the picture on the wall. The girl is a younger version of Paula.

I remember Paula telling me about her childhood, about her sister who died. And suddenly everything clicks into place.

Paula lived in this house. Paula's the twin of the girl who died. She's Ian's sister.

I run out of the basement, breathless, up the stairs.

In the hallway, I see Paula with Alice and Frances, one under each arm. Fear stops me in my tracks. She's about to take them down there. Why?

'What are you doing?' I ask.

'I…' A frightened look crosses her face, but only for a second. Now she looks determined. 'The twins couldn't sleep,' she says.

'So you were going to take them to the basement?'

'They like it down there. I wanted them to hear the music. It comforts them. And I can't play the piano at night. It would wake you.'

'Give them to me,' I say.

But Paula holds them close. 'No.'

'I know about you, Paula. I know you used to live in this house. I know your sister died here.'

'So what?' Paula looks at me defiantly. 'I've been honest with you, Katie. You always knew I was from the area. And I told you my sister died, remember?'

'You didn't tell me you used to live here. You told me all about the girl's death. But you never said she was your sister. You never said she was your twin.'

'It was all too much for me to talk about…'

I remember how calmly Paula had talked about the girl in the basement. She hadn't seemed sad at all.

'It's been difficult for me, Katie, living in this house with you. With all my memories. That's why I take the twins to the basement sometimes. I like to remember my sister.'

'But you hated your sister. You told me that before. She used to hurt you.' I remember Paula telling me she hated her, remember reading the case study in the psychiatric journal which detailed all the ways Paula's sister had hurt her.

'It wasn't always like that. There were good times, when we were younger. Before my sister turned against me, we were close. I like to think of those times. Remember her when she was nice. Coming down to the basement calms me. And it seems to calm the twins too.'

'I'm sorry about what happened to your sister.'

'At the end I hated her, but at the same time I couldn't stop loving her. You know how it is. The way I feel towards your babies sometimes when they scream.' She bobs Frances and Alice up and down in her arms and fear rises up in me. 'I hate them one minute and love them to death the next.' She half smiles, as if she's said something funny.

I need to get the girls away from her right now. 'I'll take them, Paula.'

'But I want them to listen to the music.'

'Please,' I beg.

She hands them over reluctantly, and I hug them tight, their warm bodies bursting with life. I bury my face between theirs, breathing in their baby scents and then kissing their heads.

My mind is whirring, thinking about Paula's connection to this house. Thinking about how we first met. Thinking about how Ian fits into all of this.

'Why didn't you say you were Ian's sister from the beginning?'

'Ian hates me. I know the truth about what he did. He would never have let me into the house.'

'He must have recognised you at the baby shower. That was when you first met.'

'Yes. He's a convincing liar, isn't he? He behaved as if he'd never seen me before.'

'Why?' I ask, reeling.

'He didn't want to tell you about his past. And I think he was shocked to see me.'

I remember meeting Paula at the coffee shop that first day, her coming into the house with me. She must have known Ian had inherited the house. She must have been watching from the coffee shop, waiting for me to turn up.

'You targeted me from the beginning, didn't you? That's why you introduced yourself in the coffee shop the day I arrived.'

Paula sighs. 'I used to visit my father in the house when he became poorly, and then in his care home in the final years of his life. When he died, I thought I'd inherit it. But Ian did. Ian, who never even lived here. Ian, who killed my sister. I waited in the coffee shop to confront him when he showed up.'

'But he didn't come.'

'No, he didn't. You did.'

I shiver. 'And so you befriended me?'

'Yes. I've explained that. As soon as I saw you were pregnant, I knew I had to protect you from Ian. He's dangerous.'

I remember looking around the house on the first day with Paula. How there'd already been a mattress in one of the bedrooms.

'Were you already sleeping there?' I ask. 'Is that why you had nowhere to live?'

She nods. 'I'd got in round the back. I slept in my father's old bedroom. I felt closer to him there.'

'But what did you do once I moved in?'

'I slept in the basement. We were there so often as children that I felt at home there. I felt closer to my sister.'

I shiver at the thought of Paula being in the house that first night, me sleeping upstairs with no idea she was there.

'And then you volunteered to be my doula, all so you could keep living here?'

'It wasn't just to live in the house. It was to protect you too. I was so afraid for you. I had to find a way to stay in the house with you and look after the twins.'

I feel afraid now, my heart racing. She's planned this from the beginning. Getting into Ian's house. Befriending me. Intercepting our calls. But something in her story doesn't add up. Why didn't she just tell me about Ian in the first place?

'I need to think, Paula. This is all such a shock to me.'

Paula comes closer to me, looks at me urgently.

'You do believe me, don't you, Katie? You have to believe me. Ian killed my sister.' She indicates the stone steps leading down into the basement. 'It was right here. I saw him push her down those stairs.'

21

We're watching TV in the living room when the phone rings. Mum scurries to answer it and then calls my father over.

Mum returns to sit beside us and I'm frozen to the sofa as I hear my father's voice getting louder and louder. Words like 'bitch' and 'whore' invade the living room. He only ever uses those words for our mother. Whoever's on the phone must be making him furious.

'Get out of here before he comes back,' Mum whispers to us, and we run past her and up the stairs to our room.

Dad's shouting echoes round the house as we lie, huddled together in bed, covers wrapped around our heads to try and muffle the noise. Then there's silence. He must have hung up the phone. I hear footsteps in the hallway and I pray he turns towards the living room, to my mother, and doesn't come up to find us. But then I hear his footsteps on the stairs. The sound stops when he reaches our door.

From under the covers I can hear his heavy breathing getting closer.

Suddenly he pulls the covers off us, and we are exposed. His huge red face is up close to us, his eyes bulging. A vein in his forehead throbs.

'Who sent the note to your brother?' he bellows.

I glance at my sister to confer, but she doesn't hesitate.

'She did,' she says.

CHAPTER FORTY-THREE

I look down the steps to the basement below and a shiver runs down my spine, as I imagine a girl's body crumpled at the bottom. I remember Sabrina's accusation that Paula pushed her down the escalator. I step quickly away from the basement door.

'Look, Paula, you have to go. I can't think straight anymore. And I can't have you here in the house anymore, around the twins.'

'But you need me here. To protect you from Ian.'

'We've changed the locks – he can't come in.' My voice falters. I'm afraid. But I force myself to continue. 'You need to leave.'

She looks at me, tears in her eyes. 'I thought I meant something to you, meant something to the girls.'

I feel like crying too. I'd thought the same. But I don't know her at all.

'Just go,' I say, not caring where she goes. 'Get out of my life.'

'OK,' she says, through tears. 'If that's what you want. If that's what you think's best for the girls, then I'll leave. As long as you know that I'll always love them and I'll always be there for you and them if you ever need me.'

I feel a wave of guilt wash over me. Has she just been trying to help me all along?

I follow her to the bedroom and watch her pack up her things. Then I hold the door open for her and let her out of the house, holding back my tears.

I put the girls down on the mats in the living room and go round the house, double-locking every door and window. I don't want anyone to be able to get in tonight.

I need to ring someone. Get some help. I go upstairs and grab my phone from the side in the bathroom, praying it will have dried out and be working again.

I push at the buttons urgently. Nothing. It's completely dead.

I run back downstairs, and pick up the landline in the living room, ignoring my screaming babies.

I try and ring Mum again. I know it's the middle of the night and she's on holiday, but I need her help. If I could get hold of a key to her house, maybe the twins and I could stay there, just for a few days.

The phone rings and rings but my mother doesn't pick up. She won't recognise the landline number. I leave a rushed message and then try my sister. She doesn't pick up either.

If I had anywhere to go, I'd leave now.

Instead I pick up my babies and cuddle them and then ring Amy, cradling the bulky phone between my head and shoulder. She answers in a daze. I tell her everything. About Paula, about Ian. I tell her I can't spend the rest of the night in the house on my own. She promises to come over immediately and I order her a taxi. I can pay for it with the cash I have left over from this week's piano lessons.

In the meantime, I sit down and study the newspaper articles once more, trying to make sense of everything. There's one person who might have the answers. Ian. We've changed the locks; he can't get into the house anymore. But I need to hear the truth from him.

I call him. He picks up on the first ring. 'Hello?' he says uncertainly, not recognising the landline number.

'Ian. It's me.'

'Katie – why are you calling at this time? Is everything alright? Is this about Sabrina? I'm so sorry she rung you earlier about Paula. I told her not to. She's just got it into her head that Paula pushed her. I don't know why.'

'It's not about Sabrina. It's about Paula. Why didn't you tell me she was your sister?'

'My sister?' he replies, sounding shocked. 'But I don't have a sister.'

'Just be straight with me, Ian. It's past the time for lies. Paula's your sister.'

'I have no idea what you're talking about, Katie.'

'Paula grew up in this house.'

'It must have been before my father moved in, then. And anyway, what does it matter if she did? She can't be my sister.'

'Ian. I need you to tell me the truth. Paula says she befriended me to protect me from you. Because you were dangerous.'

'She's says I'm her brother and I'm dangerous?' Ian sounds more confused than ever.

'She thinks you killed her twin sister.'

'What? I killed her sister? But I'd never even met her before. This is absolutely ridiculous. She must be getting me confused with someone else. Or else she's trying to manipulate you, to turn you against me.'

'You inherited the house from your father, didn't you?'

'Yes.'

'His name was Luke Ainsworth?'

Ian goes quiet. 'Yes,' he says eventually.

'Well, you did have sisters. There are newspaper articles in the house. Luke was accused of murdering his daughter, Paula's twin sister. And Paula says he didn't do it. You did.'

'What?' Ian says. 'You're saying my father was accused of murder? Are you sure you saw this in a paper? It's not something Paula made up?' Ian's so convincing, but then I know he's a good liar.

'Yes, I'm sure.'

'This doesn't make any sense.' There's a long pause, and I can almost hear Ian thinking, probably making up some other lie. 'I hardly knew my father,' he continues slowly. 'I lived with Mum. And he lived with his wife in this huge house. I suppose it's possible he had other children, but I never saw any.'

'How could you all grow up in the same area without knowing?'

'I'm just getting my head round this, Katie. I'm not sure if I believe it. But I didn't have much of a relationship with my father, so I don't really know what he was like. I didn't even know who he was until I was about thirteen. I tracked him down. Told Mum I was going to football practice and visited once a week. He used to make me do odd jobs for him in the garden.'

'Didn't you see your father's name in the papers after the girl died? It was big local news. You must have realised then.'

'We moved away. Mum suddenly decided urban life was too much for her and she moved us down to Kent to live with her sister in the countryside. It was too far away to keep in contact with my old friends. I would never have found out what happened. I wrote letters to my dad, but he never replied. I didn't hear anything about him again. Not until he died.'

'When did you move?' I ask. I've laid the newspaper articles out in front of me. Paula's sister died in September 1979.

'It was shortly before I went into my third year at secondary school,' Ian says. 'So it must have been 1979.'

'When in 1979?' I ask urgently.

'In the school holidays. It would have been early August.'

'Are you sure?' I ask. 'It was August, not September?'

'I'm sure. We were in the countryside a few weeks before I started at the new school at the beginning of term.'

If he's telling the truth, then he can't have killed Paula's sister.

CHAPTER FORTY-FOUR

I put down the phone, head spinning. Either Ian's lying, or Paula is. I look at my watch. I hope Amy will be here soon.

The landline starts ringing as soon as I put it down, an unfamiliar tone. No one ever rings this number. It must be Amy.

But the caller display shows a foreign number. I stare for a second and then something clicks. The German family that Paula used to work for. They must be returning my call. But it's the middle of the night.

'Hello?'

'Hello? Is that Katie?' The woman says in heavily accented English.

'Yes,' I say, my heart pumping in my chest.

'I'm so sorry I didn't ring before. I didn't get your message. You left it on my work phone and I was on holiday. If I'd have picked it up, then I'd have called immediately.' Her words come out in a rush. 'You said you were employing Paula. You need to get her out of your home.'

My heart sinks. I feel terrified for my girls. 'Why?' I ask, dreading the answer.

'She's a bad woman. She seems sweet and kind, like she's nurturing the children. But it's all an act. She hurt my girls. They're twins. They were only little. She played them off against each other, told one she was good, the other one she was evil. They're both with a child psychiatrist now. Thank god I found out in time. Otherwise it could have been much worse.'

'Oh my god.' I can't believe what I'm hearing. But somehow it all makes sense.

'How did you find out?' I ask.

'One of my girls got very thin. I thought she was too young for anorexia but we couldn't work out what it could be. The doctors couldn't find anything wrong with her. But then she confided in us that Paula wasn't feeding her. She was deliberately neglecting her, making sure she was weak.'

I feel sick. I think of Frances. How tiny she is. Has Paula been starving her?

'But why?'

'I'm not sure. But my daughters told their psychiatrist that she used to make them fight each other, egging them on to injure each other. Just for her entertainment.'

I remember what I'd read in the psychiatric journal about Paula's childhood. How her twin had joined in with her father and hurt Paula. Was she so damaged by her experiences that she tried to replicate her own childhood with this woman's twins, encouraging them to hurt each other, like her sister hurt her?

'I'm so sorry,' I say.

'You need to get her away from your children. As fast as you can.'

I feel so afraid. I don't want to go to bed, don't want to sleep without Amy here. If Paula did all of that to the German children who she had no connection to, then what has she been doing to mine, the children of a man she hates?

I feel sick and hug the twins close. I go into the upstairs hallway and look out of the huge stained-glass window at the front of the house. I can't see any headlights or hear any car engines. There's no one about. I take the twins with me to the front door to check it's bolted.

Then I go back to the box full of newspaper articles. I pull out the folder containing the psychiatric case study. I scan the case study again, reading how badly Paula was treated by her twin. Their father used to make them fight each other, the same as Paula had done with the German family. Both twins had had bruises all over their bodies. But Paula hardly fought back, and her sister got increasingly violent. She would hurt Paula just for fun. The case study expresses surprise that Paula seemed so together after everything that happened. It concludes that it's inevitable that Paula will have suffered some psychological damage from her childhood and the death of her sister, but that she seemed happy and well-adjusted.

There are several bits of paper behind the case study. Old social services assessments. At first they are glowing, saying how well Paula's managing despite her upbringing, how well she's settled into foster care.

But as the reports move through the years, there are causes for concern. Injured pets. Younger children who were terrified of her. Then later, reports of violence towards other children in care. Foster family after foster family gave up on her because they didn't feel safe with her in their homes.

22

We're down in the basement again. With Dad. He takes us here a lot these days. He makes us fight so he can see who's the strongest. He's become obsessed with comparing us, standing us side by side and commenting on our similarities and differences. He says I'm too thin, too weak, too stupid. He tells us that he should never have had twins, that he should only have had one daughter, that I am the mistake, the one he doesn't want or need.

Ever since I sent that note to our brother, the punishments have been getting steadily worse. The last few days he's hardly let me eat, taking away my food at dinner before I finish because of some tiny thing I've done wrong, like dropping my fork or forgetting to say 'please' and 'thank you'. I'm constantly hungry.

Since the note, my sister has been joining in when he punishes me. He says I'm her responsibility, that after I messed up by sending the note it was down to her to stop me from messing up again. The first time she 'helped' him he made her hit me with his belt until I bled. She cried afterwards.

But now she's hardened. She's worse than Dad. She believes him when he says she's better than me. She believes everything he says, that we are opposites, that she is good and that I'm bad. Now she hurts me just for fun. I can see from the glint in her eyes and the smile on her lips that she enjoys it. I have bruises all over. Dad always rewards her when she hurts me, with small gifts and trinkets. Today she's wearing two necklaces he bought her, the one with the tiny silver bird and a new one: a heart-shaped locket with a picture of the two of them together inside.

He's told us that whoever wins this fight won't have to go into the basement ever again. I don't believe him, but I can see my sister does.

I'm already weak with hunger. The room around me is blurry. Even if I tried to fight back, I know my sister would win. I don't know why she listens to him. I don't know why she obliges him by punching and kicking me. She must hate me.

I look at her before we start. Her eyes are completely cold, completely dead. She holds up her hand as if to hit me. Dad watches, licking his lips in anticipation.

She pauses, looks at me, and I see a moment of confusion, a moment of compassion.

'Come on, girl,' Dad whispers encouragingly. Then her expression changes to one of pure anger and she brings her fist down hard into my face.

CHAPTER FORTY-FIVE

I pace back and forth, waiting for Amy. The twins are asleep in the living room. I couldn't put them back in their cots. I have to keep them close to me. When I hear a car and see headlights light up the window, I go to the front door and wait behind it.

I hear someone get out of the car and slowly drag a suitcase to the door. When she knocks, I peer out through the peephole to check it's Amy. It is.

I hand over the last of my cash for the taxi, then gratefully let her in and explain what's been happening.

'You must be terrified,' she says, as she navigates down the hallway on her crutches. 'Have you called the police?'

'No,' I say. 'Paula's gone. Ian's not here. I just didn't want to be alone tonight.'

'Are you sure Paula's gone?' Amy says, her eyes darting around the hallway as if she expects someone to jump out of the shadows. 'She sounds crazy. She really thinks Ian killed her sister?'

I go to the kitchen and show Amy the newspaper articles. Her eyes widen as she reads them. 'Paula's twin fell down the basement stairs,' she says slowly. 'That's how she died…'

I nod. 'Yeah.'

'Do you think it's a coincidence that I fell down the stairs here too?' She glances down at her injured leg.

'Amy – you were drunk.'

'I was. But I also remember tripping over something.'

'You did,' I confirm. 'It was a box of screwdrivers. I was so angry with Ian for leaving them there. It was so careless.'

'The box was right across the top of the stairs. Almost as if it had been put there on purpose.'

'Are you saying Ian deliberately tripped you up?'

'No, I don't think so. The thing is, you assume Ian left it there, but I don't think he did. It was Paula who came down the stairs before me, not Ian. I think she left it there to trip me.'

'But why?'

'I don't know. You said she wanted to befriend you. That she wanted to live in the house with you. Well, I was in the way, wasn't I? I was going to be your birth partner. I would have supported you when Ian was away. But I couldn't because I broke my leg. Which meant she was the one who was there for you.'

I nod. I think about the way Paula wormed her way into my life after the birth of the twins. How I depended on her because there was no one else. How the psychiatric report I read said that Paula had been violent towards her foster siblings. How Paula had treated the children in Germany. And I think about how Sabrina thought Paula had pushed her too.

'You think Sabrina was telling the truth, that she pushed her down an escalator?'

'Maybe. I mean, it seems possible.'

'If she thinks Ian murdered her sister then she might have pushed her for revenge.' I swallow. If she was willing to push Sabrina, killing Ian's unborn baby, then what might she do to my twins?

'Do you think she's hurt my girls?' I whisper, tears slipping down my cheeks as I remember what the German mother told me Paula did to her twins.

Suddenly afraid, I go into the living room to check on the girls. They're still asleep.

Amy glances down at the babies on their mats. 'They're safe now. They're with you.'

I pick up my daughters and hug them tight.

'Do you want me to stay up with you, or do you want to try and get some sleep?' Amy asks.

I'm exhausted. 'Can you sleep beside me?' I feel silly asking for something so childish, but I know Amy will understand.

We go up to Paula's room, as that's the only room where the cots fit. I can't be apart from the girls tonight. I need them close to me, so I can protect them.

I feel odd lying down between the sheets in Paula's bed. Amy drops off to sleep beside me immediately but every noise makes me jump. I don't feel safe here. My mind is spinning. I tell myself everything will be OK. Paula left without a fuss. She must have been feeling guilty. But why would she leave without putting up a fight? When I talked to her about moving out because the house was for sale, she was furious. She'd said she'd be homeless. So where has she gone now?

Eventually I fall into a fitful sleep, tossing and turning as my nightmares engulf me, dreaming of unknown hands suffocating my twins until I'm jolted awake. Each time I wake, I go over to the cots and hold my hand a little above the twins' mouths to check they're breathing. Amy lies in a deep sleep beside me.

I wake to the sound of smashing glass.

I shake Amy until she stirs from sleep. 'Did you hear that?'

'What?'

'Amy – something broke. Did you hear it? It sounded like glass. A window.'

'Oh,' she says, blinking rapidly, disorientated.

Have I imagined it? 'You stay here with the twins. I'll go and investigate.'

I creep down the stairs slowly. The house creaks and groans. Outside, rain pounds against the roof.

When I get downstairs, I go into each room in turn. I'm petrified. There's no one in the living room. I check each window. They're all still closed and locked. Then I perform the same checks in the dining room. There's no sign of any break-in there either.

When I turn and go into the kitchen, I see what I've been dreading. The window of the back door has been smashed in and the door is wide open. The rain blows through the door into the kitchen.

But there's something wrong. There's no glass on the kitchen floor. I look out of the door and see the beautiful wooden baby walker that Ian bought the girls lying outside in the undergrowth. Paula must have thrown it through the window from the inside. She was already inside the house.

The smashing must have been a distraction. To get me out of the bedroom. Away from my twins. My heart lurches.

I run back up the stairs, two at a time, as fast as I can.

When I get to the bedroom, everything has been swept off the bedside table onto the floor. Amy lies still in the bed, blood oozing from a wound in her head.

The twins' cots are empty beside her. They've gone.

CHAPTER FORTY-SIX

I try and shake Amy awake, but she's out cold.

What's happened to her? And where are my twins?

'Alice!' I scream. 'Frances!'

I dash round the house, overwhelmed by panic.

There's only one person who could have taken them. Paula.

I rush downstairs.

The door to the cupboard under the stairs is open. Paula's taken them down to the basement. I can hear the faint sound of the piano music coming from the cupboard. The familiar lullaby.

Heart thundering, I peer down the stone stairs. Paula's sitting on the mattress with my babies, her face lit up from beneath by a single candle, her shadow long on the wall behind. She hugs Alice in her arms, while Frances lies on the damp mattress alone.

'Paula,' I shout. 'What are you doing?'

'I'm looking after them for you. You and Ian aren't capable.'

'You were going to hurt them. I spoke to Hanna. From the family in Germany. She said you damaged her children. You starved her daughter. Made her children fight each other.'

'So what if I did?'

I stare at her, incredulous. 'Don't hurt my girls. Please.' My heart thumps faster. I can't believe I ever trusted her with my babies.

'Ian never deserved children,' she says. 'Not after what he did.'

'I understand why you hate him. But what he did is nothing to do with my children. They're innocent. So give them back. Please.'

Paula shakes her head.

I make my way down the stairs slowly. Without my phone to light the way, I can only see the outline of the uneven stone stairs and I'm terrified I'll slip over. Paula can blow out the candle at any time and plunge the whole place into darkness. The lullaby comes to an end and I can only hear static on the tape.

When I get to the bottom of the steps I try to grab Frances, but Paula snatches her away just in time and I fall onto the mattress with a bump, jarring my elbow.

'Give her to me,' I say.

'Don't you care about your other daughter? Don't you care about Alice? Or do you only want to help your weaker daughter? The one who tore you apart when you gave birth. The one who would never have survived years ago. Who was too weak to live without medical intervention.'

'What do you mean?'

'I mean that Frances is so weak she should have died when she was born. You're clearly not cut out to be a mother to two children. Nature found a way of fixing that. She should have died.'

'You've been doing it to Frances too, haven't you?' I ask, my voice filled with disgust. 'The same thing you did to Hanna's daughter. You've been starving her.'

She laughs. 'You're such a bad mother, you didn't even notice. Didn't you wonder why Frances is so thin? Why she doesn't feed?'

'Of course I did. I've asked you about it so many times. You know that.'

'You were asking the wrong person. I've been medicating her, making her more sleepy than Alice, watering down her formula.'

'But why?'

'I wanted you to think you were doing something wrong, or that you were going mad.'

'Why? Why would you want to do that?'

'Just for fun, really,' she smirks. 'I liked watching you in pain. Like your stitches too, when I infected them with bacteria. And your labour, when I insisted you didn't need pain relief and cranked up the drugs in the drip at the hospital. Of course, I liked it more when it hurt Ian too, but when it became clear that Ian didn't really care about you, I enjoyed hurting you for its own sake.' As Paula speaks, the tape restarts the same lullaby. Quietly at first and then getting louder.

I remember how much pain I'd been in when I gave birth. How Ian hadn't been there because Paula had kept him away. She was behind it all. I feel like I might throw up.

'You wanted me to be vulnerable, didn't you? To depend on you so you could become part of my life, so you could live in this house.'

'Of course. I made sure you had the babies when Ian was away.'

'What?'

'Oh Katie, didn't you realise? That horrible examination I gave you when you thought you hadn't felt the twins moving. I induced your labour. I inserted a pessary of drugs to get it going. And it worked. I was proud of myself. I learnt how to do it on the internet. I hadn't even done a vaginal examination before then.'

Her words knock the air out of me. 'What do you mean? I thought you examined women as part of your job.'

In the darkness I can just about make out Paula's smirk. 'You still think I'm a doula?'

'Aren't you?' I recoil in shock.

'Of course not. I did a bit of nannying in Berlin, but nothing more. I made up being a doula when I saw you were pregnant. I even printed out a certificate in case you wanted to see one. But you never did. You never even checked my references. You trusted me.'

CHAPTER FORTY-SEVEN

'You're not a doula?' I stare at her in disbelief. 'You're crazy.'

'I'm not crazy. I'm damaged. I didn't have a good start in life. It was inevitable that I'd turn out bad. That's what my foster parents told me after my sister died. I guess they were right.'

Above me in the house, I hear glass smashing.

The police? But I haven't rung them. Maybe Amy's phoned them. But then I remember she's upstairs, unconscious in the bedroom. Bleeding from the head.

'Down here!' I shout as loudly as I can. 'Down here!'

'They'll never hear you.' Paula says. 'My mother never used to hear me and my sister when we were locked down here. She used to play the piano in the room above, as if she hadn't a care in the world.'

What am I going to do? I need to get the twins off Paula. And what about Amy? I need to help her too.

'What have you done to Amy?' I ask.

'Your stupid friend? You care about her, do you?'

'What did you do to her?' I remember how Amy thought Paula had pushed her down the stairs.

'I hit her over the head with the bedside lamp. I'm not sure if I really needed to. She wasn't any good at guarding your twins. I think she would have slept straight through me taking them away.' Paula laughs. 'But I knocked her out anyway, just in case.'

I need to get Amy some help. Now. But I can't leave my twins.

'Katie?' I hear a voice from above me in the house. Ian. But he sounds far away.

'Here! We're down here!' I scream out.

'Katie?' The voice sounds like a whisper now, even further away. When I strain my ears I can still hear the rain outside. He won't be able to hear me above the noise.

'Ian!' I scream even louder. My babies scream with me. I remember the night I woke up and thought I could hear my babies crying, but they sounded far away. Paula must have had them down here. I could hear them from the hallway. If only Ian would go into the hallway.

'Ian!' I scream again.

'Katie?'

In the dark, Paula clamps her hand over my mouth. I fight furiously, biting her hand and pulling away, but she lets go of the twins, dropping them onto the mattress, and pushes me down, then lies across me, her hand still over my mouth. I try to shout to Ian but my words are completely muffled by her palm.

But I can hear footsteps. They're getting closer.

A shadow blocks the doorway at the top of the stairs.

Ian.

Paula jumps off me, but before I can grab my screaming daughters and run away, she has them back in her arms, close to her body.

'She's got our babies,' I call up to Ian. 'Call the police!'

Then Paula's hands circle Frances's neck. 'The police won't get here in time.' She smiles calmly, enjoying every moment of my agony. 'Get Ian down here where I can see him.'

'Ian!' I shriek, as I watch Paula's hands tighten around Frances's neck. My throat is raw from my screams.

Ian runs down the stairs towards us, stumbling over the uneven stone, coming to a rapid stop when he sees the candle next to the mattress, sees Paula's grip on the girls.

'The prodigal son returns.'

'Paula—' I've never seen Ian panicked before, but as he stares at Paula I can see fear in his eyes. 'What are you doing with my children?'

'My nieces, you mean. I'm their auntie.' Paula is completely calm.

'Katie said you were my sister. But I didn't even know I had a sister. You have to believe me.' Ian stumbles over the words.

Paula laughs as Alice cries in her arms. Under the sound of Alice's whimpers I can hear the tape still whirring, playing the same haunting lullaby over and over.

'You really are an accomplished liar, Ian. You know you had two sisters. Twins. Just like yours. Twins must run in our family.'

'They must,' Ian says distractedly, and I know he's thinking what I'm thinking. We have to get the girls away from Paula. I scan the darkness for some kind of weapon. All I can see are the girls' soft toys and the tape player, the reels still turning. Could I throw it hard enough to knock Paula out, or at least knock her off balance? I try to catch Ian's eye.

'Did you know that we were locked down here in the basement when you visited my father?' Paula continues, her voice cold. 'Sometimes we heard you, laughing and joking with Dad, while we were down here in the dark and the dirt.'

'I had no idea.'

'He preferred you to us. He told us. He'd always wanted a son, and there you were. He didn't want two girls.'

'I'm so sorry,' Ian says. He sounds sincere, as if he's genuinely moved. 'I really am.' He shuffles closer to Paula and I think he might be able to grab our babies. I pray that he does. But she squeezes the twins tightly. Too tightly.

'After you started coming round, everything changed. You know why we were first locked down here? Because we waved at you. That's all we did. And that got us locked down here.'

I stare at the picture of the children on the wall, thinking of them shut away down here in the basement. I can't imagine what

Paula suffered, first at the hands of her father and then at the hands of her sister. They both used to beat her up down here.

Ian speaks quietly. 'What our father did to you – it's not my fault, Paula. It's not my babies' fault either. Let them go. Let them be happy.' The twins are quiet now, and I'm worried Paula has squeezed them too tightly, forcing the air from their tiny lungs.

'Do you think they'll be happy in this house? They should never have been living here in the first place.' Paula's voice rises, her anger filling the room. 'I should have inherited the house.'

'Is that what this is about? The house?' Ian takes a step forward.

'I was the one who suffered in this house. I was the one who lost my sister. I grew up here. I endured that childhood. Why should you inherit it? You never even lived here.'

Ian glances at me and then at the tape player. 'You're right,' he says desperately. 'The house should have been yours.'

I know what Ian's doing. He's trying to distract Paula so I can reach the tape player. It's our only chance.

'I was the one who visited Dad when he was ill,' Paula continues. 'I went to see him in the care home. Even though I hated him, I did that for him. I thought I'd get my reward when he died. You never even saw him. And yet, despite everything I did for him, you were still his favourite.'

I take a step closer and Paula glances up at me. Her cold eyes meet mine and all I can see is pure, unadulterated hatred. She pulls the twins away, but the cassette player is almost in reach.

'Look – you can have the house,' Ian says. 'You can have anything. Just give us our girls back.'

Ian meets my eyes. I'm inches from the cassette player. If I just stretch out my fingers, I can grab it.

Paula looks down at the babies, considering Ian's offer. I take my opportunity, lunging towards the tape player. My fingers grip its cold metal and I lift it into the air. I throw it as hard as I can at Paula.

CHAPTER FORTY-EIGHT

Paula ducks and the cassette player flies past her head, crashing to the floor. The tape doesn't stop, the reels turning and the piano playing through its speakers.

Paula lifts her head up slowly and meets my eyes. My babies' screams echo around us.

'So that's how you really feel, is it, Katie? After everything I've done for you.'

My breathing is ragged and heavy from the exertion of throwing the tape player.

'You've hurt my daughter,' I say through tears. 'I thought you loved my girls. I trusted you.'

'You don't know what it's like to be truly hurt. Hurt the way I was.'

'I read the newspaper articles, Paula. I read how your father hurt you and how your sister joined in. How she beat you up. I can't imagine how awful that must have been. Your own twin.' When I first read the stories I felt sorry for Paula. But not anymore. Not after I realised what she's been doing to my family. 'What happened to you was awful. But it's nothing to do with my daughters.'

'But it's everything to do with their father.' She glares at Ian. 'My sister died because of you.'

'What do you mean?' Ian asks.

'You might not have known about us when you first started coming round. But you knew at the end. We wrote you a note and put it in your bag. We asked for your help. But you ignored it.'

'I didn't. I never received anything.'

'You did, Ian. You must have. You showed it to your mother and she called my father and told him all about it. And after that the violence got much, much worse.'

'What? My mother knew about you? She had your note?' Ian pauses. 'She must have found it in my bag. I used to pretend I was going to play football when I came to see my father. I'd change afterwards and she'd go through my bag to wash my kit. She must have found it then.' He pauses. 'That must be why we moved away so suddenly. She knew I was seeing him.'

But Paula's not listening anymore. She's lost in her memories. 'That was when he started making us fight each other. If you had just helped us, that would never have happened.'

'Look, Paula,' I say. 'You need help. If you just give us the twins, we can get help for you. Help you get over your childhood. Come to terms with everything that's happened. We don't have to mention anything that's happened today.'

'You think it's that easy, do you? I'm afraid that's not how it works. Ian didn't help us when we were locked down here. And only one of us came out alive. That's what happens in this basement. One twin lives and one twin dies. Because of Ian. And now your twins are down here too. History repeating itself.' She laughs. 'It's so appropriate, don't you think? Ian kills my twin, and I kill one of yours?'

I realise that Paula is truly unhinged. She doesn't have any compassion left in her. It was all beaten out of her as a child.

'Paula, please,' I beg. 'Just let my girls go.'

'I'm so sorry, Paula,' Ian says desperately. 'I truly am. I never heard what happened to your sister. I was in Kent, starting a new life with my mother. I didn't read the papers. I didn't even know I had a sister, let alone that she died.'

'I don't believe you. You're a compulsive liar. And your twins are going to pay.'

Paula puts the twins down roughly and I see the slither of a chance to grab them, but before I can reach for them, she picks up the candle and holds it over the old mattress. I can't come any nearer. If she lets the flame touch the mattress, the whole thing will become a bonfire with my babies on it.

I can't stop myself. My screams fill the room. 'Help! Help!'

Paula watches me gleefully, the whites of her eyes shimmering in the candlelight. Seeing her like this, I think she's actually prepared to kill us all.

I look up at the wall, see the photo of my twins with Frances's face scratched out. In exactly the same way Paula's twin's face is scratched out. As if she was always planning to murder her. As I stare at the flickering candle, I realise that I still don't know who killed her sister. It wasn't Ian. I'd assumed it was her violent father. But now the pieces of the puzzle are starting to come together in my mind. Paula's horrific childhood. Her sister beating her up.

'You snapped and killed your sister, didn't you? She was hurting you and you retaliated. You pushed her down the stairs.'

Paula smiles serenely. 'I wondered when you'd work that out. I pushed her. I had to. It was her or me.'

I stare at her, disbelieving. She's capable of killing her own flesh and blood. Her twin. And she has no remorse at all.

'There wasn't space in the world for both of us. Just like there isn't space in the world for both of your twins.'

She holds the candle up high, dripping hot wax on the mattress, so close to Frances's face.

I have to get her on my side, have to pretend to understand her, so she'll give the girls back to me.

'You were just a child. No one could blame you. Not after what you'd been through. Of course you snapped. Your sister was violent towards you. Again and again. No one could cope with that. Of course you pushed her.'

Paula laughs as she plays with the candle, hot wax dripping so close to my babies. 'You still believe that my sister abused me?'

I frown. 'I read the psychiatric reports. They explained what had happened to you when you were young. How your sister used to hurt you. How it affected you later on when you went into foster care.'

'Yes, well, that's what I told the psychiatrists. They lapped it up. It was exactly what they wanted to hear. Poor little me. Abused by my father and my twin. With a dead sister to boot. I became quite in demand in medical circles. Lots of them wanted to do case studies on me. Analyse how such an awful childhood had affected me.'

'So you made it all up?'

'It happened. Just not the way I said. Think about it logically. There are two sisters. One of them is stronger and cleverer than the other. One tortures the other. Which one do you think would end up dead at the bottom of the stairs? The weaker one, or the stronger one?'

'What are you saying?'

'The weaker twin doesn't end up alive. She dies. I was the stronger sister, and I survived. I was the one who tortured my sister.'

23

The fight is over. She has won. I'm bloody and bruised on the basement floor and Dad is finally satisfied. Every bone in my body hurts.

'Well done,' he says to her. 'Well done, Paula!'

I haven't fought back, and she is uninjured, her pretty face unblemished.

Dad starts up the basement steps and my sister follows him. I crawl up behind them. I want to get to Mum. I hope she'll help me. I can't stay down in the basement on my own, not like this.

When we get to the top of the stairs, I stand shakily.

'What are you doing?' my sister asks angrily.

Dad turns. 'Didn't you hear me? Whoever wins the fight gets to leave the basement. You have to stay.'

He turns to my sister. 'Make her go back down.'

'Go back down the steps,' Paula says to me. 'Please.'

I can barely see, barely stand up. But I need to get out of the basement.

My father is losing patience. 'OK then, if she won't go back down, then you'll both have to stay down there.'

'No!' my sister says.

And then she turns and I see her hands flying towards me. She pushes me with all her might.

I fall backward. I feel my head crack against the first stone step, see my legs above me, tumbling over me.

And then nothing.

CHAPTER FORTY-NINE

Ian stares at Paula incredulously. 'You were abusing your twin? And then you killed her?'

She nods. 'She didn't deserve to live. She was too weak.'

Ian chokes back tears. 'She was *my* sister.'

'Don't pretend to care now. You never even met her.'

'Sabrina was right, wasn't she? It *was* you who pushed her down the escalator. You killed my sister and then you murdered my baby.' He stumbles over the words, shocked.

Paula laughs. 'I didn't want you to have a baby. I didn't want you to be happy. You didn't deserve it.'

Ian looks like he might throw up. I see fury in his eyes. He takes a step towards Paula and she holds up Alice's toy caterpillar next to the flame of the candle. The flame laps towards it, but it doesn't catch.

'What do you want, Paula?' I ask desperately. 'We'll give you anything you want. Ian's said you can have the house.'

Paula smiles serenely. 'I'm not in the mood to negotiate,' she says. 'I'm enjoying this far too much.'

'Paula, please.'

'OK,' she says. 'Seeing as you're being so nice to me all of a sudden, maybe I can cut you a deal.'

'What?' My heart leaps. 'Anything you want.'

'I'll have the house. Ian will take it off the market and sign it over to me. You won't tell anyone what happened here.'

'You'll give us the twins?' I reach out my arms, but she places the candle over the twins once more. Wax drips onto the mattress beside them.

'I'll give you one twin,' she says, smiling. 'I'll let you choose which twin comes out alive. And after we're done, you can tell the police it was all a terrible accident.'

'No!' I scream.

In the distance I can hear footsteps. Voices above us.

Suddenly there is the sound of feet thumping in the cupboard upstairs.

'Hello? Katie? Are you down there? Are you alright?'

'Mum!' I scream out in relief, as her shadow appears in the doorway.

'What's going on? I flew back from France as soon as I got your message. I found Amy upstairs. She's been attacked. But I couldn't find you or the twins anywhere…' She stops mid-sentence, eyes adjusting to the candlelight.

'Paula?' Mum says, confused. 'Why does she have the girls down here?'

'She wants to hurt them. She's been starving Frances. She's going to kill her.' The words tumble over each other urgently as the candlewax drips closer to Frances's face.

Before I can even blink, the basement door slams shut. The rush of air blows out the candle and I hear light footsteps speeding down the stairs.

The dark is so pure that I can hardly make out a thing, but I see a glint of metal rising up into the air and then coming down hard and fast. The tape player. The music stops as the metal cassette player hits its target. There's a sickening crack as metal hits bone. I gasp.

Paula's agonised scream joins my babies' hysterical crying and the noise is deafening, bouncing off the walls and engulfing us.

Ian dashes over to the mattress and there's a scuffle, a jumble of bodies rolling on top of each other, as the cries continue.

With Paula incapacitated I lunge towards the mattress, desperate to reach my children. Ian wrestles with Paula, my mother caught somewhere underneath it all. I snatch Frances from the mattress into my arms, and then pick up Alice. I walk towards the basement steps, overcome by relief to be holding my babies, to have them close.

I feel a hand on my ankle, fingers digging hard into my flesh, pulling me back.

I try desperately to keep my balance, but I can't. Suddenly I'm falling. Frances and Alice are in my arms; the ground is coming up to meet us.

I try to twist my body round to land on my side, but there's no time. I see movement, a flash of red. I land on something both soft and hard, a jumble of arms and legs and flesh.

It's Mum. She's thrown herself underneath me. She's broken my fall. She's put me and the babies before herself once again.

The twins scream louder in my arms, and I worry they've been hurt as I hit the ground.

My mother moans in pain, and I try to manoeuvre off her, without harming the twins, but Paula's still gripping my ankle. I pray that Mum's OK.

Ian is there in a second, dragging Paula off me. Her grip loosens and she falls heavily onto the mattress, her breathing ragged.

I hand Frances and then Alice to Ian and he holds them close and smothers them in kisses. Their screams are quietening, becoming less hysterical. I shuffle off my mother, who stays flat on the ground.

'Are the twins OK?' she whispers.

'I think so – are you alright, Mum?'

'I've survived worse.' She half smiles.

I turn to look at Paula, as I get up unsteadily onto my feet. She's mumbling to herself on the mattress, blood flowing from a gash on her head.

EPILOGUE

Six months later

I sit in the coffee shop opposite the house, watching the builders put scaffolding up and remembering the first time I came here.

'They've started work, then?' Mum asks.

'Looks like it.'

'I'm glad you moved away. You were never happy there.'

I nod sadly and reach out to touch Mum's hand. 'Thanks for letting me move in with you.'

'It's no problem. I love having the twins around.' It's like she's got younger since we've been living with her, always chasing around after them, joining in their games and laughter. She's happier than I've seen her in a long time. She's still occasionally bothered by her headaches, but fortunately the doctors have told her they aren't a sign of anything sinister.

'Ian will be here in a minute,' I say, looking at my watch.

At that moment, the bell above the café door jingles and Ian wheels the double buggy in. I lean over and kiss both babies on their cheeks. Frances looks at her sister with a cheeky grin and her sister grins back. They look so similar now. Frances gained weight rapidly once she was being fed properly. I shiver with guilt when I think that I didn't know what Paula was doing to her.

'Hi,' Ian says warmly.

I stand up and kiss him politely on the cheek. 'How's it going?'

'Really well,' he says. 'Jessica and I are moving into the flat in a couple of weeks. It's nearly ready for us.' He beams with excitement. He's used the proceeds from selling the house to buy a flat nearer to the centre of London, and he's going to live there with his new girlfriend. He thinks the flat will be the first in his property empire. I'm just glad I've got nothing to do with it.

'How's Melissa?' he asks.

'Good. Bought herself a new flat too,' my mother says proudly.

'And Amy?'

'Same as ever,' I smile. Luckily her head wound wasn't serious. She's turned her injury into a dinner party piece and now she brings out the story of her brush with death at every opportunity.

Ian's phone beeps and he pulls it from his pocket. 'Jessica's nearly here,' he says. I swallow. She's coming to the coffee shop to meet the twins for the first time. I wanted to meet her at the same time as Ian introduced her to the girls.

The bell rings again and a blonde woman steps nervously into the café.

She holds out her hand and introduces herself and I try to smile. She's well-dressed and seems friendly. She could be worse.

She leans over the buggy and coos at my twins.

My heart beats faster and I feel like I can't breathe.

Just a panic attack, I tell myself, focusing on a spot above the counter and trying to slow my breathing. I have them a lot these days.

'I'm going to have a lot of work to do once we move into the flat,' Ian says. 'And I thought Jessica could look after the twins when I'm busy.'

I grit my teeth. 'On her own?'

'I love babies,' Jessica says, as she reaches out to tickle Frances. 'I used to work as a nanny.'

The panic rises in me again. 'No,' I say to Ian, firmly. 'That won't be happening. They're your twins and you have to look after them yourself.' I can't trust anyone to look after them who's not family. Not anymore.

The police and the ambulance had arrived soon after we'd rescued the twins. Paula's being held in a secure psychiatric hospital now, awaiting trial for charges of child neglect, but I still don't feel completely safe.

Ian is protesting about Jessica looking after the girls, saying that we can trust her, that she's very reliable. I stand up quickly, grab the handles of the buggy and leave the coffee shop without saying goodbye.

When I get back to Mum's house, I hold the twins tight to my body, feeling their chests rise and fall against mine until they drift into contented sleep. I look down at their tiny, delicate bodies and think of the years ahead, of nurseries and schools; strangers looking after them. I wonder if I'll ever be able to let them go.

A LETTER FROM RUTH

Thank you for choosing to read *The Woman Upstairs*. If you enjoyed it, I'd be very grateful if you could write a review. I'd love to hear what you think, and it makes a huge difference by helping new readers to discover one of my books for the first time.

If you want to keep up to date with all my latest releases, just sign up at the following link. Your email address will never be shared and you can unsubscribe at any time.

www.bookouture.com/ruth-heald

I wrote the first draft of *The Woman Upstairs* in the final weeks before my son was born. I was terrified of giving birth, having had a traumatic experience the first time round. At the hospital, in labour, you are completely at the mercy of the midwives, nurses and doctors working there. Sometimes they are kind and caring, but not always. I've heard story after story about how women weren't listened to while their bodies were examined, cut open and acted upon. I wanted to write a book that examined the harm that could be done if a woman was badly influenced during those vital moments of labour, birth and the first weeks as a new mum. It seemed to me that a live-in doula would be perfectly placed to take advantage of a new mother at her most vulnerable.

My protagonist, Katie, is level-headed and strong, but she's in a precarious position living with two newborns, in a house owned by the absent and untrustworthy Ian. I hope you've been able to empathise with her struggles as she tries to make her new life work as it literally crumbles around her. I also hope you enjoyed the final showdown with Paula, when we see the impact of Paula's corrosive childhood and Katie sees her own mother in a new light when she selflessly jumps in to save the family.

I'm always happy to hear from my readers – you can get in touch on my Facebook page, through Twitter, Goodreads or my website.

Best wishes,
Ruth

 RJHealdAuthor

 @RJ_Heald

 www.rjheald.com

ACKNOWLEDGEMENTS

Lots of people have supported me during the writing of *The Woman Upstairs*, but first I'd like to thank my husband, who not only provided feedback on the book itself but also did so much more than his fair share of the housework and childcare when I was locked away with my manuscript, working to meet my deadline.

Family and friends have provided help and encouragement. My mother always set me a good example of persistence, without which I would never be published. Although she is no longer with us, that will always stay with me. My children are a source of joy and their endless curiosity encourages me to see the world through new eyes. My in-laws have been very generous with their time, looking after the children when I desperately needed time to focus on the novel. I'd also like to thank Charity Khoo, who advised me on twin births, my friend in the police force who helped me work out what might happen to Paula, and my online writing group, the Neons, who were the first to see the opening chapters of this book and provided valuable feedback.

I'm very grateful to my editor, Christina Demosthenous, for being a diplomatic sounding board for my ideas and providing insightful editorial comments, which have taken the book up to the next level. Noelle and Kim at Bookouture are the dream team for publicity, and I'm constantly in awe of their passion and enthusiasm for book promotion. Thanks also to the Marketing and Insights teams, who get my books into the hands of interested readers, and to the rest of the team at Bookouture, a highly talented group who work tirelessly on our books.

And finally, thank you to everyone who has taken time out of their lives to read my book. One of the greatest pleasures for me is knowing that there are people out there reading and enjoying my work.